The Lady Orangutan and Other Stories

Sources for the petroglyphs:

Jornada Mogollon: (pages 3, 22, 118, 156, 177, 266)

Chaco Canyon: (Frontispiece, Preface, and pages 167, 215, 225, 293, 297)

Una Vida: (pages 15, 34, 37, 39, 44, 57, 59, 83, 108, 110, 180, 202, 204, 306)

Albuquerque: (pages 10, 18, 30, 68, 71, 75, 87, 90, 96, 124, 218, 254, 279, 288, 289)

The Lady Orangutan and Other Stories

Jane Wodening

Sockwood Press • Nederland, Colorado

Each story complete and unabridged, chosen and arranged
by Jane Wodening

Most of these stories have been published before, some
more than once; a few have never seen the light of day until
now. A partial list of publishers: Baksun, Granary, Grackle,
Rodent, Invisible; anthologies such as "Sites of Insight" by
James Lough, periodicals too numerous to mention going
back into the past, such as Whole Earth Magazine and
Rolling Stock. Some changes and updates, but very few, by
J.W.: "The Flock" was changed quite a bit, thus the name
change to "My Flock". Another "Vision of my Death" was
added, and "Gaits and the Canyon" was edited as well.

Sources, early collections by Jane Wodening:
"Lump Gulch Tales"
"Mountain Woman Tales"
"The Inside Story"
"Book of Gargoyles"
"First Presence"
and some until now unpublished

Cover photo by Ron Ruhoff
Petroglyphs copied from the rock by Jane Wodening

Published by
Sockwood Press
PO Box 706
Nederland, CO 80466

ISBN: 978-0-9790171-6-2

Printed in the United States
1st Edition

Table of Contents

PREFACE

Four manuscripts have been sitting around the house not getting published and when I noticed that I was going to be eighty in a couple of years or so, I realized that if I didn't get these made into books, they would probably never be made into books. One has to do things or they don't happen. I wanted to collect some of the more solid short pieces from earlier publications and align them as a sort of train of thought through a lifetime. So I have begun with this collection, naming it after the lovely orangutan who made me realize that there were things that I needed to tell people because, although they seemed obvious to me, others didn't find them so.

As I have gone about the Southwestern United States, I have always stopped to see the petroglyphs and copy as many as I could down into a notebook then, at my leisure, I would work on them, wanting to bring out in my copies what I had seen on the rock: that viability, that love of life that includes the community of people, the air, the land, and all the life and all the lives in the environment. "All my relatives," they say, and they mean really everything, every atom, every living thing. Some were made high on a cliff and others on low boulders, some in sun and some in shade. I do not know what each petroglyph means. Nor can I define the Mona Lisa or The Art of the Fugue. But the creative passion is there, personal creativity, tradition, whimsy, and a connectedness to the world around. I would like to include some of my copies here and respectfully ask the spirits for permission.

Paul Keller has read just about every short story I've written, and remembers them all, too. He and I shuffled through the stories together and picked out the ones that belonged in this book.

There was a scam that happened in the process. A proofreading company in Ohio charged me an enormous fee to create a book of useless blather that made me feel like a foolish wasted life, and there could be no reason to publish the stupid thing.

Then Janette Taylor heard of my plight, and carefully, and at long labor, went back to the stories as I had written them, took out the typos and other glitches. Then Julian Taylor, who had just finished his second edition of "The Flying Crossbeam," created Sockwood Press just in time to bring out the two books together.

These three magical people I thank with all my heart.

-- Jane Wodening
May 28, 2014

THE BUMBLEBEE

The sun shone in the big window that morning. I had the top of the Dutch door open, and I was sitting by the window in the big chair, reading a book.

And then into the house came a big furry bumblebee, and she started hammering herself against the big window, making a horrendous noise and disturbing my reading.

I do not swat flies, generally speaking. For one thing, I see a lot of personality in flies. On the other hand, I consider flies to be one of the best of bird foods, and I love birds. And then, of course, if you kill the flies you leave a smudge on the window. So what I do is I have a clear plastic cup that I keep on the windowsill, and a white card the covers the cup's mouth. When a fly comes in, I catch them with that cup on the window, slide the card under and lock them in, carry them to the door, and release them.

Very slowly and cautiously I took the cup and started chasing that bumblebee. But the bumblebee didn't want to be caught. She got behind things. She would tear across the window from one hiding place to another. Finally I told her. "I'm doing this for your own good." I said it aloud.

Expressing fear or making a sudden movement will make a creature attack. Everyone knows this. Mostly insects are unaware of us huge creatures until we chase them with a flyswatter or a cup.

1

Since I continued so slow and inexorable, the bumblebee did not go into attack mode until I did finally get her in the cup and sealed up. With her belated rage screaming there in my hands, I walked to the door and reaching under the top half of the door, I released her and watched her tear off into the woods.

I was exhausted.

On the following morning, the sun shone brightly in through the big window, so I opened the top half of the Dutch door and settled in the chair to read a book. In through the open door came the great bumblebee, and she started hammering herself against the window, disturbing my reading. Well, I knew what to do. I took the cup and with slow cautious movements I caught her with very little difficulty. I was amazed to note that she did not go into attack mode on the occasion of being caught but walked calmly on the clear plastic. Reaching the the top of the Dutch door, I released her again and watched in amazement as she took off into the woods.

It was so peaceful.

On the following day the sun shone brightly in through the big window, and so I opened the Dutch door and settled down in the chair to read. I was in an exciting part of the book so that the sound of the bumblebee came to me dimly at first. But I finally looked up and I saw her. She was hammering herself again and again – not at the window, but at the plastic cup.

I reached my hand to the cup. I was unafraid. She flew to the middle of the big

2

window, and I gently placed the cup over her and slid the card in slowly. She walked onto the card.

I studied her through the plastic. She was calm and assured as I walked to the Dutch door and released her. I watched her fly off into the woods.

I never saw her again.

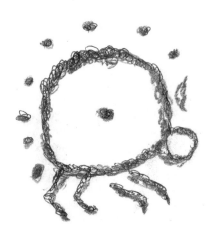

TRANSFORMATIONS

It was when I was eleven I gave up the human race, just set it aside. Until then I was a shy little girl with pigtails, wetting my bed in a sweet little suburb of Chicago. When I was eleven I moved with my parents to a tough copper-mining town in the Rockies and the culture shock was too much for me. I hadn't been very successful with people up until then anyway, sucked two fingers so hard I had calluses on them where my teeth gripped them, thought of what to reply several days after I was spoken to and then was too embarrassed to chase the person down and tell the answer I'd thought of. But moving to the Rockies was the end. There was simply no way, no way at all. When people spoke to me I didn't even know what they were saying, let alone what to say back.

So I took up with dogs. I ran with them for several years. I'd go through town like the Pied Piper, sometimes taking half a dozen or so on a walk. Running with dogs got so big in my life I remember seeing a human neighbor on the street and searching my mind how to say "Hi" in English.

It was only natural that I'd get a job working for a veterinary hospital, hosing out kennels, barbering poodles, and handing over the scalpel and the sponge. There was a dog there who was a stray the doctors had gotten from the pound to use as a transfusion dog. At that time, you'd have to kill a dog to give another a transfusion.

4

So they had her there in case they needed her blood. She was a swell dog. She'd go around with me while I was doing chores in the morning before the doctors came in. They did suggest I take her home, but I had a dog at home already, so I didn't.

I was twenty-one, and all the inevitable things happened at once. A female dog friend of mine in my neighborhood came into heat, and a neighbor man went out and shot her and a couple of friends of mine, dogs who were naturally following her. He said they were forming a pack. A nasty whippet with no soul needed a transfusion, so my dear friend at the office was killed. The dogs started snarling at me, even biting me, all happening within about a week. From that time, something changed in my chemistry. Dogs who never attacked anyone else would attack me. I had to quit my job. I was afraid to get out of my car or walk into, or out of, any house. This went on for several months. But then I got married, and as soon as I did that the dogs stopped attacking me.

We spent the next seven years driving across the country looking for the right place to live, meeting a lot of artists (the man I married being an artist), and experimenting with birth control methods. At the fifth child we stopped, exhausted, in a gulch in the Rockies and put down roots. It was as good a place as any. After the fifth child was weaned, we managed to stop having them and a good thing too, because I had a greenish pallor and my hair was getting shorter at a great rate. I felt terrible about stopping having babies because

5

it was a true and basic great thing to do, and I was good at it. But it was becoming a self-destructive self-indulgence. At the same time, what could I possibly do beyond that? I felt as if my life was over.

But two disparate wonders occurred which I used to encourage myself. One being that I began playing the recorder and discovered the magical delight of making music. The other was that I acquired a donkey who had spent two years entirely alone, with only unfeeling care and yet had survived with his sensibilities intact, greeting every passing bird or butterfly, every shift of wind and sun, with heartfelt recognition and honor. I was extremely touched by his excitement and respect for everything around, and I have tried to live by his philosophy ever since.

It may have been at this time or earlier that I was sitting on the rock overlooking the gulch, basking in nature as a place empty of humanity, when I heard my neighbor staggering home, drunk, and singing off key again. My immediate reaction was repulsion, that he was spoiling nature. But then I argued with myself thus: "Humans," I said, "are a very interesting species of great ape that would be good to study, and I happen to have a lifetime membership."

From that point on, I became more involved in humans, starting shyly by playing the recorder with them, expanding from there.

There was a woman I used to know. She and I used to say we'd send each other our writing when we wrote it. But neither of us ever wrote

6

anything, and then we didn't see each other for many years. Then I visited her as she lay dying. I looked at her in awe and spoke clumsily and stared and then left. That night I woke in wild terror and my head on the pillow was her head on the pillow, and for the first time in my life I knew I would die someday, and if I didn't do something, I would die without having done anything.

There was only one thing I could do that night, I could write about her. So I did. I have written a lot since then. I've written about what I want to know about — people and other animals and how things happen. Writing suits my temperament well because, although it's a very sociable thing to do and I am a sociable being, I can do it in the integrity of solitude.

At this point, I thought this piece was finished. But two days later, my husband of thirty years left me. For several months I worked with all my energies to get him back, but he couldn't bear the thought of it. Again I had to transform. I sold the house and started driving around the country. I drove and lived in the car for nearly three years. After twenty-three years in one place, deep-rooted, I began to look at places I'd never known existed. Sometimes I would see a road and it would call me and I'd go up it. Sometimes I'd stay there for weeks, live a life, leave again, weeping.

I got a cabin, then, higher up in the Rockies, and wished to pull myself together into a singularity, an individual person. At the cabin I watched nature in action all around me. Living things never stayed still, even the plants. Things kept happening to them. Other lives impinged on them, or the weather shaped them, or they were too close together and competition became the first urgency, or they outgrew what they had been. So, of course, I could see that, although I was — and in fact had been since birth — an individual person, I was part of all of life and would therefore be inevitably always transforming.

There are legends in the olden days of people transforming into all sorts of things: a frog, a dove, a white oak tree, or a grain of wheat. They'd do it to escape from each other in wild games of god-tag, in which the incredible vitality of transformation would flash and glitter in the tale. And then one of them would get stuck or caught in one or another character and have to wait perhaps for years, or centuries, for the prince to kiss the princess. Or for the witch, transformed into a chicken, to eat the grain of wheat and then, nine months later, give birth to and even love and care for her erstwhile enemy. It's a hard thing to do, transforming is, but sometimes it's necessary if you want your life to be anything after a blow or when the environment changes or when a realization comes that what you've been doing is no longer a viable identity.

KNUT NEVERSETTER

You know that tin house standing down by Mahaffie's bridge? There was a young man lived down there, his name was Knut Neversetter. He had a snug little log cabin, he was a real nice fellow but crazy as a tick. It came into his head that what he wanted more than anything else was a tin house. The problem with that was that although he owned the house he didn't own the land it was sitting on, I guess that's called Squatter's Rights. He went to the county officials and asked them if he couldn't build another house and they told him no, he couldn't, he'd better be content with the cabin he had.

Knut stewed about that quite a bit and then he went back to the officials and said, how about if he added on a room of tin to his cabin and again they said no, he couldn't do that either.

So he came back and he was miserable. You could see him there, sitting on his front stoop, whittling, and the Summer was about gone and he hadn't got any wood brought in for Winter.

Then he got another idea, he went back to those officials and he asked them if it would be all right if he simply covered the cabin he had with tin and they said sure, he could do that but he couldn't make it any bigger or add anything.

It was then that there was a big change in Knut Neversetter. He gave over his whittling and he was hauling tin around and whistling and

9

working on his cabin, covering it top to bottom with tin. By the time the aspens dropped their leaves, Knut's cabin was finished and it gleamed and glittered in the sun as the snow started to pile up around it and that Winter he kept himself warm burning the log cabin in the stove.

THE BEETLE

I was talking with Betsy on the phone, fiddling, as one does, with the spiraled cord, poking absently at the dust collected on the dial and at the stack of books on the footlocker which serves as a telephone table, when I saw a little gray beetle clinging to the top edge of a book.

"I won't be able to come up tomorrow either," Betsy was saying, "Beth has this endless cough."

I mumbled something about how insidious the latest flu was. What was a beetle doing here in February? Where could it have come from? Had it been in the house all this time? Had it perhaps been wintering over in some obscure crack and then gotten disturbed by the Saturday morning cleaning? How could it expect to gain sustenance on the telephone table?

"But I'm definitely counting on Wednesday. It's been three weeks since we've had a proper Wednesday."

I reached out to the beetle, trying to get it to walk onto my hand. It seems to be getting hard for me to get a clear view of insects these days. So helpful if they get on my hand so I can arrange the distance and the light to suit my needs.

"Okay, I'll see you Wednesday for sure," I said. Placing the receiver on its cradle, I touched the beetle gently. Instantly, it loosed its hold on the book and hung there by a cobweb looking like an empty shell, a long-dead little beetle, relic of a spider's gluttony, long forgotten. Possum. There are many insects who play possum. I've seen it many times before. Spiders themselves do it often. I had never seen it quite so convincingly done, though, as this beetle achieved it. Dark gray, covered with dust, hanging shriveled and inconsequential in a cobweb. I was taken aback.

I reassured myself that I had been extremely gentle and couldn't possibly have hurt the little creature and, with a faint hope that she might be interested in eating some of my aphids, I resolved to carry her up to the greenhouse on the roof. "Maybe she's hungry," I muttered to myself hopefully. I imagined that she was a female in hopes that she would populate the green house with aphid-eaters.

Carefully, I picked up the book and stood up. The cobweb must have been attached to something else, for the beetle fell with a slight sound to the floor as I stood and I saw her lying on her back, waving her legs feebly in the air. I stooped down with my book, gently slid the paper cover under her and picked her up. She rolled down it to the inside, the great squashing maw between the cover and the title page. I put my finger in there to hold the book open, went out into the snow and up the icy ladder to the greenhouse

carrying the book and its precious cargo. Somehow
I got through the door and into the greenhouse
without dropping her, then looked around for the
best source of aphids to place her on. I settled
on the young Greek bean plant, just setting out
its real leaves although it was a foot high
already. These were compound leaves, each with
three newly opening leaflets. Carefully, I spread
out the book. She was there and she was on her
feet, crawling slowly across the page. I placed
the tender young leaf in front of her but she
changed course to avoid it. She certainly
mistrusted me. It seemed she had it in her mind to
go to the edge of the page. I put the book so that
the leaf was just below the end of the book in a
line with the direction of her course. She came to
it and stopped, waving her antennae in intense
interest for awhile while I tried to hold still.

The leaf passed muster and she slowly pulled
herself onto it. There was an aphid there but she
walked past it, not seeming to notice. She looked
old and withered and frail. "Maybe she needs
water," I thought.

I stuck my finger in the barrel of water
near the Greek bean and let a drop fall on the
other leaflet where it curled, barely open, beside
her. The blow shook the young bean like an
earthquake. I watched with concern as the beetle
slid and clung to the underside of the leaf. She
seemed, however, to know how to cling to a leaf.
Ancestry, no doubt, little hairs or microscopic
suction cups. I watched with relief as she climbed
delicately back up on the top edge of the leaflet.

Then I saw her notice the pool of water contained in the other one beside her. Hastily, eagerly, she stretched herself across the gap, clinging still with one back leg to her original leaflet, curling her four front legs around the edge of the one holding the pool of water. The other back leg waved frantically in the air, scrabbling thoughtlessly for some purchase where it could help to hold her body in balance as she bent with her mouth solemnly still against the water. That back leg was the only part of her that moved as she absorbed the water in passionate immobility.

For long minutes I watched her as she drank and drank, watched her unattached leg gradually calm down, then jerk occasionally with rapturous satisfaction. Her shriveled body swelled, her thorax stretched forward, her head reached out, her abdomen filled. As she at last walked away from the water, her color had changed from dark dull gray to warm brown. Spots of gold appeared on her thorax, her chin turned to a luminous maroon. The under part of her abdomen which had a few minutes before been drab and dusty was now a beautiful blend of tan and pale olive. She who had been frail before now walked in glowing golden strength.

She went purposefully to the top of the little vine where the second pair of real leaves was in bud and I watched carefully as she explored it, looking, no doubt, for higher and bushier reaches where she could lose herself in greenery. Her antennae were going constantly. She stopped to clean a bit of something white off of one front

14

foot. She had an awful struggle with it, scrabbling at it with her mandibles and her antenna. At last she got it off her foot but it was then stuck on her antenna. She worked away at that for awhile then, pulling it down through her mandibles again and again. I feared for her antenna but I needn't have. She finally got rid of the thing at last, gave up the effort to find a way further up the beanstalk and walked down the long stretch of stem to where the big seedling leaves came out.

She stopped there and I craned and peered at her, trying to see what she was doing. There were newly hatched aphids there and she was among them. I don't know if she was eating them or not. I couldn't get a proper angle to see her mouth to be sure. After a while, she went on down to the ground. She blended wonderfully with the soil, walking with sure steps over pebbles and under pine needles, until she was lost to view.

THE LADY ORANGUTAN

The way it happened was we were there in the
monkey house and it was Stan and me and Myrrena,
who had just learned to sit up. We were reading
the sign by the orangutan cage and the orangutan,
who was an old female with wrinkled, pendulous
breasts, came up to the corner of the cage where
we were and she was looking at Myrrena's feet.
Stan had Myrrena on his shoulder and it was a hot
day so there were her bare legs and bare feet
sticking out of the diaper and that was all the
orangutan could see of her. This lady orangutan
had one of the most beautiful faces I've ever
seen, expressive brown eyes with wrinkles all
around so that seeing her face was a revelation of
tenderness and passion and sensitivity and she was
looking at those feet waving on Stan's shoulder
and her face shone and her eyes burned with
eagerness and she pinched up her lips in an "ou"
and kissed the air and leaned against the cage
bars and her whole face was saying, "Oh, the
little darling," so I told Stan, I said, "She
wants to see the baby," and we like to humor each
other unless we disagree (it tends to make two
people doubly effective rather than half as
effective), so he promptly took Myrrena off his
shoulder and sat her down on the railing facing
the lady orangutan and she was delighted. I mean
the orangutan was. Myrrena was a little startled
and stared at her but the orangutan went into

16

ecstasies and screwed up her face and wiggled her
fingers at the baby like little old ladies do on
the street when I'd let them see Myrrena and
they'd have this exaggerated look of tenderness
and she had it too. I never did believe in those
old ladies before, it seemed too overdone to
believe, but there was this different sort of old
lady doing it too and I realized it must be
something more than upbringing and presumed
expectations, it must be a real feeling, so I
watched her carefully then to see if she would
explain to me what those old ladies were up to.

She started rocking her arms then, like
people do when they're saying "baby" in sign
language and then reached her arms through the
bars toward Myrrena and I said to Stan, "She wants
to hold the baby," but he vetoed it and rightly so
because you never know with strangers, but I felt
a little bad about it because then she got
frustrated and I could see in her eyes a
desperation, and then she turned away and ran and
leaped around in her cage screaming and hollering
and beating on the walls and it was very
impressive and people came from all over the
monkey house to see her, but they didn't
understand what she did after that, because they
hadn't seen what went before. What she did was
this, she came back to us and she stood there and
slowly slid her hands down her belly to her crotch
and then slowly and gently lifted an imaginary
baby out from between her legs and tenderly placed
in in her arms and rocked it. Somewhere I have
seen or heard of women doing this in tribal dances

17

when they want to have a baby. She did it several times, very slowly with wonder in her eyes mixed with intense passion. Suddenly, she turned again and leaped and screamed and beat on the walls again and then got down on the floor and lay on her back and thrashed and threw her arms around with her legs apart and bent at the knees and I saw her straining and pushing with her abdomen like we do when the baby is on the way out, then she got up and squatted and pissed on the floor and her face was grim and fierce and angry and there was no more she could think of to do but climb up to the highest shelf way in the corner and sit there with her back to us and her face to the wall.

SOCIAL GRACES

There had been a tea of some sort. I never got it clear what the gathering was about. Letty and Adelaide were on the committee. They always were and they always would be because they could be counted on and they could cook. So Letty was helping to dish out the cake while Adelaide was in charge of the coffeepot. Early on, two women had come in to the kitchen and one of them asked which cakes were homemade. Letty told them that those with the whipped cream on top were homemade and the two women said didn't they have any without whipped cream and Letty said here these over here didn't have whipped cream but the two women said oh no they had to have homemade and those weren't homemade so they took two pieces of the homemade cake and one after the other they went to the sink and dumped the whipped cream in the sink. Letty said she'd never been so mad in all her days.

"Have you ever heard of anything as rude as that?"

Letty poured a cup of tea for me and I reached over to the tray to get it. As I brought the tea to my chair, I whanged my arm on the arm of the chair and sloshed tea into the saucer. Actually it was an act of incredible gymnastics on my part not to slop the whole thing onto the floor, which would have left Letty in the ghastly position of not enough tea to go around and would have left me having done it again.

But I didn't quite spill it, or not much of it, and Letty graciously covered the tense moment by going over the story again.

The two women of the story had been around for a couple of years and pestered everyone no end, always coming into the kitchen and wanting the first chance at everything and then always staying in the kitchen in everyone's way. 'Why do they act that way?" Letty asked. "Why did they throw the whipped cream into the sink?"

Letty remembered a previous gathering when Margaret was putting the cookies on the plates and took the job very seriously, putting just enough of each kind of cookie on each plate. And then these same two women started eating off of Margaret's perfection before the rest of the people had even arrived.

And the time when dishes of nuts were put out and the two women, who always seemed to be there early, were eating all the cashews out. "Maybe somebody else would like some cashews too," Letty had said.

It seemed a long time since I had come into the room and seen that chocolate cake dripping with thick rich brown frosting. When Letty had begun to gesticulate with the cake knife I had been encouraged, but it seemed that her intense concentration on the matter of these two women and their vulgarity made it impossible for her to apply the attention necessary to the task of cutting the cake.

And as Letty waved the cake knife in the air with her eyes snapping, she told the story again.

20

Again, with every moment savored and enjoyed to the full, she described the two women entering the kitchen, walking as Letty mimicked them, like ladies in the nineties, swinging their bodies to take tiny steps. Letty minced her mouth into the little pruney shape that people use to show a mouth that tries to be a rosebud and fails. She waggled her head so that I could almost see parasols and lorgnettes promenading into the kitchen where Letty and Adelaide and other real women, mountain women, were doing real-life things like pouring coffee and cutting cake, putting a dollop of strawberries on and then a dab of whipped cream.

Letty and Margaret had tried to get these two women out of the kitchen. "There are places for you at the table," Margaret had urged. But the two had preferred to eat their cakes in the kitchen doorway, deepening and prolonging Letty's wrath and being very much in everyone's way.

"They came into the kitchen," Letty said.

"Which kind of cake is homemade?" Letty minced prunily.

"Well," Letty quoted herself, and by this time, I could have recited it in unison with her. "These with the whipped cream are homemade."

"Haven't you got any without whipped cream?" When she quoted the two women, she raised her already surprisingly high voice even higher and never neglected to waggle her head. Another gesture she used to characterize them was stiffened fingers and almost grotesquely bent wrists.

"Well," she was quoting herself again now and her gestures were refreshingly her own, "these pieces over here have no whipped cream."

"Oh, no," (the two women squeaked, waggled and gesticulated), "those aren't homemade. We couldn't have those."

"So they took two pieces of the homemade cake and, one after the other, they dumped the whipped cream in the sink! Can you imagine?"

Adelaide told me last year's big story about the lady who always liked real cream in her coffee and made a big fuss every time she was offered any of the synthetic powdered creams. So at their next gathering the hostess mixed up the powdered stuff with water beforehand and put it in a pitcher and the hoity toity lady was delighted. "Real cream! How wonderful! How delicious!"

But this year's story was clearly the winner.

"How could they do that?"

"Some of these people from the city think that we mountain folk have no upbringing at all," said Adelaide. ''They think once they get up here they can do just anything and we won't know the difference."

At last the cake came and Letty picked up her fork and we all ate the chocolate cake with the chocolate frosting and drank the tea And when that was through I had an almost ungovernable urge to lick my saucer or ask for another piece but I didn't.

SUBMARINE

There are two Missouri lakes visible from the Peak-to-Peak Highway, tiny things. If you put the two together, they'd still be a fraction of the size of Thoreau's Walden Pond. A little stream ripples past the school house and under the road through a pipe into the bigger one we call Missouri Lake. That empties into Little Missouri which is a stock pond for cattle, and that empties down a gully with a pretty waterfall and then it goes on down into Clear Creek. A nice little area and now there's a subdivision there.

But that's not all there is. Missouri Lake is a hotbed for legend. I suppose the reason is that it's bottomless. Over on the western side, it goes to about ten or twenty feet deep with a gentle enough slope, Then it drops off suddenly toward the middle and nearly to the bank on the southeast side to a depth beyond where anyone has been able to measure. You can buy any length of rope you'd like, tie a rock on one end and watch the rock pull the whole rope through your hands. They say the Indians had a legend of a dragon in there that came up every century or so for a bite to eat. I heard there were divers who went down in the Fifties with heavy diving gear and they got down a hundred feet or so and couldn't go any farther because the bottom curved into a downsloping tunnel they didn't dare go into.

23

Sure they found stuff, I heard that too, I heard they found a coach and four on a ledge at about fifty feet and left it down there, bag, baggage and bones. But there's no record of any coach falling in.

A lot of what you hear isn't true and a lot of what people scoff at is, so you never can be sure. And of course everyone knows that truth is stranger than fiction.

There used to be a stage stop at Missouri Lakes and the horses could water there after the long pull up the hill from Black Hawk.

People who have swum in it say it's cold enough in the shallow part but if you go out where it's got no bottom, a blast of cold hits you like you fell into the Arctic Ocean.

The strangest legend about Missouri Lake is the one about the submarine. And although everyone who might have remembered it is now dead and it never got into the newspaper back then, there's no denying that one. I've seen the submarine with my own eyes. It still exists, locked out of sight now in a shed in Central City.

In the Summer of 1942, someone in Black Hawk thought they'd try running a mill by water power with a siphon down from Missouri Lake. Naturally, the lake level went down and that Winter when the kids were skating in the protected cove where the wind didn't whiten over the surface of the ice, they saw below them a long massive shape, very mysterious.

In the Summer of 1943, Fred de Mandell got a couple people to dive down and see what that mysterious thing was and what it was was this. It was a cigar-shaped hulk about seventeen feet long coming to a point on each end. There was a round hole on the top, two metal bars sticking out on either side, one in front of the hole and one in back. And the thing was full to the brim of round river rocks. It was made of tin in strips neatly nailed with roofing nails to a curved wooden frame.

Fred de Mandell was fit to be tied. He ran a little museum and gift shop in Central City and he felt that this thing must be in his museum. I don't know when they realized it was a submarine. Fred had the men wrap chains around the hulk so that in Winter when the ice was thick, they could raise it straight out with a winch and he could have it as the prize of his collection.

The plan was to put an A-frame over the hulk, chop a big hole in thick ice, winch the thing straight up, then drag it with the winch across the ice to a flatbed truck and haul it down to Fred's shop to see what they had and what needed to be done.

It was the following January that they did it. The whole community knew about it, it was a festive occasion. John Jenkins the mayor was there, maybe forty or fifty people all told. And as the half dozen or so workers made sure everything was in good order, the high school band went through its entire repertoire, reserving "Columbia, The Gem Of The Ocean" for the emergence.

Fred de Mandell was a careful man. He had planned this out in every detail and in spite of the thing's tremendous weight, they pulled it up. The only hitch was that when it came out into the air there was a crunching sound that mixed in with "Columbia, The Gem Of The Ocean" and one of the chains did bite into the rotten old tin and boards but the men slid the thing carefully across the ice and onto the flatbed truck. Over the next few months, Fred got it put back into shape.

I don't know when and where they took out the river rocks but they estimated there were about four tons of them in the thing.

It was the following Summer that Fred got into trying to research what it was all about. Everyone was sure it was an experimental submarine. And obviously, it was old. There were foot pedals inside which might have been connected to the two horizontal bars so they'd turn and it seemed pretty clear that there had been fins on those bars that could turn and guide the submarine in the water. And eight long bolts protruded vertically, top and bottom. Who knew what they were for. But they found no engine.

Sometimes people get lucky. When Fred was asking around about it, an old guy he'd never seen before overheard him. "I knew the man who built it," the old guy said. "I knew him as well as anyone here did." And that afternoon, Fred got out of that old guy all that we know about the man who made the submarine. You know how there are times in history when there's something just crying to be invented and here and there all over the world,

certain people are having insomnia and struggling
in basements and wood sheds to invent it. That
happened with the telephone. Alexander Graham Bell
was just barely the first one to the patent
office. It happened with electricity too. There
was an amazing genius named Tesla in Colorado
Springs who discovered how to harness electricity.
He just didn't have business sense like Thomas
Edison did.

Well, the same thing was happening in the
late 1890s about submarines. Actually, the dream
of submarines had gone on for centuries. Robert
Fulton, the one who later invented the steamboat,
had gone so far as to submerge a small orchestra
in a submersible boat in 1856 which played the
Russian National Anthem under a few feet of water
in honor of the coronation of Tsar Alexander II
which was also going on that day. They say the
music could be heard on the bank.

A wheelwright in Suffolk named Day in the
1770s had, with the copious use of tar and
ballast, sunk himself thirty feet in Yarmouth
Harbor. He sat down there for twenty-four hours
and came up again, then got a local gambler named
Blake to stake him for a hundred-foot dive, ten
percent of the winnings, set himself up in a
converted fifty-ton sloop with a hammock, candles,
timepiece, biscuits and water, went down in
Plymouth Harbor and was never seen again.

Ben Johnson talks about one in the 1620s,
greased leather over a wooden frame, twelve rowers
and room for passengers. It was made by a man by
the name of Cornelius Drebble who had a mysterious

27

fluid in a bottle, a few drops of which could revitalize the air. (He carried the secret of the contents of the bottle to his grave and no one knows to this day what that fluid might have been.)

There was Bushnell's "Turtle" in the Revolutionary War whose crew tried to attach explosives to the "Eagle" but was thwarted by copper sheathing. There was the "Hunley" in the Civil War, propelled by manpower, which sunk The Housatonic and then, from damage caused by gunfire from The Housatonic, was lost with all hands. There were several steam-powered, ironclad "Davids" then, too.

But in the 1890s, there were people in Austria, Germany, England and the United States working on the submarine and every one of them was called crazy by his neighbors and one of them was named R. T. Owen and he lived in Central City.

Mr. Owen built his submarine in the back of a blacksmith shop on Eureka Street next door to McFarland's Foundry. It took him the better part of a year.

He was a quiet, retiring, secretive sort of guy and across that one Winter, while most of the other miners were scrounging and carousing, Mr. Owen was working away, hour after hour, week after week, soaking those boards and slowly bending them to shape, bolting them piece by perfectly curved piece to each other, getting together the metal parts, the metal bars, the fins, the foot-pedals, rimming out the hole on the top then trimming the tin to fit smooth, tacking it on with roofing nails, a dab of tar under each. A very tidy job he made of it, hundreds of nails close together like fine stitching on a quilt. Undoubtedly he made a cockpit too, the same slow care going into that as he had put into the rest of it. And whatever those vertical bolts might have been for.

Mr. Owen kept his own counsel. The old guy who talked with Fred de Mandell that day didn't think that Mr. Owen had ever gone down into Missouri Lake in his submarine. It may have been that after working with stolid determination and infinite care for most of a year, then one fine warm day he hauled it up the long hill by horse and wagon, stood on the bank of Missouri Lake there on the southeast side where the rock juts up and the cold cold water is deep beyond reckoning, stood there alone and a cold sweat seeped around his eyebrows and his legs went all wobbly and he knew that for all those months he had been working on nothing but his own elaborate coffin. It may have been that he decided not to do it. Practically everyone around here thinks he didn't do it and they could be right.

But there are things that bother me about that image. There is that eight thousand pounds of river rock hauled up that hill and carefully and exhaustively put into the sunken hulk until it was full. Fifteen feet down in the cold waters of Missouri Lake. How did he get that rock in there? He could, I suppose, with a whole lot of horses, and a structure similar to the one used to haul it out, have filled it on the bank and winched it out to where it was.

29

All I'm trying to say is that putting river rock in it took a lot of doing and seems to me to suggest he was preserving the submarine in the best way possible in the care of the best friend he had: Missouri Lake. And it says he considered it to be a valuable secret.

I think he went down once. For years I've tried to imagine him standing on that bank with his submarine gleaming in the sun beside him, a silent and secretive dreamer, all the tedious care he had put into it culminating in... chickening out at the last moment? No, his style would have been to get in the thing, to test it cautiously in the shallows first, test the seals and the fins and whatever else was in it and on it, whatever those eight vertical bolts were attached to or did. I'd imagine he knew how to swim.

I would concede that he might have contented himself with testing it in the shallows. He did, after all, survive.

OF THE UNKNOWN

Driving west, following the Sun, everything
Stan and I owned packed in the back of the station
wagon, level, blankets laid over smooth, the
cradle on top rocking the baby as we drove, the
dog beside. At night, we slept back there, put the
dog in the front seat. It wasn't too comfortable,
but it was cheap and we had time. We stayed on the
back roads, New Jersey to Colorado, took us two
weeks but there was privacy to sleep and eat and
nurse the baby. And we saw the country.

Following the Sun. We didn't even have a
map. If the road turned north, we'd take the next
left. Sometimes we'd end up at a farmhouse and
have to go back.

There was one road, dirt. We did dirt roads,
lots of them. This turned out to be one of those
roads that start out wide and solid and dribble
down to nothing in a couple of miles or so. It was
two or three days along, somewhere in
Pennsylvania. We weren't sleeping well. The night
before had been particularly bad. We had pulled
over at a kind of turn around place between farms
and somehow a cop had materialized, empty road and
a cop shows up. We had cooked a can of beans or
something on the camp stove and I was sitting in
the back on the blankets nursing the baby. He
shined his flashlight on me. I was trying with my
long hair to cover my socially unacceptable naked
breast that the baby was working on, and to make

31

an innocent face as I was being blinded by his flashlight beam. "It's not a good neighborhood right now," he told us. "I want you to move out of here early in the morning. You can stay here," he said, "for tonight, but be long gone by ten in the morning." We couldn't get an explanation out of him. We slept badly that night and we didn't dawdle comfortably over breakfast as we liked to do. When we started out that morning, we felt not so much like we were going west but that we were wandering through an indistinguishable maze of undefined wickedness.

And then it developed into one of those real hot days. That's one thing I've never been able to cope with is heat, and this day was one of those days that are so hot they seem to buzz. I suppose maybe it's insects, but no, I think it's the heat that makes it buzz. About noon, we took that dirt road and went along a few miles through vegetation so lush and wild it seemed almost a jungle and then the road, as I said before, dribbled down to nothing, finished up in a little clearing. I think there was a quarry over at the other end. We didn't get out of the car to look. Even the dog didn't want to get out to take a leak. We put together some bread and cheese and ate it there in the front seat and after we finished we both felt a horrible lassitude, almost as though the bread and cheese had been drugged, which I guarantee it wasn't.

We slept.

I woke with a feeling of gnawing terror, looked at Stan who had just then awakened and his face was tense and pale with sweat shining on it. The dog was crouching silent and stiff on the front seat. I looked into the cradle. The baby was lying there wide-eyed and still. Babies don't usually lie still when they're awake. They're usually waving and kicking and chattering at best, but she was lying wide eyed and still. If my terror was from a nightmare, we had all had it and we were none of us making a sound.

I looked around the clearing. The light had changed. It was mid-afternoon. The buzzing of heat had stopped. No bird sang. No insect chirred. There was no breeze. It was silent. There seemed to be a thickness to the air, a blue-gray shimmer filling the clearing.

Together, Stan and I lifted the trembling dog onto the blankets in the back. He wouldn't move by himself. The station wagon was not an easy car to start, never had been. I don't know how many times we'd had to call old Mr. Schwing mornings back in New Jersey to come and start it for us. For a moment we sat, Stan behind the wheel, his foot poised over the starter, and we were thinking about two things, one that Mr. Schwing was not available to start the car, and the other that as soon as Stan stepped on that starter, it was going to make a noise and we both felt, sweat pouring now down our faces, that silence was our only way to buy time. The blue-gray shimmer was getting thicker. Breathing was becoming difficult. Two branches across the way jerked. Gnashing his teeth together, Stan stepped on the starter.

I jumped at the sound and looked wildly around the clearing. The same two branches jerked again. The dog stared at them, his eyes glazed. Stan tried again. I watched the branches, too. The air developed a yellowish tinge and seemed to be quivering with the expectation of something about to happen. On the third try, the car started. It was difficult backing around. There was the slope of the ground in the beginning and Stan's sweating hands slipping on the wheel. There was the mud puddle which almost dumped us in the gully and, when it failed at that, nearly succeeded in stalling the car. We made it around then and drove into the green-black depths of the jungle-like vegetation. Strangely, as soon as we crossed the edge of the clearing and entered the forest, our fears disappeared. The dog licked my ear and sighed. The baby commenced to whimper and I brought her up into the front seat. We opened the windows. Sun flickered through the branches onto the windshield. A light breeze brought the scent of flowers and rich earth. We were away.

VERA'S MEN

When Vera came from Kansas to visit her sister Annie Murray, everybody could see she was a good-looking girl and everybody knew beforehand that she was unmarried. Now, although there were a number of unmarried men about, the most eligible bachelor in the Gulch was Tom Gill. Jesse Williams, who concerned himself with such matters, couldn't resist playing cupid so he announced that he was going to have a dance at his house. He got Annie and her husband Jim to play, Annie on the organ and Jim on the guitar and, people being shy as they were here then, when Jesse saw both Vera and Tom sitting out, he sent them to the kitchen to make sandwiches so they might get acquainted in their own way.

Tom Gill was ruddy, handsome and energetic almost to the point of being blustery. He knew what Jesse was up to and although he appreciated the opportunity to meet Vera, he expressed his embarrassment by strutting and stomping around the kitchen in a most boisterous manner. Vera found him too cocky for her taste as she told her sister Annie the next day.

But Jesse hadn't figured on getting them to the wedding bell stage in one evening so he threw another party and another, he kept having parties and as often as he could, he put the two of them together one way or another and after a while even though Tom drank too much, Vera felt he was worth saving and she went to work to stop his drinking. To do this, she had to keep an eye on him so she consented to go out with him and by the time the snow was falling off the roofs in great thundering hunks in the Spring, Tom and Vera were very much in love and got married.

The love between Vera and Tom became legend from Nevadaville to Nederland, partly because they were such a handsome couple but also because they never could seem to keep their hands or their minds off each other and Tom, who had been as heavy a drinker as anyone, didn't drink a drop after the wedding.

Several years went by and though they never had any children, Tom and Vera were as close as ever if not a good deal closer. Tom was working in the Hoboken Mine up on Baldy above the War Eagle and in the morning, before he'd leave, he'd always take Vera in his arms and give her a big goodbye kiss. But one morning, whether one of them was tied up doing something or he was late or what it was nobody remembers, but the fact is he didn't kiss her goodbye and he set off into the snow and half an hour later he was back and he gave her a big kiss and went to work late. And that day in the mine Tom Gill, although he was not yet forty years old, had a heart attack and died before they could even get him out of the mine.

You can imagine how bad it was for Vera and pretty soon she went to Illinois to live with some relatives she had back there but she couldn't stand it and after a few months she wrote to her sister Annie and said she was coming back here and when to meet her at the train in Rollinsville. As it happened, Annie couldn't meet the train nor could her husband Jim but a young fellow named Mike Neal was able to go. He had arrived in the area about the time Tom Gill died so he got the full force of the legend of Tom and Vera's love and the horror of his death without ever actually meeting either of them. Mike was a sweet and gentle guy, a good steady worker, not a drinker at all, and when Vera stepped off that train, small, slim, strong, her dark hair piled high above eyes filled with grief mixed with a powerful will, Mike Neal fell in love.

Vera didn't think anything about him at all but he courted her slow and proper until she at last had to acknowledge that he was doing so and finally he came to her and said, "I know you'll never love me like you did Tom Gill but I love you and I'm a good man and if you'll consent to be my wife, I'll be a good husband to you."

Vera married Mike Neal and they both lived happily into their nineties. Vera always said she'd married the two finest men she'd ever met.

HOW JOEY FELL IN

Willard C_____ was a strange fellow.
Very often it was his fault and he wasn't blamed
and sometimes he was blamed and hadn't done
anything but this time there seemed to be no mix-
up, he was totally to blame and everyone knew it.
But they all slapped him on the back for it with a
big smile so it came out backwards anyway.

What it all started with was when Joe Greene
gave Willard a homing pigeon that he'd brought
from Nebraska and Willard and his brother Joey
were going to use her to send messages back and
forth between the house and the Hoboken Mine.
Willard was carrying her under his arm when he
went out that morning to the outhouse. Now at that
time, the outhouse didn't have a seat, just a bar,
so the pit was open. Later they put a seat there,
a real nice four-holer, but just then it was a
bar. There was no problem with a bar at all, one
could do everything that was necessary with no
trouble and sprinkle the lime on with more
accuracy than when the seat got built so there
wasn't a smell problem either.

So, it was a bar, and when Willard went to
unzip, the pigeon slipped out from under his arm
and went down in. Happily Joey wasn't far away and
came running when Willard called but they looked
in and the pigeon was a sad sight, she was mucky
with dabs of the morning's collection and in an
effort to rise out of the slime she was beating

her wings as fast as she could, whacking them on the sides of the hole and raising a thick cloud of lime. Whether the bird was going to die of breathing that cloud or breaking her wings or of simple disgust was hard to say but that she was in a desperate situation was clear to both Willard and Joey and they decided that Willard should hold Joey's feet as Joey went in headfirst after the bird.

Then, as Willard lowered Joey in, the pigeon managed to struggle her way up the shaft and Willard, seeing his valuable pet getting away, made a grab for the bird and dropped Joey as he was into the mire.

And thus it was that no one was watching as the pigeon circled higher and higher cooing as she went, then getting her bearings, headed back to her home in Nebraska.

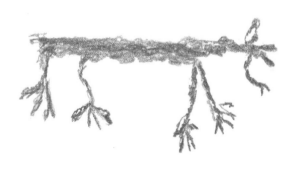

WHY DON'T I WRITE?

I want all my writing to be jewels. In fact, I feel that any book I write would be only a straw on the flood. No book, no body of work, could affect the progress of civilization. It would be like crying out, "Be reasonable!" to six billion stampeding, red-eyed buffaloes.

I think that the realization that books have degenerated, even across these few decades of my life since the 1930s discourages me. I fear that books are soon to become as obsolete as carriages. Reading has always been an odd, constrictive, mind-rattling set of eye movements. But it seems unthinkable that books would ever become obsolete because we've all been trained to read. I suppose we'll have to go on reading from the computers, but Ivanhoe and Winesburg, Ohio become mere history, exotic, irrelevant, and tame beyond meaning to a sedentary urban people accustomed to tremendous speeds and enclosed space.

"What do you do in the mountains all day?" people ask. "Oh," I say, "I chop wood, dig outhouse holes, haul things about, hike, feed the birds, talk on the ham radio. And I read a lot." I don't include writing in this list, because I've not been writing ... even though I've been saying over and over that if I don't write, I'll die or crack up. But my mountain activities are delightful. I get outside a lot. My muscles are strong. In the winter I ski or snowshoe. It's pleasant to watch the sun go across the sky, the birds swirling around me. And I keep close tabs on the moon.

"Don't you think it's time," my income tax man said, "to quit calling yourself a writer?" He was desperate. I hadn't made a cent from writing for over a year. And added to that, I haven't been writing.

I have such a lovely book to write. Two lovely books. I keep all my notes in milk crates. Then there are the other books I've already written. But the taxman's viewpoint is that if the stuff stays in the milkcrates, it's not a profession but a hobby. And I can see his point. What earthly interest would it be to the Internal Revenue Service that I fill milk crates with writings? "Prove yourself!" says Society. I have milk crates full of proof. For a while I papered the wall with rejection slips till the sight palled. Did I say I could sell? Selling is not the same as writing.

"Are you ready to die?" the man asked as his fist crashed onto my mouth. "Are you ready to die?" He kicked me violently in the abdomen. A relevant question. Have I given up on that project-my life, my writing, my perspective? Why am I asking these questions in this tone of voice? Why am I in this position? Why did that man beat me up?

There is no way I can persuade myself into writing to sell. Writing is hard, soul-searching work. Writing to sell would have to be tucking bits of articulate wisdom into a lot of pap. Like worm pills in the dog food.

Look at Emily Dickinson. Look at Jane Austen. They had sisters who demanded excellent writing out of them constantly. But they died middle-aged. I am middle-aged. Maybe in some ways having a sister to care and listen is unhealthy. Limiting. Maybe one comes to a place where one either dies or goes on starkly alone into an area of the mind which could be profound or could be insane, it seems very hard to tell the difference.

I could, yes, join the local support group of writing ladies who wouldn't dream of saying anything bad and are (as I would be also) only there to be heard anyway. I could make another big push, clean up several old manuscripts and search again for an outlet, collect a few more rejections. I could tour America again living in my economy car and demand that friends set up readings. I could get involved with a man or some other project and try to forget about writing. I could simply get to work here, keep filling those milk crates.

I should write like a dairy animal produces milk or as a rosebush blooms, to fulfill my being. I should write because there are things in me crying to be articulated.

The reason I don't write is because I suspect that what I write will be jeered off the playground as I was as a child on those rare occasions when I got others' attention. Too odd. Not with it. From Elsewhere. "Keep out of our way!" I don't write because if I present my writing and succeed, I expect to be trampled by the other kids.

Once I went, sad and alone, to the zoo. I had heard of wolves looking into the eyes of prospective meals to see if it was their "time to die." And there in the zoo was an exquisitely beautiful black-maned lion who looked into my eyes. And immediately I realized that this was the test. His wondrous wild calculating eyes told me to jump! To run! To flee his unquestionable murderous power so that he would have the delight, the satisfaction, of the pounce.

I stood my ground. There was, I admit, glass between us which gave me courage. I dove into those great joyous killer eyes in which the love of killing and the love of life were one. Fire and ice were one. And in those eyes I struggled for life. And watched that magnificent creature amicably struggling for my death. Not kindly, but hopefully, he let me study his eyes for many seconds. Then I saw his developing discouragement as I refused to give him the game. "You're no fun," he seemed to say. He turned away from me with an appearance of disgust. I tried to catch his attention again. I loved him, loved his murderous vitality. But he had no use for me. He turned his back on me. Rejected me. I had won the stare. I was not yet ready to die. Perhaps, if I want to write -- and I do -- and to write well and a lot, I should create a fantasy. Instead of considering Society as six billion stampeding red-eyed buffaloes, I should consider it to be a great black-maned lion with wild eyes of fire and ice. I should persuade myself that, sometime, that lion will come to my milk crates, and whatever's in them he will take into himself, and it will become part of him and part of the future. And I should prepare the contents of the milk crates for that encounter.

PILGRIMAGE (LONG'S PEAK)

I remember driving to the foot of the mountain shortly after dawn and coming to a curve in the road where there was a good view of it, massive, majestic, magnificent. "We're going to climb THAT?" I thought, "Lord save us." But there was the parking lot, full, the big sign and the path into the woods. Hundreds, maybe thousands of people climbed it every year. Sort of a twentieth Century pilgrimage, backpacker-style, a test of strength and nerve in a place where the world can only be admired.

There wasn't much to speak of below timberline. There was the path, well-trod, the tunnel of trees, there were flowers and birds, and people, pleasant, greeting us, quite a few of them coming down in the afternoon as we were going up. We strolled up the path all day.

Toward the end of that first day, the sun long gone behind the mountain but the light still strong, we came to timberline and looked up over snow-patches pink with algae, at tiny clumps of gnarled Lilliputian trees, on up to the massive rock face still above us. An immense dragonfly came and landed on someone's arm and we gathered 'round to look at it. It glowed with luminous green, blue, rust and orange, it had huge eyes, it was bigger than my hand and I bent down to look into its face, a gentle wild fearless face with no sense in it of what we were. Its huge delicate

45

wings quivered rainbows. People coming by stopped to look, then passed on. A long time it honored us with its presence and its beauty. I wondered if it knew we were alive. It seemed to emanate concerns and attitudes that at first I called innocence but then realized that in saying that, I was only saying it was not human.

One of us knew of a good place where we camped above timberline, and when the light faded the cold crept on us all. We huddled into our bags and soon slept. The stars hung over us thick and gaudy. Soon after sunrise we were off. Other people all over the mountain were moving also. The day was, for that altitude, balmy.

The boulder field was full of people waking up, readying themselves to go on to the top. Marmots were begging handouts, their rodent whistles sounding shrilly in the clear thin air. I was amazed at the mass of people, and amazed at how I then accepted them. This was not solitude in the wilderness. The people, however, were all smiling and excited and I didn't mind them too much.

We decided to separate and go at different paces. None of us would be isolated -- there were so many people. Anyway, I walk slowly up mountains. By the time I got to the cleft between two rocks called The Keyhole, the others were far ahead on a crumbly dirt path that wavered across a slope that would have been too steep for trees even if it were below timberline. I stood shocked in The Keyhole. The view was magnificent: mighty mountains gleamed in the early morning sun,

misting into the distance in every direction. The
steep slope in front of me, occasionally dotted
with pillaring boulders, cut across by the thin
gray path, with a few people strung out on it, was
uninviting in the extreme. Although the air was
cold, my hands were crawling with sweat.

I have lived in these mountains for thirty
years and my fear of heights has grown over those
years as deeply entrenched in me as my love of
their magnificence, their awesome richness and
vitality, their unfathomable mysteries. Why the
fear has grown along with the rest, I don't quite
know. Across those years I have seen again and
again the pitiless harshness of mountains. "One
false move and you're dead," the mountains say,
often. And this mountain was saying it now.

It was shame, I think, vanity, which made me
step out onto the path at last. All these city
people were walking out onto it bravely. Or was it
fearlessly? I stepped out fearfully, pulled my
eyes away from the mountains across the way, the
depth of the gorge below, and the towering heights
above me that I was this day supposed to climb to
the top. I narrowed my vision to the path before
me and walked slowly and with care. Fear caused my
heart to race and my pace slowed to balance it.

Perhaps around the bend the mountain
wouldn't be so steep. No, the next bend revealed a
face just as steep as the previous one. And the
next and the next. People passed me cheerily. I
found I was clutching rocks as I went. Going from
one rock to the next. I was sweating all over with
fear now. What were these people made of that they

47

were so cheery? I smiled wanly at them. I chose
grim determination to keep me going. One step
after the other, on and on up this gray path. My
daughter up ahead, who today for the first time
had passed me by on a mountain, walked along this
tortuous path with surefooted delight. My little
half-grown nephew had said, "This is the sixth
time I've been up here and it's boring, boring."
Ah, if I could have such boredom, I could have
pride with it; I could raise my eyes to look
around me.

At the base of a big rock I saw a small
hole, the entrance to a burrow a few inches
across, a tiny path leading out from it. "Pika," I
thought. I dibbled a few sunflower seeds in front
of the hole, backed away and sat on a rock looking
intensely at it. "Here," I thought, "is someone I
could believe if he'll come out and speak to me."
In a few seconds he came out, ignoring my
offering, running across the seeds to another rock
near me. He sat on top of his rock as I was
sitting on top of mine, and he gazed across the
gorge with a look of warm contentment. "All my
life I've lived here," he seemed to be saying.
"All seasons, all days, wind, sun, raging
blizzard. I was an infant here and I have raised
infants here. This is my home and that is my
view." Tremulously but obediently, I raised my
eyes from the comfort of his self-assured posture
on the rock to the heady task of looking at his
view.

Magnificence beyond measure. Sunlit mountain
peaks misting into infinity, massive earth rising

rocky and wild above trees, above clouds.
Mountains upon mountains, earth blatantly showing
itself supreme, powers even greater than life
itself. The gorge below now so deep it was purple
with the mass of thin air between us and the
bottom. Lakes glittered down there, stringing out,
amoeboid. I imagined marshland with beavers. I
imagined being down there, the air damp, looking
up and seeing the great mountain above me. I
imagined being down there imagining I was up here,
sitting with a pika, on my way to the top. How
grand it all was, what a blessing to be alive. I
looked back at the pika. "It is an honor to live,"
he seemed to be saying.

     There was more he could tell me, much more,
and my mind was whirling to find a question to ask
him, but the sound of muttering voices behind me
distracted me, footsteps approached. The pika
heard them too and dashed into his hole.

     I went up the mountain with a sense of pride
in myself and in the mountain but still I was
clinging to rocks. The gray dirt path sloped on
and on. Again, to keep my balance, I looked only
at the ground a few feet ahead of me. Foot by
foot, I progressed. People passed me cheerily,
sympathetically, encouragingly. They all seemed to
be nice people and they were all going along
better than I. I wanted to be superior to them
because I lived in the mountains, but in this
situation I seemed inferior. But I would not turn
back. If I turned back, how could I face a
mountain again? Or a pika? Or myself? I laughed
dryly inside myself to think that the only way to

honor was through the hypocrisy of not acting on my true feeling, which was terror.

Well over an hour I was going along this path, and at every turn it stretched across a steeper, sheerer slope. Three times I came to places where I had to scramble, dangling over space, and all three times there were smiling people there to help me across. One of them, his back muscles swelling under my terrified clutching hands, I remember clinging to a second longer than I should have, fervently wishing that he'd help me along the rest of the way.

The path ended at the bottom of a rockslide and I stood in astonishment watching people clambering up the slide. Must I do this? I told myself I must. Going up the bottom of the slide on hands and feet, I dodged pebbles rolled down inadvertently by others above me. I remembered a hilarious sequence in a Buster Keaton movie when he dodged and danced magnificently up an avalanche of enormous boulders. I sneered at myself as I crawled up, moving timorously aside as a runnel of pebbles rolled down beside me.

I was in fact trembling in the temporary and unsure safety of the downhill shadow of a large stationary boulder when I heard a woman above me screaming. Peeking around my boulder, I saw her walking down, two men attending her. It was a perfect example of hysteria. She was sobbing, throwing her head and arms around wildly, shouting things like "This is horrible!" "I don't have to do this!" as the two men helped her down. Cowering behind my boulder I watched her, envy rumbling in my gut like hunger. Everything she shrieked was true. She was the small boy in the story of The Emperor's New Clothes, who said, "He's naked!"

Nonetheless, her decision, for so I'll call it, could not be mine. Her feelings were much like mine. How I would have loved to have two strong men solicitously hand me down the mountain. But as I cowered there, I saw her future. The men who were helping her would not honor her. She had chosen the truth of the fear within herself above the truth of the glory of the mountain. Fear is true, but also true are the home and the view of the pika. Such a confusion of contradictoriness is truth. She must have been one of those who overtook and passed me smiling, I thought, maybe the one with the big receptionist's smile that had looked so incongruous. I couldn't tell. She wasn't smiling now.

The main thing was, I didn't want to allow my fears to govern my life. I wanted to be led more by admiring, even hopefully by understanding the world, rather than by the anguishes of internal imaginings. Finally, in spite of the obvious truths she was saying, she had, it seemed to me, lost touch with the ground she walked on. Cowering as I was, I chose against her choice. The mountain was too important to me to reject it. There was no way to conquer it. Any mountain climber knows that, though few say it. The thing I was doing or trying to do, and I suspect so were the others, was to be able to think and see and love through the fear, in spite of it. I had no problem acknowledging the fear. But what I wanted

51

to do, and what was harder, was to acknowledge the mountain.

As the sound of her cries dimmed around the bend, I went on up the rockslide, now worrying about both being hit by rocks coming down and setting them rolling myself. I was amazed to see that everyone around me was walking upright while I was on hands and feet. But I didn't care if I looked funny.

At last I got to the top of the slide. The only way to go on was through another slot between rocks. People were there, peeking through and admiring the view. I joined them. It was an incredible sight. The world was there spread out, miles of mountains and valleys reaching south, the Continental Divide curving down through them like the backbone of a living thing, vast and magical. "I live there," I said. The plains lay eastward misting smooth and immense. Could I see the curve of the earth or was I imagining it? I could see Denver, a cluster of tiny jags off to the south, smaller towns, too, scattered across the plains. From here, they seemed miniscule but interesting, worth exploring. There was Pike's Peak, miles and miles to the south, Arapahoe, distinguishable by its smoothness among its jagged companions, Mt. Evans, looking from here inconsequential.

The mountain on this side was no longer a steep slope. It was a sheer cliff. The path ahead was a narrow shelf in a nearly flat rock that plummeted several thousand feet. I couldn't believe I was expected to walk on that. I stood there awhile seeing others step out onto it and walk till they were lost to my sight around the bend. Beside me a small boy about nine years old looked at it and whimpered. His father said, "We can make it." An old man came up and stood, his back straight, eyes gleaming. "I'm 76 years old," he said, "and this is the tenth time I've been up here." He stood awhile proudly, catching his breath. The air was very thin here. No matter how long I stood, there would be no way to stop gasping for breath. But the thinness of the air only accentuated the fact of that shelf. The old man walked smartly out onto it. I followed, pressing my sweaty hands to the rock face.

Around the bend, the shelf narrowed. The old man was nearly out of sight ahead of me. Fear made my legs wobble. The dearth of oxygen in the air didn't help. The shelf was not steeply rising but the trembling weakness of my own body caused me again to resort to all fours. Looking only at the narrow span of rock between my hands, I crawled blindly along. Tears came to my eyes and dripped down onto the rock where I was looking and I crawled on over them. ''This shelf couldn't well go much farther," I remember thinking. "Shelves on cliffs don't usually go more than a few yards." But this one went on and on. And on and on I crawled, my vision staying between my hands. Then my head bumped against rock. I looked up. Sure enough, the shelf ended right there. A rock face was there and I could go no farther. I looked at it in amazement. There was no mistake about it. The shelf ended.

The rock from there on was smooth and perpendicular.

I think at that point, I nearly fainted. Or it may have been the lack of oxygen that caused me to be unable to answer, or even ask, where all the people had gone that had been ahead of me. I may have stayed there on hands and knees for some time, I don't know. But I was awakened to the sound of a child whining, a man's voice murmuring below me. I looked down and there was the nine-year-old boy and his father on a path below me. I had taken a wrong turn, gone up a dead end. They passed me and the father glanced up briefly at me, then looked quickly back at the shelf he was walking on, whether in embarrassment at my insane plight or in care for his footing I don't know.

There was no way for me to turn around. I had no desire to stand. I realized I would have to crawl backwards the length of the blind path. The fact that the whimpering child was ahead of me, and doing much better than I, increased my determination to go on. As long as that child went up, I was going up also. "Come on," I heard the father's voice say. ''You can do it."

I did it. I crawled backwards for yards and yards, dry-eyed now across my evaporated tears. Then I stood up on the path and walked after that boy and his father.

The shelf went amazingly on and on and on around the peak. At every bend I first yearned for something less horrifying, then came to see that it continued just as it was. Slowly, agonizingly, I walked on, my hands pressed against the wall.

Some people passed me in places where there was a
slight widening, their bodies swinging seemingly
fearlessly out over the abyss. Things went through
my mind. I recalled a sequence from a Jean Cocteau
film in which the hero crawls clutching along a
wall. I remembered that I had heard someone say,
"Hardly anyone falls down this mountain, though
several have frozen to death up here." I realized
that every step I took up, I would have to take
down again. And what would I do if the wind
started to blow? After the shelf, they had said,
would be the home stretch. I wondered what that
would be like.

    I came to a point then where there was a
confusion. The wall beside me slanted away from
the perpendicular, there was another rockslide
ahead of me, and there was no path, no shelf
anywhere. A man crawled up beside me from the
abyss below me, panting, his face rosy. "Where, in
God's name, did you come from?" I demanded. "South
face," he said, blowing. Someone else crawled up
after him and then a third. I gazed down. It was
too steep even to see the rock face over the edge.
"It can't be done," I said. "Oh," he waved his
hand deprecatingly, pride in his eyes, "lots of
people do it." Then the three of them scampered up
smooth rock beside me and I watched them going
impossibly, gracefully, carefully, and strongly
up. There, several hundred feet up, was the top,
turreted with massive boulders upon which people
were standing or sitting, eating sandwiches. And
I, of course, was to scamper up also and join
them. The home stretch.

It wasn't perpendicular, I grant that. That it was steep, however, no one could deny. Nor could anyone deny that it was smooth, that it lacked hand or foot holds in some places where it was the steepest. I looked it over in dismay. There was a sort of cranny maybe halfway up. I was now looking for anything I could clutch. If I could get to that cranny, I could lie in it and clutch it for a little while and feel, for a few yearned for moments, safe. Back on my hands now, though not my knees, with my feet straining all over the rock for tiny holds to push me, often on my belly, with my canteen clanking beside me, the buttons of my jacket scraping between me and the mountain. Foot by foot I wriggled till I came to the cranny at last and clung to it intensely like an infant to its mother.

Something called my eye upward and there, hanging above me like a nightmare kite, was a man ape shape, backlit against the brilliant sky, arms dangling. It leaped and cavorted about on the sheer rock above me like a monkey raging gloriously in a tree. I clung to my niche and watched in open-mouthed shock as this image of primate ecstasy joyed toward me and appeared, as he came nearer, to be a young man in a shabby jacket, his healthy face glowing in a glory of unabashed happiness. What my face expressed to him I can't imagine, but as he got closer to me, he smiled at me, danced a complete circle around me as I lay there and said, "just call me your friendly neighborhood Spiderman." I may have laughed, I don't know. I do remember asking him where he got his boots. "Salvation Army," he said, gaily. ''Ten dollars!" And, his arms waving, hair flying, he cavorted away down the cliff and vanished around a boulder.

Soon after that, I left my cranny and crept and slithered up where the Spiderman had danced down. My daughter, my bored nephew, all of them were there. "We were worried about you," they said. "What took you so long?"

''Terror," I said. "It slows one down."

I remember, on the way down, through the tunnel of trees, smiling at people who were heading up like those others had smiled at me when I was heading up. I kept saying to myself over and over, "I don't ever want to do that again.""I must remember never to go back up there." I suppose I knew I would some day have this mad desire to climb that mountain again. It was such an intense experience.

SAYING HI TO MOON

Lots of times I talk with him. Especially when he gets big and I can see the expression on his face. "Hi, Moon!" I say, so happy to see him always, "What's up?"

And I focus quickly on his expression and he tells me what's coming along in my life. It seems like he likes me particularly, or he wouldn't show sympathy like that. The subtlety and diversity of his expression amazes me. He achieves it with rock . . . light . . . air (humidity, barometric pressure, pollutants) . . . and my psychological state.

Or is it me projecting psychic knowledge on an inanimate object?

November I spent in the desert and I watched the phases, how he grew a little every day. Or shrunk. How he always rose a little later. Mostly he doesn't speak. No need. But one night that November he blurted out at me, "I'm mortal too!" Then he whispered, "I will die someday!"

I understood. I wept. For him. For him sorrowing at my death and the deaths of others he knew and loved across millenia as I have known and loved dogs, goats, birds, flowers. Each one gone now. "Your goat, Tree, thought you were immortal," he said.

"Was she wrong? What is Truth?" I asked him.

"Which perspective would you like?" he
asked. "Until now you thought I was immortal."
We stared at each other tenderly.

TALKING WITH DRUMS:

CW's* Ragchewing* Side, By AAØZR*

(There is a glossary at end of story!)

Even on my dear old 2W* HW8* which was my base rig for the first five years of my ham radio life, I ragchewed a lot. My QTH* is a tiny cabin in the mountains with only a couple of solar panels to keep the radios going. I ragchewed from 5wpm* to 13wpm - using the little straight key given to me by NØBLU*, the one he had learned on at the age of twelve. "One QSO* a day and you'll be up to 20wpm in a year," said Tom, N2CO, who sold me the HW8 in 1991.

My CW learning was done alone and vigorously. Springs would fly. So that when I emerged in the Colorado QRP* Club as Charter Member Number 9, when my call was KBØHPH, they watched my keying and laughed. They called me "The Hammer." Bill, K5IMP, made a workable key out of an actual carpenter's hammer and they presented it to me in a grand ceremony. A picture was taken and I got into QST's* Forum in September of 1996.

CW is so fun. Even at 5wpm with the sweat running down your brow from the effort, there's the achievement itself and the blatant magic of radio - "Oh! His name is John! He lives in Dallas! And I'm 559*! I wonder what he looks like? What he does for a living?" As the speed increases, so also do the possibilities of finding out about each other.

One friend I made at this time was Wes, KEØNH. With Lou Gehrig's disease and other complications, he lived in a wheelchair and was often having medical emergencies. At one point for several months, he was unable to talk so Larry, NFØZ, put together a gadget which would allow Wes to do CW at 25wpm and the words would come up in a little window attached to the handle of his wheelchair. Thus he could talk with the nurses, and with slow-code friends like me when we'd visit.

I'll never forget my first great ragchew at 13wpm when I could finally talk about the pain and horror of divorce. Using CW, one is obliged to be succinct. Blather has no place in CW. And so there's a clarity that can be found nowhere else. With that ragchew, I realized that real communication could happen in CW. And it was then that I determined to increase my speed.

And Larry, NFØZ, was my Elmer* for CW speed. Sparkling humor and fascinating info would rattle rhythmically at 13wpm, slowly increasing to 15wpm. Then one day he said at 15wpm, "I'm going to 20 now." "Well, make it short," I said, in considerable terror. And I listened with everything I had. And I copied* it.

"What's your favorite flavor of ice cream?" he asked at 20wpm.

And I cannot describe to you the pride and joy with which I answered -- at 15wpm -- "Double chocolate." It was like receiving a medal.

After that, a world opened up that I could hardly believe. Calling CQ* at 25wpm is asking to speak with people who have been through a lot of trouble to learn this form of communication -- for whatever reason.

Some of the best fists* are WWII vets:
"Where were you stationed?"
"Guam."
"What was Guam like?"
"Hot, and lots of bullets."

I'll never forget talking with a Lakota Indian named Chuck in California who seemed to be wheelchair-bound. "When the bands are bad, I do beadwork," he said. I asked him about the great porcupine quill patterns in the Lakota tradition and he was pleased that I knew about that. He also had a friend who was setting up a solar house in Colorado. When the band changed and I lost him, I about cried.

There was a fascinating guy in Canada who, after a long and delightful CW QSO, informed me that he had a degenerating condition of the ears so that now he could hear and converse only in CW.

One of my most interesting single QSOs was with a man who owned a fishing boat in the North Pacific (the antenna up the backstays, of course). He loved the ocean and cared a lot about sea life so he had worked for a while for Greenpeace, but it was too scary, he had to stop.

I've been a member of a weekly sked* for a few years now. Every week a few of us get together on 80m* and gab about whatever is going on in our lives. It was on that sked that I was given complicated instructions to a picnic at 20wpm and got there on time. Then I knew I could copy code.

That sked has taught me too some of the ethics and graces of CW that keep good CW ops* from bumping into each other. Good manners take time to learn and good manners are a lot of what differentiates ham radio from the free-for-all of CB.

Some other friends I've made on CW I've met again and again and gotten to know them. It began, I think, when I was driving up the East Coast and found myself on a ferry going to Cape Hatteras. Naturally, true ham that I am, I spent the entire boat trip in my car, calling CQ and signing AA0ZR/MM* -- something I 'd always dreamed of doing -- and I gabbed the whole two hours, with half a dozen or so different hams. And at least three of those hams kept track of me on the rest of my trip -- we still keep in touch.

When the ferry docked at Ocracoke and I got out of my car, a man in a car near me asked how fast I was going? He had World War II written all over him. Big smiles.

"About 25," I said.

"A bit too fast for me," he said, "but I could tell you were just having a lot of fun."

"Oh gosh," I said, still aglow with all my new friends, "If I'd known you were listening, I'd have slowed down!"

The personality shines out through the fist. I learned the bug* partly because of the wonderful musicality of AI8Z Mike's fist with the bug but I now stick with the keyer* because I can go faster on the paddle*. I feared I 'd lose my fist, my identity, with it, but somehow a lot of personality still shows through. I can tell Tom W6XF of Reno NV from Jim WIXU of Payson, AZ within seconds, even if they're going 40 wpm talking to each other. (I can't send at 40 yet. Although my ear can often differentiate the dits, my hand can't.) The cleanest fist I know I think is Mike of Tucson, N7FC. Next time I find him on 30m, I'll have to ask him if he plays the drums.

I've always thought of it as talking with the drums, ever since I first heard it, slow and smooth and a fantastic rhythm, on my HW8. CW seems to me to reach straight to the heart and straight back to pre-history when information was sent across the land via drums and beacon fires. But with ham radio, and good CW ops, the drumming flies around the world.

A lot of the joy of CW is musical.

Sometimes it feels like flying. Often, after a good QSO, I think of all the 'no-code Extras'* I know, and wonder how many E-glets* just sit on the edge of the nest and never spread their wings to learn how to fly!*

TALKING WITH DRUMS:

Glossary for "Talking With Drums"

CW - stands for 'continuous wave,' a misnomer for Morse code.

Ragchewing - gabbing; casual conversation. Particularly in Morse code. Some ragchewers go on for hours.

AA0ZR - This is my ham radio license moniker or 'call sign.' We are distinguished by our call signs and are supposed to 'ID' with them about every ten minutes.

0- zero. The line across shows it's not an 'O' but a 'zero.'

2W - Two watts. Try to imagine that in a light bulb.

HW8 - a low-power four-band radio sold as a kit during the 1960s.

QTH - location. In this case, my home station location.

wpm - words per minute.

Straight key - a Morse code key that you tap for each dit and dah.

N0BLU - Another ham 'call.' Naturally, everyone calls him 'Blue.'

QSO - conversation.

QRP - low power (i.e. under five watts output power). Such a rig can broadcast around the world but it takes finesse, a good antenna, a good location, and luck.

QST - (means 'attention all hams!') the big ham radio magazine.

559 - a measure of readability, signal strength, and tone. The best of all signal reports is '599,' so the central number '5' instead of '9' shows that my signal strength is weak, although the other two numbers show that tone and readability are just fine.

Elmer - tutor in ham radio.

Copied - received and understood.

Calling CQ - CQ means 'I'm seeking you'- 'you' being anyone who's listening. It's a general call for a QSO with anyone who can hear you.

Fists - each person doing Morse code sounds different from every other and that recognizable difference is called that op's fist.

Sked - a schedule, or a time and frequency chosen beforehand for two or more people to meet.

80m - The eighty-meter band. Somehow, when I realized that these radio waves were over eighty yards long and gallumphed through the air at frequencies of 3.5 MHz, that is to say over 3,500,000 of 'em per second, then it seemed to me that I was in touch with the cosmos.

Ops - operators. Also we use 'op' for 'name.' So that by way of introduction, one might say: 'DE (from) AAØZR (that's me, my call) OP JANE QTH MTNS WEST OF BOULDER CO K' (The 'k' means "It's your turn to talk now')

AAØZR/MM - my call plus /MM - the slash (/) says 'plus' and the MM says 'maritime mobile.' One M means 'mobile,' which is interesting enough, and something I've done only while driving through quiet country. But if you're /MM, you get a lot of attention.

The bug - another form of Morse code key. This one has balances and weights, so that although each 'dah' still has to be keyed (i.e. struck with the finger, like the keying on the piano), the 'dits' can be set to rattle at whatever your speed is. This gadget does speed up the wpm somewhat. And it has a recognizable slurry rhythm that only a musical ham can make really copyable.

Keyer & paddle - an electronic device set up so that one can run both the 'dits' and the 'dahs.' Thus, '73' '||... ...||' (which means 'Best wishes') can be keyed in four moves instead of the six a bug would take or the ten on a straight key.

'No-code Extras' and 'E-glets' - The highest level of ham radio license is the 'Extra Class' license. To achieve this license, the ham has to pass a 20wpm code test as well as a big theory test. But there are so many interesting facets to ham radio that many hams, although they want the honor of the top-class license, don't want to use Morse code. So they get their 'Extra,' or 'E' licenses and then let the code go. Thus the image of E-glets with all the potential of 'flight' but never taking the plunge.

* Within a year of my writing this article, CW has become no longer important in ham radio; the 20wpm test is no longer given and people are getting Extra-Class licenses with only a 5wpm code test. CW has been legislated out! It remains to be seen if it will be allowed to keep its places on the bands. And I doubt that potentially serious code people will be given much scope to develop the skill.

CABIN FEVER

When it would get into Winter the folks all knew about the problem of cabin fever and did a lot to guard against it. Cabin fever is a condition that doesn't happen much in this time of telephones and snow plows but in those days, even in the thirties, it was a serious thing. Simply put what it was, when the snow piled up around and there was finally no way to go anywhere until Spring – even though there was plenty to eat, lots of firewood, and everything in good shape – after a couple months or so stuck in that, people tended to go berserk. It's human nature.

So about once a month throughout the Winter, they'd have a dance at the schoolhouse. Some people would ride up in sleighs with bells jingling but most of them would walk through virgin snow to get there. They'd come from all over the gulch and beyond. Some of the ones furthest out would have to set out early in the morning to get there by nightfall, so there would be food laid out, somebody sawing on a fiddle, maybe a banjo or a mandolin, and Bill Rosner on the guitar. They'd go on 'til dawn, dancing, eating, drinking, gossiping, fighting, mainly rubbing up against each other. Nobody wanted to leave until dawn because they needed the light to go home by.

That Bill Rosner who played the guitar, he was a quiet sort of fellow, too poor to even stake

69

a claim. He arrived in '28, and he had The Fever bad. Came in from Iowa and you could see it burning in his eyes. That's the Gold Fever he had. But he never could get enough money together to stake a claim. Maybe it was only that he never found the spot. What he did, day after day, he panned the creek and got enough dust that way to stay at the Boarding House. One Winter he stayed in Old Jake's cabin up on Colorado Creek and it was there, predictably, with the snow howling around, that he made his big invention. What he invented was a panning partner.

When you pan, the way you do it is you take the pan, scrape up some sand from the bottom and some water and then you squat there by the creek and shake that pan, you shake it fast and light and then every few seconds, you give it a good jump. That gives the gold that's caught up in the middle a chance to fall to the bottom and then as you shake the pan some more, all the dust rattles to the bottom and you start pouring off the plain sand, and there's the color at the bottom.

That Winter when Bill Rosner was living up at Old Jake's cabin, he got together some old gears that Jake had left lying around and he put them together. He attached a six-inch hose so that when the snow melted in the Spring, he could put that hose in the creek upstream, the water would come down the hose and move the gears. The prize gear was about a foot and a half in diameter and it had a lot of small teeth on it. Part of it was a big hunk taken out. So the water would move the little gears and they were attached to the big gear and on the top,touching the big gear, was the pan. As the big gear slowly moved around, it went bumpety-bump on the bottom of the pan and it would shake that pan perfectly as it should be shaken. Then the big space on the gear would come along and give the pan a wallop...thunk, like you have to do to be sure the gold doesn't get stuck in the middle.

That next Summer, Bill tried out his new invention. He'd shovel out a dip for the machine and a dip for himself and there they'd be, the two of them side by side just a-shakin' and a-thunkin' away companionably and Bill was a happy man. Not that it increased his income a whole lot; there was the necessity of setting the machine in place and the hose, then feeding it, scooping out the empty sand, so it slowed down his own panning a bit, but it was his own invention and he was proud of it until he died in his nineties.

DUSKY BEAUTY

There were three things I liked about going to my grandparents' house. One was crossing the streets with my mother and father on either side of me. Sometimes, when I was little, they'd let me swing between their hands. But when I got bigger, they stopped. They said I was too heavy, I hurt their arms.

My parents were very reserved, and they thought I shouldn't be cuddled and spoiled. How my brother and I turned out the way we did, I suppose I shall never fathom. Mom says it was Daddy who did it, teaching us to love nature the way we did. He used to take us to Bemis Woods and we'd walk and then he'd say, "Oh!" and point to a bird or some other creature and stare at it for a long time with a look of wonder on his face and his mouth open.

The second thing I liked about visiting my grandparents was my grandfather. He lived in the den, which was a little room with leather overstuffed chairs and books in glass cases all over the walls. He seldom came out of it. But when we'd go to their house, he'd let me visit him in his den. This was a great honor. He didn't like children clamoring around in there. But I'd go and smile shyly at him and he'd smile shyly, too. We didn't talk much but there were two little ditties about Jane that he would sing to me often and I could sing them to you now-off-key, as I learned them from him. And he would blow smoke rings for me, too. That was very dramatic. He would be sitting in one of the chairs and I on a footstool at his feet, and he would lean his head back, draw on his cigarette, then, with a second of hesitation that was like a drum-roll, he would arrange his mouth and the smoke in it. Then there'd be a jerk of his throat and a smoke ring would emerge from his pursed lips and rise expanding, followed by another and another. And I would look at them in wonder with my mouth open. Then, as often as not he would cough, not a little cough, one of the racking kind where he would bend over and couldn't catch his breath. Then my aunt would come in and scold him for smoking and take me away. But as I was being taken away, he would twinkle his eyes at me between coughs and I knew he was saying with that twinkle that he'd rather blow smoke rings for me and then cough and be scolded than not.

My aunt and uncle and two cousins lived with my grandparents. The two cousins were all right, though one was too old and the other too young. My uncle was never there, he was always working. But my aunt was the queen of the house. She liked beautiful things and the whole house was in good taste with beautiful things which harmonized with each other. She always laid an elegant table with flowers and fine linen and fine china. She and my mother would chatter about flowers and nutrition and rationing and recipes and then, invariably, my aunt would bring out the prune whip in beautiful stemmed glass and it was brown and bubbly with some pretty things on top like whipped cream and fruit and I always hoped that this time it would be chocolate, but it was always prunes.

The third thing I liked about visiting my grandparents was my grandmother. In the Winter she would be sitting in a pink flowered overstuffed chair in the living room, and in the Summer in a chaise-lounge on the porch. And I would go to her in trepidation because she was sad. She was very fat, and her head was in a cloud of fine white hair, and getting out of a chair was a tremendous amount of work for her, so she seldom did it. But when she saw me, she'd smile tenderly at me and it seemed as though she knew everything about me. It seemed she could see my life in the future, and it was something like hers because I was something like her. "How's my dusky beauty?" she'd say, because I stood out in the family for being so dark-skinned. Olive, they called it. "Like a little Italian child," my mother told her sister when I was born. But I was a pretty little girl in a dusky sort of way, with full lips and big brown eyes I'd look up out of with my head shyly down, smiling. "How's my dusky beauty?" she'd say.

Later, she wrote me a letter. We had moved away. My grandfather had died already. "Take care of yourself while you're young, my dear," she said. "Until I was thirty, I was full of life, but then I let myself go." I was then fifteen, and thirty was old beyond imagining. "Now I'm walking on two canes," she said, "and haven't done what I wanted to do." I was still composing an answer when she died.

At the time of writing this story, I'm fifty. I've taken care of myself, more or less. Thirty seems immature to me. I've had five children, all grown now, bearing children themselves. I went to join my daughter last week as she bore a child. The father, a gentle, sensitive idealist, is a black man, and I was curious what my fifth grandchild would look like. "We'll name her Rose Harmony if it's a girl," they said.

It was a perfect birth. I snapped a lot of pictures, told my daughter how well she was doing, watched the father to see he didn't faint.

And there was the baby. Such a beautiful infant I had never seen before. Rose-colored skin, full rose-petal lips, high, arched brows. A girl. I took her in my arms, tickled her belly. "How's my dusky beauty?" I said.

THE BIRTH OF GODOT

Fruehling came to us a month before she was due, bulging with pregnancy. There was the usual difficulty about moving a dairy goat to a new place. Often they'll quit eating for a few days and if they do that in the late stages of pregnancy, sometimes they die. I took twenty pounds of grain from her previous home and weaned her gradually onto my grain.

But it was a cut on her footpad that really brought us together. It wasn't a serious cut, but it hurt to walk on and with the added burden of her pregnancy, she was limping rather badly. I tried for a couple of days to chase her around with a spray bottle of Bactine, but it was ridiculous. So one morning I went out and spent several hours creating a stanchion big enough for her so that I could hold her steady and properly medicate that sore foot.

Extra feed in the new stanchion. She got in it just fine for that. Locked her in. Then I took her foot and gently and carefully washed and medicated it. The medicine cut back the pain as well as the germs and Fruehling noticed the difference immediately.

The next afternoon I went out again at the same time and she went gratefully to the stanchion. A few days of this and her foot was so much better, I thought I'd skip a day's treatment. I looked out the window at her an hour past the

76

usual treatment time. I made no sound going to the window but she saw me right away. She looked at me sideways, raised her sore foot in the air and held it there, looking at me. Needless to say, I rushed out with feed and medicine. But, you see, from that point on, we were friends. And, having a friend in her new place, she kept eating and she lived.

She kidded at 2:30 in the morning. I was ready. Neowyn and Ethan were visiting, asleep in the back room. Neowyn and I were taking turns checking up on Fruehling across the night. She was so big, we knew there would be more than the usual two kids.

The night was cold and windy. I woke Neowyn and Ethan by plunking a squirming, bleating, slimy, leggy, newborn kid in the middle of their bed, then running out again for the next one, who came soon enough. Then, leaving Ethan to clean and warm the new kids, Neowyn and I went out together, cups of cocoa to warm us, and sat with Fruehling as she labored on the third.

But the third would not come out. We milked her and left her alone awhile so we could feed the two kids who were, through the night, wobbling to their feet in the kitchen. Hours of cocoa and coffee and sitting in the straw with Fruehling, desultory talk. And then a bag of waters bulged out and broke. So we knew there was another in there. But nothing more came out. Dawn came and still the job was unfinished. And Fruehling labored on.

She wasn't working that hard. But now and again she'd stop and push with an attitude that seemed to say there was nothing achieved in the pushing, but yet there was something left to push. And we all knew it was so. There was, at least, no placenta out yet.

At nine, I called the vet who was busy and said, "Soap your arm and go in after it." I knew that already. Feeling like a fool, I filed my nails so there would be nothing to snag on. I had always been ready to "go in after it", but I never had. Being ready is one thing and doing it is another.

I scrubbed my hands and arms and smeared jelly all the way up to the elbow. Ethan and I went out and shut Fruehling and ourselves in the old car we used as a goat shed. Fruehling lay down. Ethan knelt at her head and held her collar, whispering sweet nothings to her as I sat at her rear.

Tiny little closed hole. But I had watched kids coming out of it. Kids at least as big around as my fist.

Slowly, I slithered my greased fingers into that tiny hole, slowly went up that slimy tunnel. Fruehling, feeling something in the birth canal, contracted hard, squeezing my arm till I felt my hand swell. But I stayed where I was and Ethan kept her lying down with his gentle voice soothing her – soothing me, too. "Take your time," he said. "Feel out the situation. She's being really good."

All my senses vanished except the sense of touch in that hand. I was transformed from a human being to a hand. It was a transformation like death, like birth, or, to be more accurate, like returning to the womb. Inside her, at first I struggled to feel, to name things. Tubes and strings of flesh were lying along the bottom of the birth canal under me. They must have been umbilical cords from the other two kids. Who knew what else. My hand was me and I could feel top and bottom and sides of this tunnel I now was in and there was no gravity pulling me to put weight on the tubes and strings. I touched them and left them alone. I was a weightless, groping, five-fingered creature creeping up a long tunnel to the chamber I knew was not far ahead. I went deeper.

I went deeper and came to the cervix, the entrance to the womb, then through it into the great cavern-ridged, vaulted walls and ceiling like a church, like a cave chamber deep in the earth. And lying crosswise inside the entrance to the great cavern, a furry body, ribs under wet fur. Slowly, carefully, I felt the body. Ribs and more ribs. I searched for a heartbeat, any movement, but I found nothing. I felt, groped along the furry thing. Of course. It was crosswise, its side to the tunnel. Fruehling could push till she dropped and never get that kid out.

I groped to feel out the little body. I plunged deeper yet into the cavern and found the head, triangular, its nose pressed against the far wall, the forward part of the womb, closest to Fruehling's heartbeat.

The best way for a goat to be born is head and forefeet first. But this little troglodyte seemed to want to go out the front or stay in there, one of the two. At the same time, I had no sense of it being alive. It was, in my mind, a dead kid, a buck, no doubt, as the other two were does. This seven-pound clinker of fur and bone was a serious threat to the life of my lovely new friend, Fruehling. I had gone into this cavern as a hero goes on a quest to save the life of a friend.

But oh! The place! The vaulted cavern! The moist, warm, quiet safety!

But I hadn't gone in there in search of a home. I was there to move this dead kid into a position so that Fruehling could push it out.

My hand was me, and where it was I was, so that only distantly, like a half-forgotten dream, I noted the crick in my back, the gentle voice of Ethan droning in Fruehling's ear, Fruehling herself lying quietly, trusting me to do everything possible to save her. That outer world nagged like a conscience. I realized I had to realign this little corpse who, though I still couldn't figure out quite what shape it was in, was my closest companion.

The second-best way for a goat to be born is hind feet foremost.

I moved back along the kid's neck, groped across the ribcage again, felt further away from the head across a mass of wet fur that seemed shapeless and endless. The pinpoint flashlights of my fingers could find no sign, no instructions as to what to do. This is silly, I thought. I know what shape it is. Lots of leg with hooves at the end. Desperately, I searched for a recognizable piece of anatomy. Finally, I found it, the little stub of a tail. "The tail!" I said to Ethan, my voice hushed and soothing to match his.

I knew where to go then. I felt down along leg bones to the little horn hoof, wrapped my hand over the hoof to protect the delicate inner wall of Fruehling's womb, those ridges I knew were more fragile than lips and tongue, and slowly forced the leg around so that the hoof was pointed out the tunnel my arm was in. It took strength to fight stiff bone and flesh, and it took gentle care to avoid hurting that membrane cavern wall. By the time I achieved it, sweat was running beside my eyes. "Now I have to get the other one," I groaned to Ethan. The other leg was underneath and harder to pull around, but, my fist wrapped solicitously around the hoof, I gently and smoothly wrenched it around to lie beside the other in the birth canal.

Slowly, exhausted, and with relief, I pulled my hand, my very being, out of the womb, suffered a parting, hand-swelling squeeze from Fruehling on the way out, and looked around me.

Ethan was exhausted, too. Gentling a worried animal who's having something strange done to her is hard, concentrated, internal work. You have to silence every twitch, every tension or insecurity, every personal discomfort. You have to make of your whole self an instrument of hypnotic calm, an image of trustworthiness that overwhelms any caprice the animal might have – and the word "caprice" means "goat-likeness." If Fruehling had made one move questioning my activities, it could well have killed her, scratched the inner surface of her womb, wrenched the placenta prematurely from the wall. But she didn't. She had lain there, soothed by Ethan, touching him with her nose, her eyes listening, listening trustfully to the work I was doing to save her. The eyes of any mother in labor always have a listening look. It's an internal concentration, the sense of the importance of the activities going on inside one's own body, one's own womb being finally the real world — more real than any problem in daily life or any social crisis, more real even than sun and wind and rain.

Ethan and I got up and slowly stretched cramped muscle, dusted straw from our clothes. I wiped slime from my hand and arm. Fruehling, too, stood up and we saw the two little hooves sticking out under her tail. She still had that listening look in her eye. It was a long wait. Fruehling was the most exhausted of us all by far. She stood, accumulating strength. Ethan and I smoked, stretched, and murmured.

"Why don't we just pull it out?" he said.

"All the books say to let her push it if she can," I said. I was doing it all by the books. The books all spoke of tearing things, things I had felt in there, fragile ducts and tender innards. The most powerful muscle on Earth is the womb. So say the books. More powerful than the biceps of a weightlifter, the jaws of a wolf. I bowed to the experience behind the books, but also to the yearning I could see in Fruehling's carriage. That great cavern had to contract sometime soon. It couldn't stay big and open like that. And Fruehling yearned to clamp it down and feel the little body slither out.

We were startled when it happened. Like an icicle falling from the roof. Whoosh. Out it came.

And it squirmed.

I reached for it, the "dead kid", my unmoving companion in that wondrous place. I wiped mucous off that nose and heard the first bubbling breath. I looked under the tail, that tail that had led me to the work I was to do. "It's a girl!" I said. I picked her up in my arms. Slimy, leggy creature, jerking and wiggling, she cried a shrill bleat, snorted.

Company came that day. None of us had had any sleep to speak of, but we weren't tired. The placenta had come out whole soon after the kid. Fruehling was walking about, eating, milking out sticky colostrum. "What shall we name her?" I asked.

"Name her Godot," Windy said. "Because you waited for her so long."

JIM MURRAY

He was a good-looking cuss when he came out
in the 'teens with his wife Annie and he'd
prospect or he'd work in the mines. There was
still work going on even in the 'teens and Jim was
hard-working, big, broad-shouldered and steady
except one day he'd up and quit doing one thing
and start another.

His wife Annie was slim, small, dark-haired
and pretty. She was real close with her family
back in Kansas and gave him some trouble now and
again to get him to go home again but he'd say,
"Wait till I hit pay dirt, then we'll go back
there, build us a twenty-room house, hire us some
servants and live like we should."

Annie loved Jim and she'd smile when he'd
say that and wouldn't trouble him for a while but
after a couple years she managed to get her sister
Vera to come up for a visit. Vera was slim and
dark and pretty like Annie and it wasn't very long
until she'd married Tom Gill and everything was
working out nicely.

Then Jim got a job down in Denver doing
construction and he and Annie lived down there for
a few years and then Annie died and when she died
the light went out of Jim's eyes and he went deaf
but he was a strong and healthy man and though for
a time he wanted to die, he didn't. He came back
up to Lump Gulch and built himself a cabin out of
an old one that had fallen in.

The cabin that Jim built was small with two rooms, frame, with a good solid foundation, built so solid that so far, and I'm talking forty years later, there has never been a mouse inside that cabin. On the front of it he built a little porch and across the middle of that he put his name etched in a board, "Jim Murray".

Behind was a nice little outhouse and over beyond the little meadow beside the Old Timer's place next door was Jim's own spring which he fixed up nice with rocks in a circle and you could see down to the bottom anytime. In the Winter, of course, he could melt snow. He had a stove in each of his two rooms and he'd go out every day or two, Summer and Winter, to get wood for his stoves.

In 1953, the schoolteachers moved in to the Old Timer's cabin next door, Ester and Betty. They were also from Kansas and they spent their Summers in Lump and went back to Kansas to teach school the rest of the time. Jim was by this time nearly eighty and his appearance had degenerated somewhat. He was still big and broad-shouldered. He was still a good-looking man with a strong chin and a well-molded face on a powerful body. But after Annie died, Jim didn't take care of himself and he'd come over to the schoolteachers' place sometimes in the evening to visit and although he never chewed in their house, tobacco juice would have dried on his chin and shirt-front and they'd put "It's A Long, Long Trail A-Winding" on the wind-up Victrola as loud as it would go and he'd rock hard and fast in their rocking chair and whistle with the record. Sometimes he'd sing to them songs he'd made up himself and sometimes he'd say, "When I hit pay dirt, you girls can give up teaching for life."

Then every Saturday Vera and her second husband Mike Neal came and got him and his dirty clothes and took him to Rollinsville to get groceries, not to mention drunk at the Stage Stop, and to their place in Moon to make him shave and bathe and feed him supper. And this went on for a number of years.

Whenever visitors came to the schoolteachers they would have to go next door and see Jim's cabin which he always kept tidy. One time the schoolteachers had a visitor named Murray who was looking for a long lost relative and thought maybe Jim was it but Jim said that he didn't know anything before waking up in a hospital bed with a concussion and that name on a letter in his pocket but somebody else said he had a brother named Pat over Georgetown way so it's hard to know.

One afternoon in the Autumn of the year Jim was claiming as his eighty eighth year, it was clouding up real thick and Jim went out to get some firewood for his two stoves and he didn't come back. The schoolteachers were already gone to Kansas but Bill Rosner was living at the old boarding house and when he saw Jim didn't have his lights on he called Vera and Mike on the phone and pretty soon though the snow was coming down fast there were twenty or so people out looking for him and calling all over the Gulch but he didn't answer.

It snowed all that night and all the next day and people were slogging around on snowshoes and skis that day and the next and the next. They looked for him every day for two weeks but the Winter came early and wet and the snow was so deep they knew there was no use and in the Spring people started wondering about him and kind of looking around the gulch but it was over Gamble Gulch way the Lurchs found him and the way they did was they saw his ax hung up in a tree and knew he always sat under his ax and sure enough there he was, sitting under the tree, his old brown cap with the ear flaps, his gray overcoat, his mittens, his galoshes, all covering his mouldering bones.

THE FISHERMAN'S TALE

"There are two kinds of fish in this river, the salmon and the steelhead trout. And they're all but identical. It takes someone who knows to tell them apart. Now and then you'll catch a male steelhead with a bit of a rainbow on his side but mostly they're chrome, just like the salmon. Pink meat, fins the same, taste, everything. Only the salmon are oilier, better for smoking. Steelheads you eat fresh.

"The big difference between the two kinds is their love lives. The salmon, everyone knows, they only breed once, they breed when they're dying. They feel death coming over them, they swim home and breed. For them, sex and death, they probably can't tell them apart. And the males are real horny. You'll see a male salmon waiting at the mouth of a little side stream, a female will go up it, he'll follow her and they'll spawn. Then he'll go back and wait for another. After a couple of days or so, he's the shabbiest-looking wreck you can imagine.

"But the steelhead, they mate. They pair off, two by two and they're true to each other, take care of the eggs together, go back out to sea, come home ready to spawn again the next year. To the steelheads love is part of life.

"There was a tragedy in this river twelve years ago. Two friends of mine drowned.

88

"There were always the three of them, ever since they were little children the three were always together. Kenny and Zia and Dan.

"When they grew up, Zia turned out to be an amazingly beautiful girl and she chose Dan as her true love. Kenny sang and played the electric guitar in the band. I played the drums and Long Tom the keyboard and the electronics. And Zia and Dan would always come to hear Kenny sing and the three of them were always as close as anyone could be.

"It was a full moon night on New Year's Eve at the Inn right over there, that place with all the windows gone now and the paint peeling. But it was a lively spot then, twelve years ago on New Year's Eve.

"I never saw Kenny so happy as that night. He kept dragging people out onto the porch there and pointing up at the moon. 'Look at the silver moon!' he'd say. But Zia sat with Dan at a table and all night she was saying, 'There's something terribly wrong.'

"But finally very late we packed up our gear. Kenny and I put it all in my new van and I headed for home. The others all piled into Kenny's car, Long Tom in front with Kenny, Zia and Dan in back. Kenny took off and when he got to the bridge, he missed the turn and went right over.

"Long Tom fell out before they hit the river so he was saved.

"But the car landed on the driver's side and Zia was on the bottom. Dan found an air pocket and he was saved, too. "But Zia and Kenny both died.

And the strange thing was that Zia had her arms so tight around Kenny that they had to break her arms to get the two of them apart.

"It's troubled me a lot. Dan's still alive last I heard, but he's a bum now, really on the skids since then.

"I don't know what happened to Long Tom. He went away.

"I haven't played the drums much since then. I couldn't do it now. Too old. I fish a lot in the river here beside the Inn. Or up above the bridge.

"The Inn closed down within a month after that and no one has started it up again.

"The part that troubled me the most was that I felt so strongly that Dan was her true love. And never understood why she died with her arms so tight around Kenny.

"Until one day fishing it came to me. That she was a steelhead for Dan. And a salmon for Kenny."

DEAR EMMA,

I don't even remember what the correspondence was about. I only remember that I was just starting out to do the business – sales, distribution, arrangements – and I was excruciatingly unsure of how to do it. I tried to be brave. One of the first places I wrote to was a museum. Emma wrote me back, and she was human and kind and she taught me how to deal with people in business.

Just be yourself, she said, and say what you need to say, briefly, humanly. There are people in every office, she said.

I don't think she ever said those things. We were, after all, doing business. But she knew I didn't know what to do, knew I was in an agony of shyness. She knew every thing about it. She was shy, too, agonized by shyness, too, like I was. And I could recognize her as shy, desperately so. I imagined her, there at the museum, in a back office, behind the door, hiding, doing her work, and able to keep her senses open in the peace of that seclusion.

How my first letter got to her, I can't imagine. But she answered me promptly, kindly, sensitively, in such a way that I could write back. And I did: I wrote right back. And she answered me and I answered her, brief letters, little things, like alpine flowers. I remember I would go eagerly to the post office for her

letters and that they'd be there and I'd open them
with joy. My friend. I had found a friend.
Quickly, gently, and with complete understanding,
she taught me how to do what I had to do in
business, how I could be shy and still do it
right.

There weren't that many letters between us.
Neither of us proposed to talk of other things.
"Do you like dogs?" "Where were you born?" "What
do you do on your time off?" "What books do you
read?" No, nothing like that. It was strictly
business. It would have been against the training
she was giving me to talk about our lives. And so,
it was soon over.

As it turned out, there has been no one I
have ever encountered in all my business
correspondences that could hold a candle to Emma.
I could handle them, though, because she had
taught me how. There were all kinds. There were
the gruff and there were the mechanical; there
were the misguided, the hilarious, the brusque,
the bureaucratic; there were even shy ones. But,
except for Emma, there was no gentle
understanding. She was the shyest of all and she
understood that I was, too.

Many years went by and in all those years I
assume that Emma stayed in the back office behind
the door and that she did her work well and that
in the peace of the back office and the quiet and
orderly routines of her life, whatever life it
was, she kept her senses open.

But I, in those years, had to meet people
face-to-face, had to shake their hands as though I

weren't shy. Or so I felt. But I was shy. I was as shy as Emma. And I did, I put a smile on my face and reached my hand out boldly, shook their hands firmly, and said, a carefully composed, friendly twinkle in my eye, "How do you do?" And people would tell me how I looked so poised and natural, but it was a mask that hid every feeling I was having. And as the years went by the mask got stronger, the feelings more hidden. I was safe behind the mask as Emma was safe behind the door in the back office.

The feelings were there, the sensitivities, the knowledge that Emma had given me, that there was a person in every office. Thus there was one behind every face in every public scene, too. And in the privacy I had composed for my self behind that friendly mask, I looked at them shyly, tried to understand them as she had understood me.

To a certain extent, I succeeded. I did see them. I saw their feelings. But I couldn't reach out truly as she had done from her clearer vantage behind the door. The mask hampered my natural expression. It was, in fact, extremely limited in expression. There wasn't much the mask could say. Certainly, it would never say what I was feeling, in my shy solitude behind it. Never ever that.

A clumsy thing, the mask. I wore it in all kinds of situations. There were times when my face would freeze into a pleasant expression even though violent emotions were going on inside me. I remember with shame the smile I had frozen on my face at a friend's deathbed. Fond feelings, anguish, unsaid messages, terror, yearning for a real connection, for knowledge, all boiled, roared silently behind a frozen, insipid smile that I could not take off, could not change, though I sat there on the edge of the bed, my dying friend's hand in mine, wanting with all my heart to tell, to ask, to relate truly, deeply, but the smile would not move. There was no opening, no word, no way through.

After the brief correspondence with Emma, there were other times I corresponded with the museum. But it was always other people, people in front offices. I gave up on ever finding her, forgot even which institution she had worked for. Then one Spring came the trip to the big city, the visit to the offices of the museum, prearranged, where we would meet all those front office people, go out to lunch with them, and talk.

The mask was on solid: hair, dress, shoes, and friendly twinkle in place as we rode the elevator and entered the office. And there were the introductions, all those people who did the various work of the museum, people who had written to me. I greeted them all, each one thickening and firming up my friendly twinkle, my warm handshake. "And this," said someone, "is Emma." There she stood, behind a desk, blinking, squinting, as though the light out here in the front office were too bright for her, glowering even, as though she might bite, as though she had been dragged out of her burrow against her will. Her office clothes and office hairdo didn't hide her. She stood, sensitive, seeing, thinking, wide open, her feelings exposed there on her face and in her stance. She wanted to run away, but she was fascinated to see me. Most of all, blatant, loud, overwhelming, as though she were wearing it in red letters on a sign across her chest, as though she were saying it over and over as she was being pulled forcibly out from behind that door, the bitter lament of the teacher who is used and then discarded, "she won't remember me."

Again, like a demoniacally obstreperous machine that cannot be controlled, the mask hid emotions that I had not learned to formulate: shock, excitement, knowledge that here was a rare and precious thing, an honestly sensitive being, a warm friend, a real friend, someone who would settle for nothing less, nothing more socially acceptable than the truth. The mask was firmly in place. The show must go on. Thus I rationalized. After all, how could I express in word and gesture that which I had worked hard to hide? The emotions behind the mask were powerful but the mask hid them entirely. Hid them behind the friendly smile, the hand reaching out to shake hers, the inane and meaningless, "How do you do?"

Did she refuse to take my hand? I think she did. Mask or no, I could still see. I could see her disappointment, could see her loss, could see her thinking, "she doesn't remember me!"

The mask was that good. Even she couldn't see through it. None of them could. To cover the embarrassing moment, the other lady led us away, into the adjoining office, where the head of the department was. I saw Emma standing, alone now, giving me another chance. I looked at her through the door. She was looking off in some other direction, desperately shy, with the shyness that's often called "pride," thinking how she had come out here from her burrow and she could go no farther. I had to make the next step. And I looked at her, and everything was gawky in my mind, and I couldn't walk through that door, couldn't trust the mask to act decently to her. What would I say, anyway?

Then she turned away, started walking toward the maze of the back offices. "Emma! Don't go!" I shouted, but it was only inside. I made no noise, even my lips didn't move. Her back, as she walked away, expressed her feelings - grumpy, disconsolate, disgusted with me for forgetting her, and with herself for caring.

Shyness can be cruel. I let her go. She had told me that she remembered me. And she had told me again to just be myself, that there were people everywhere, people with honest feelings somewhere, inside.

THE GOLDEN GLOBE

Godot stood in the sunlight, her head high, bulging belly tightening and loosening under gleaming black fur. When a contraction came, she would lower her head a little, her golden eyes glazing in internal concentration. Between times, she danced around, chasing chickens and cats. A string of mucus hung down across her bulbous udder. The other goats watched her, the old one lying in the sun, joying in the birth through slitted eyes, the younger ones dancing about. She'd chase them off if they got too close.

Then she lowered her head, her eyes not seeing, and under her tail a golden globe emerged, golden with a greenish tinge, and with a thin, thin red line, jagged and branching across it. And inside the globe, two hooves swirled for a second or two, then vanished back inside her, but the globe remained, darker, smaller, and Godot moved about the yard, carrying it there under her tail.

She stopped moving about and the globe swelled, the two hooves emerged again into it, then a golden head, eyes closed, muzzle arched, an ancient looking image, solemn, primordial, above the hooves, and for a long moment it hesitated like a flower does in full bloom.

Godot gave a mighty heave and the primordial head burst the golden globe, leading a golden body which slithered to the ground coated with glittering slime, long legs sprawled in every direction, head wobbling now, sneezing.

INSTRUCTIONS

(For Windy while we're away)

Chickens

In the morning around eight or nine at the latest, get the food together. For the chickens, a pan of scratch from the second bin from the right by the outside door in the boys' room. Mix the pan of scratch with one handful of whole corn and one of the bird seed. Open up the chickenhouse, lean a cinderblock against the door so it stays open, scatter two-thirds of the seeds around on the ground outside, and put the rest down in the pan. If you can think of a chicken song to sing, they like that. Neowyn has always given a slow, repeated, rising whistle. Check around for eggs. Put down a fresh bucket of water, first tossing what's left in the bucket over the fence to the garden. The water faucet is in the corner of the yard between the kitchen and the girls' room. Fill a couple of white plastic bottle-bottoms with water and lay one inside the chickenyard, one outside. The birds are now ready for the day.

Goats

-- Getting set:

Put one pan of food in the stanchion, then tuck the white milk bucket into the top of the

corner of the fence just to the left of the
stanchion. There's a nice place for it there. Open
the stanchion by pulling down the baling-twine and
unhooking the bottom hooks, then pull it aside so
that Tree can get her head in there easily. Climb
over the fence. There are two places it's easy to
do, one just to the left of the corner where you
tuck the white bucket and the other at the truck
tire. Open the door of the old car we use for a
goat shed, letting Tree out while you give the
second pan of food to Daffy in the car. As soon as
Tree's out of the car, shut Daffy in with her
food, and never mind her yowling. Tree will run to
her stanchion and start eating. Put the stanchion
back in its place, over Tree's neck.

Pull the baling twine up as tight as you
can, hook the two bottom hooks, sit down on her
table facing her rear so she's on your right. This
puts you where you can reach up to get the bucket.
Put your right leg under her middle, sticking out
the other side, sweep off her udder with your
hands, and you're ready to milk.

-- Milking:

Put the little bucket not right under her
udder, she's liable to tip it there. Put it rather
closer to you, between your legs. What you must
realize is that the milk is made in the udder and
she lets it down into the teats. The udder is a
big pair of complexes with tubes and whatnot, but
the teat is a sack with a big hole at the top and
a little hole at the bottom. What you have to do
is close off the top hole of each teat with the

top of your hand and squeeze the milk out the bottom hole.

The first squeeze is the hardest because the milk has formed a plug in the bottom hole so that you have, in effect, to pop the cork with the first squeeze. You should squeeze the teats as hard and fast as you can. Don't pull down at all, just squeeze hard. Pulling down is harmful to the udder, but you can't possibly hurt it by squeezing the teat with your hand. The main rule for successful milking is never let a drop of milk go back up into the udder. Get a nice rhythm going between the two teats -- two strong hands, two teats, open one hand and feel the milk bubbling into that teat while you get all the milk out of the other teat, back and forth. Pretty soon there will be less, and if you've ever seen a kid or a lamb nursing, you know what to do: punch the udder with your fist. So for awhile you punch squeeze, punch-squeeze. Then even that doesn't work. But you must empty that udder every day because if you don't, she'll make less the next day and less the next. So punch with your fingers between the two halves of the udder -- go ahead and do it, she likes it and you'll find more milk in the teats. This works a few times, then you're through milking. Don't stop milking for anything until you've got it all out. If she gets out of the stanchion before you're through, bribe her back in with the rest of the food or a rye cracker. Keep your vibes patient. Don't let her drink the milk. She will, too, if she gets the chance. It's the baling twine that keeps the stanchion solid. Keep it pulled up tight.

Hang the bucket on the hook that's right over the gate. You have to stand on the bottom pole of the fence to reach it. Then undo the stanchion and let her out.

-- Hay and Water:

From the hay shed in the garden, get a couple of small flakes of alfalfa, about a sixth of a bale total. Put it in two piles: one in the goat-shed there by the garden, and one to the left of the gate. Take the bucket that's by the slab fence and go through there to fill the bucket at the faucet. Close the gate to keep the goats from following you. Give them a full bucket of water, place it carefully so it won't tip, be sure the handle is down. Then the goats are fed.

-- Tree, Psychological Problems:

Tree has been known to be nasty and irritable with people. The best way to handle her is with patience and bribes. She may tend to sit down on her udder while being milked. There are two ways to deal with this. Usually, if you take your hands away from the udder for a moment and lean back a bit, she'll stand up. Or you can punch the middle of the udder. If all else fails, prop up her ribs with one knee and the pelvic bone right behind the udder with the other knee and continue milking. Vibes are all-important. Relaxed, amiable, on-top-of-it vibes are the best. Don't fight her, she'll only get worse. Give her something to eat. She has a way of rubbing up against people, then jabbing them. If she does this, I apologize. All I can say is that she's never drawn blood and what she seems to be after is dignity and honor. Also, if either she or Daffy is in heat, she's worse.

-- Finishing Up:

After you've fed them, climb back over the fence -- do not use the gate -- fasten up the stanchion again, take the bucket of milk (you can reach it by climbing on the rock under it) to the basement. Then pour a quart of whey from on top of the bin in the pantry into another bucket and give the whey to Tree. Then strain the milk through a cheesecloth in the kitchen and do with it as your imagination dictates.

Greenhouse

Some time in the morning, water the greenhouse. Dip the water out of a barrel into the gray pitcher, or use the green sprinkler and give some to each plant. Don't miss any of the hanging plants or those in corners. Don't water any with wet dirt. It ought to take about half a barrel. After you've watered them all, fill the barrel again. The faucet is behind the door. You can miss a day if you want to, but two days would strain some of them.

House Plants

On Saturday, you should water the plants in the house. There are some in every room. It takes a couple of gallons or so. Don't miss the ones hanging from the ceiling or the ones upstairs.

Dogs
-- On Chains

The dogs are very amiable and discreet unless there's a bitch in heat, then they're demanding. Probably the best thing to do is to take them out to their chains before you do anything else. Never leave a door open or stand in a doorway. They can open screen doors. Never take or let them out except on leashes, they'd be likely to be shot by our insane neighbor. So first put on the leashes, then open the door, take them out to the chains, fasten the chains, then take off the leashes. If they bark, bring them in. They usually do bark pretty soon; they don't like to stay on the chains long, especially Peter. Sometimes we bring Peter in if he barks, and leave Scamp out.

-- Walking:

At around noon, take them on their leashes for a walk out the back, past the aspen grove and through the woods. Look at the direction of the tree-shadows to keep from getting lost. It's best not to go among the houses -- the dogs are more tense and adventuresome there. Normally, they both dump once on the noon walk and once on the afternoon walk, so give them every opportunity to do so. They generally like to place it on bushes or low branches and never closer to the house than the far side of the aspen grove. They're quite good about trying not to tangle us up in the trees. But if they go the wrong way 'round a tree, a tug on the leash and the use of their names will remind them to rearrange themselves, unless there's a bitch in heat. Then they have to be guided around like blind idiots.

-- Feeding and Afternoon Walk:

At around five in the afternoon, the dogs should be fed. Each one gets a quarter of a can of canned dog food on top of the dry food. The cans are on the landing on the way to the pantry. The dogs should never run out of dry food. It may be found in the big bin in the boys' room to the left of the bin with the chickenfeed. And there should always be fresh water. They should be given canned food only once a day. Give Scamper his food first, in the pan by the old coal stove, then feed Peter under the radio. Wait half an hour after they eat, then take them on another walk.

The half-hour wait expedites their dumping. After the afternoon walk, keep them in the house till morning. They like to hang out in the girls' room quite a bit. Peter can open the little door into the kitchen but Scamper can't, so prop it open with a dustpan or something.

Rabbit

Ruby the rabbit should have the dry rabbit food and fresh water at all times and a hunk of cabbage every day. He's very nice and can be let out in the house, but I don't entirely trust

Scamper with him when nobody's there. Scamp has never attacked him but he has killed rabbits in the woods and squirrels in the house, so just be there if you let him loose. Ruby can also be put out in his pen by the boys' room door but it's all right to just leave him in his cage.

Pigeon

Fanny, the pigeon, may want to stay out with the chickens and if he does, let him. If he wants to come in, he'll be by the front door, and if he gets up the nerve, he'll fly onto your head. If he does, just walk into the kitchen (being very careful of door frames), then go over close to the little shelf by the mirror, and he'll get onto that shelf. Or onto the fridge. If he's in, be sure the food and water on top of the fridge are fresh. His food is under the window seat by the fridge (NOT the popcorn). In the morning, unless it's wet or cold out, he'll want to go out again. He attacks with a great display sometimes but don't pay any attention. His bite doesn't hurt much. Just mind your eyes and grab him by the body (gently but firmly), including the wings, or let him walk onto your hand, biting the while! If he demands to come in and then gets on the table, he may want a bath. Put the large frying pan (not the Dutch oven) on the dishwasher half full of cold water and leave it there for half an hour.

Snake

Sparkle, the rainbow boa, is in a box in the boys' room. Because she needs to be at 80 degrees at all times, she needs to have her light on all the time, so check it every day. And the blue bowl should always have water in it. Otherwise she needs nothing. We'll feed her before we go, so she'll not need to be fed till we get back. If the lights go out or if for any reason you have to or want to mess with her, reach in slowly, talk softly, pick her up gently, and wrap her tail around your arm to give her a sense of security. When her tongue comes out, she's being curious. Only if she rears her head back like a cobra will she strike, and even if she does, her bite is not poisonous. She's a constrictor. She enjoys crawling around on people if they're quiet and gentle.

Evening
-- Putting to bed:

When it starts to get dark, the birds will put themselves away, usually in their proper places. Check with a flashlight in the chickenhouse. There should be a guinea fowl, a striped rooster, a big red hen, two dark hens and a tan and gray halfling, six in all, plus Fanny the pigeon, if he's out. They can all be easily picked up, especially in the dark. Around the body, including the wings. Gently. Or, if the vibes have gone awry, you may grab them by the neck. Gently though firmly. If they aren't all there, look around the yard in corners and hideyholes. The guinea is usually the last to go to bed. He makes a tour around the house.

Check all around for eggs. Don't feed them in the evening. When you've got all the birds into the chickenhouse, close the door. Wrap the chain twice around the door-handle and snap it to the padlock loop, then lean a cinderblock up against the door. For the goats, take two pans of the grain mixture, place them far apart inside the old car, and shut the goats in there.

Then, if the goats are in their car, the chickens in the chickenhouse, Ruby back in her cage, Fanny in somewhere, the dogs in the house, Sparkle's light on, all is safe and well. Lock the basement door and the two doors on the porch. Never use the back door in the girls' room. In the evening, you should check all lights, stoves, and doors throughout the house.

Troubleshooting

Keep your eyes and ears open to any sort of calls for help (trying to ignore the insane neighbor and his dogs). If Tree's bloated, i.e., if she's fat suddenly and her droppings aren't in pellets anymore, or if she can't chew her cud properly, or if she (or Daffy) suffers any trauma, give her a pan of several handfuls of bran moistened with warm water.

If anyone gets cut, get a leaf or two of Aloe Vera, open it and spread the juice on the hurt area. If you want to kill germs, use the blue lotion on the ground by the stanchion. If any of the birds get to sneezing, you can give them the tiniest bit of Terramycin. I usually wet a tooth pick and get a little Terramycin on it that way, wash it into a half a glass of water, and give whoever needs it a dropper-full of that water. The Terramycin and the dropper are by the white bucket on the shelf in the kitchen.

If the goats get out, use the rye crackers or kitchen garbage to lead them back through the gate. If that doesn't work (it will, though), grab Tree by the good horn. You can do about anything with her if you take her by the horn, even put her head back in the stanchion. Daffy follows her, so all you have to deal with is Tree.

If the dogs get out, take the leashes and look for them among the houses, calling their names and whistling a single rising whistle. If there's a bitch in heat, they won't come home. If there isn't, they ought to be back in twenty minutes or so... if they haven't got shot.

Well, help yourself to any food in the house, greenhouse or garden. There are plenty of books to read. And I sure hope you enjoy your stay here.

HARRY AND LOU

Back in the old days there were two kinds of
people in this gulch, there were those who were
grubbing for gold and those who were avoiding the
law. Fact is, the ones avoiding the law were very
often the nicer people.

There was one fellow, John Goff, he was a
moonshiner from Kentucky, he had four or five
stills dotted here and there all over the Gulch.
He was a real nice man and hospitable as they
come. There was one thing made the kids a little
nervous about visiting him though, and that was if
you'd knock on his door, he'd raise his .45 and
point it at the door and say "Who's there?" He'd
ask it only once and if you didn't answer it right
away, he'd shoot through the door. That John, he
was such a good shot with his .45, he could kill a
running mouse -- draw, aim, shoot and kill it in
the time it took for the mouse to run from one
hole and just only think about getting to the
other.

Hank Brady was one of the quiet little gold
grubbers. He lived in the little cabin by the
creek down below, where you can see just the roof
from the road. He found enough gold on his little
claim to keep him and his wife Ada in beans and
ham. After he died, Ada stayed on, then Lou
Dapplemeyer came along and jumped Hank's claim.

Lou Dopplemeyer and his sister seemed to be
a pair of ruffians who knew no law but they both

knew how to shoot. Lou started digging away and there wasn't much Ada could do, only the one sheriff at that time, and he was fairly busy as you could imagine over in Central, never came to the north end of the county.

Well, Ada got really miserable, so the neighbors got together and decided to do something about it. It was Harry who went and talked to Lou. They stood there a long time. I don't know what they said. Harry was a quiet, soft-spoken man but he could persuade a knot out of a barn door. After that talk, Lou went and made a legitimate claim over Gamble Gulch way and left Ada alone.

Some years later, Harry and Lou got to be friends and one time Lou said to Harry, "Harry, there's maybe one thing you didn't know about when you talked me out of Ada's claim, that all the time you were talking to me, my sister was standing behind a tree with her .22 aimed at your head."

Harry looked at Lou and he said, real quiet-like, "Well, there's one thing maybe you didn't know too, and that was that John Goff was behind a rock across the way with his .45 aimed at your sister."

DEATH WATER

June. White water time. And that year, after a particularly snowy Winter, the creek was so white it was brown: silt and mud swept up and brought down and roiled around in the white. It roared and screamed at us as we drove on the road safe above.

Very exciting, all that natural power crashing down there. I like that sort of thing. Thunderstorms, hail, waves, high winds, glaciers, deep cold, white water. Not to mention the overwhelming forces I haven't had the pleasure of experiencing. Avalanches, sandstorms, seventeen-year locusts, hurricanes, storms at sea, depths of jungle, massive thundering herds.

I saw a tornado once but it was several miles away. But I don't enjoy danger at all. I cringe at speed and heights, all that stuff, so when my eight-year-old son Bear, staring long out the car window at the creek below, said, "I could cross that," I said, "That's death water," and I told him there'd been two deaths in that creek already that year and it had been high only a week and a half. I knew he didn't hear me really and it disturbed me. Why does man always have the urge to pit himself against, prove himself upon, and fling his foolish life into the powers? I spoke to him very sternly on the subject but no matter what I said he sat silently and I heard his stubbornly heroic thoughts.

That was the day that Carolyn and little Geoffrey were with us. To change the mood, Carolyn and I tried to remember old songs, and the main one was "Sweet Violets." Between the two of us we got the first two verses. It took us half the way down the canyon to do it and then the girls all wanted to learn it so we went over it a few times.

I don't recall what we did in town. I only know it was on the way back that we stopped at The Falls. It's not a thing I do unless goaded. The water was so fierce and with the way Bear had been thinking, I didn't want to stop, but I couldn't think of a good reason not to when Carolyn asked me to. So we did stop, and I held Bear's and Rarc's hands and kept the girls close and we walked down the little path, two women and six children. The Falls are the last dynamic display of North Boulder Creek before it merges with Middle Boulder Creek, which comes down from the dam and along beside the road. A quarter mile below The Falls the waters join and double and leap and crash over rocks and rapids the last few miles to town. At least in June the water leaps and crashes. Other times it rolls quietly around the base of those same rocks that it covers in June. ·

There were a lot of people there. They were all over the rocks above The Falls and there were a few hippies sitting in the shallow overflow below the path. It was a hot day.

The Falls were roaring so loud that we could only shout into each others' ears. The water crashed over the cliff rudely, lacking grace. I didn't like it. I clung to my children and glowered.

112

DEATH WATER

Across the creek was a rock wall, wet to
several feet above the level of the water, and I
was looking at the mosses flourishing in the
crannies, lichens gleaming orange and pale green on
the smooth face. Then I had an impression of
something wrong in the creek below the rock wall. I
looked down and saw the wet blond curls of a young
woman who had been down by the bank. She was caught
up, rushing down the frothed current in the center
of the creek. I was amazed that she could keep her
head up in that crashing tumult, but I knew, I knew
from the repetitive headlines, from the annual
gossip, from the particularly violent whiteness of
this year's creek, that she hadn't much chance to
survive. I clutched my children around me and
screamed, "She's dead!" I don't know if I was heard
by any but the children over the noise of the
water. Why I said that, I don't really know except
that "death water'' was running through my mind.

One of her companions pushed past us. He was
tall, thin, pale, delicate. Miraculously, the girl
caught herself on a big slimy rock midstream that
rose black above the water. I heard a faint cheer
behind me. "Maybe she isn't dead," I said. Her body
was trembling all over, her arms and legs clinging
with amazing tension to the slippery surface of the
rock. Her blond curls clung to her neck, her wet
translucent clothes wrapped against her body, her
large breasts lay over the rock as though also
clutching it. The delicate young man stood on the
bank beside her and reached out a lean frail arm
toward her. She hesitated a moment, then reached
out her hand toward his. We all stood open-mouthed

113

and concentrated as their two hands poised like the hands of God and Adam in Michelangelo's fresco, straining, strained to touch. Failed to touch. For a last chance, she lunged at his hand, giving up her grip on the rock. She missed. The current grabbed her, sucked her down and away behind the rock, out of our sight.

Rarc saw her fall in. He was fresh out of first grade then, and eight years later as I wrote this, he remembered something I had forgotten. There were bad minerals in the water coming over The Falls, something the creek picks up from old mine dumps up above. I don't remember what. Was it arsenic? Anyway, you were not supposed to drink the water and I had hollered at those very people when we first arrived and saw them drinking the water, "Don't drink the water," I had yelled at them over the noise of The Falls. "It's bad." But they had shrugged and drunk it anyway. "Nyaaa," they said and waved their arms at me.

It had been a hot day. Rarc remembered every detail. He had been watching them. The thin delicate young man had been lying down with his mouth to the water and the blond girl had crouched at the bank where it was rushing down fast and she had been dipping it up with her hands. The roaring and the rushing of the stream must have made her dizzy; she had lost her balance, fallen forward and reached back with her hand so that the young man would catch her. But he had been lying down and couldn't reach her so she had lurched sideways into the creek. By the time she'd raised her head, she was right in the middle, and that's when I had seen her.

I clutched and counted my children and clutched and counted them again. "Maybe I still have that rope in the car," I said and started to gather my brood to go and see, though I felt no hope that I could catch up with her. I could not let my children be more than a yard away from me — it was a physical impossibility. We started up toward the path. "My shoe's untied," said little Geoffrey and I stopped, knowing that it was too late for the rope, too late for anything, the girl was probably dead. Carolyn knelt and carefully retied Geoffrey's shoe. I looked around. There were no people. Even those who had been above The Falls were gone, running on ahead down the creek to reach for the girl with sticks, with clothes, with whatever they could find.

"Maybe," I thought, "there'd be another place before it joins the other creek."

Slowly, hysterically cautious, we walked the children along the path where just before us many people had raced, bent on rescue. The creek rumbled fierce below us. By the time we got to the road there were no cars but ours and one other, and a young couple weeping in each other's arms, at which sight I gave up entirely, grimly shoved everyone in the car, and silently drove up the canyon.

I stopped in Nederland and called the Boulder police. "Two bodies were found," a hard but pained woman's voice said, "five miles below The Falls at Blanchard's Lodge."

"I had my children with me," I said, groaning with guilt.

"One female," she said, "and one male." "He went to rescue her," I said.

MINE HOLES

The mine holes around here are really
dangerous, the danger being mainly that it's hard
to know how they're shaped or how deep. One can
sometimes tell that it's just a pothole because
the mound of dirt around it is not much. A pothole
is a test hole, dug maybe ten feet or so, to see
if there's something down there. And that's all
there is. There are potholes in this gulch all
over the place.

But then some holes that look like potholes
aren't. Some places there are lines of what look
like potholes but if they're in a line, they're
not to be trusted because that's most likely an
adit that goes along underneath maybe twenty or
thirty feet down and comes to the surface once in
awhile for air. Most of these have fallen in and
look to be only a few feet deep, but as the dirt
falls in often some rock or timber catches it and
it lays there with a considerable cavity
underneath. All it takes is the weight of a human
jumping down on it or only a wet Spring for it to
fall in further and there's the real hole gaping
fifty feet down.

And you can't trust an adit ever because any
moment it might send down a shaft. I remember
reading a sign tacked to an adit over above
Tungsten that said, "Danger! About fifty feet
inside this tunnel is a vertical shaft that goes
about fifty feet down. Our beloved dog Rex is at

MINE HOLES

the bottom. Our true and faithful friend for many
years. May he rest in peace."

The Victoria was the biggest mine in the
Gulch. It was truly successful. It was Johnathan
Crane had that mine and he ran it like it should
be run. He ran it till the vein was cleaned out.
You can still see the double chimney standing in
the gully where the Victoria Mill was. The dump
from the mine stretches out and piles high on the
slope. The way to tell the age of a mine dump is
that the raspberries come in fifty years and the
strawberries in a hundred. Well, the Victoria has,
in the last couple decades, managed a few
raspberries down the northwest side. Hard to
imagine what they're feeding on, dry sharp pebbles
and mostly shade. It's as though they're there to
show that it's been fifty years.

Harry knew Johnathan Crane, they were good
friends and one year Johnathan got very sick and
he was dying. Harry went and visited him every
day, brought him things and sat awhile to talk
with him, tell him the latest news, talk about the
old days.

Then came the day when Johnathan could
hardly speak and he beckoned Harry toward the bed.
"There's no use me keeping this secret to the
grave," he said, "There's free gold in the
Victoria yet." Harry watched in dismay as the
dying man seemed unable to continue but then he
did.

"At the bottom of the main shaft is an adit
that angles up south." Here Johnathan had a
coughing fit which nearly carried him away. "At

117

the top of the adit," he whispered, and Harry could barely hear what he said, "is free gold at grass roots." Harry sat up. "Grass roots?" "Black dirt," Johnathan Crane said, "Black dirt," and then he died.

Not long after the funeral, Harry went down into the Victoria alone. The Victoria is over three hundred feet deep but he went down and at the bottom was an adit that angled up south. He crawled up that adit. It was a long way. But at the top of it was solid granite.

Harry went up that adit several times. The last time he went he was about half-way and he heard rumbling above him. He scooted down that hole faster than he'd done anything before or since, with rocks and gravel at his back catching up. He got out all right but though he lived to be eighty-six, Harry never went into the Victoria again.

"FIFTEEN YEARS," I SAID

"Fifteen years," I said, but seven had come to mind. It's creepy how much we know about each other, stuff we wouldn't dream of telling, usually not even to ourselves.

How it happened was that Stan was bragging on me that I knew things, how I knew when Sirius the dog would die in January and other things I can't remember, and I was diddling with the doily on the chair arm like anybody does when they're being praised. And the whole scene was silly, I mean it was like telling ghost stories.

Yuseph was sitting there in his big chair that nobody else sat in and Ellen was in her straight-backed chair so she'd be ready to jump up and serve somebody anything and Stan was bragging on me about knowing when somebody would die and stuff like that.

Now, my feeling about why he was carrying on like that is that he was having mixed feelings about the things I knew, and he wanted to see how they sounded when he told them. It was like a combination of "See what a remarkable creature she is." "Help! I've married a witch!" "Can you believe this?" "Should I encourage this?" and "Here's a Sibyl if anyone wants one."

Yuseph took up on the latter. "How much longer have I got?" he wheezed, and I gasped and looked at him. His face bagged hugely, skin so thick with broken capillaries from drink that it was rosy,

119

hiding a blue-green pallor almost completely. His vast belly sagged bloated over long, thin legs. And yet I had never thought of him dying. His energy was intense. He had an incredible power, his charisma shouted, "Here I am! I have done great things! I am brilliant!" And it was all true. It was partly his brilliance that gave him power. Though I've met brilliant people who didn't pour it out, as he did, as passionate life-loving energy. My feeling is that brilliance tends to bring out a person, makes the soul articulate.

Anyway, there he was right in front of me. "How much longer have I got?" he said. And he kind of believed but he didn't believe, at least that's what I thought I thought.

Scientists don't believe. Scientists need proof. And yet he'd been raised in Rumania. I imagine there were "wise women" in Rumania and you could ask them a thing and they'd tell you the answer. But then he was looking down at me, humoring me. I was young. Young and very shy. Could a "wise woman" be twenty-five years old and pregnant for the third time? Naturally, he smiled down at me like an adult allowing a child to show off her new piece on the piano. Well, maybe he acted that way because he, too, was shy. Such a thought didn't cross my mind at the time.

I gasped when he asked me that and I looked at him in a way to see the number he was asking for and in a second or two it came to me. Seven years.

That was it, seven years. Seven times to see the lilacs bloom, seven times to swelter through Summer, seven leaf displays as school started, seven changes to Winter tires, seven years. It wasn't enough. If I said seven years, he'd be scared, he'd be haunted, he'd lose power from fear. If I told him seven years and he did die in seven years, I'd have appeared to have cursed him, I'd have seemed to have done something to him. I didn't want that burden, that seeming responsibility. Now I see why people don't tell the things they know even to themselves. Few were there when Relativity was turned into The Bomb. Knowledge can be used easily to destroy. What's hard is figuring out how not to do that, how to use knowledge benignly. I didn't want to be involved with his death. I didn't even want to make him feel bad. I liked his power, I didn't want to weaken it. Would I have weakened it? I thought of Ellen, smiling at me, too. She was thinking, "What a thing to ask her and so shy, poor child. What will she say? What is there to say to such a question?" Something like that. I looked at her, slim, bright, full of grace, a delicately aging elf. I looked at her and I thought, "I'll say fifteen years."

So that's what I did. The whole thing took about four seconds, two to see the seven when I looked at Yuseph and two to look at Ellen and think fifteen and then say it.

"Ah, well!" he said and looked highly pleased. His face flushed, he rubbed his hands, leaned back, spread his arms, crossed his left leg back over his right. "That's more than I expected!"

And then I knew that he knew it was seven. He was, as I say, brilliant and intuitive and he knew it was seven and wanted to know if I'd confirm it.

121

He knew it was seven and he was already scared and I had given him a hope that his hunch was maybe inaccurate. A scientist wants proof to back his intuitions.

Now I'm not wondering about right and wrong. I'm just saying what choice I made and trying to understand why I lied. I had enough to deal with without the time of his death ticking along after both of us. I gave him a lie and I believe I could see he recognized it was a lie. He appeared to accept it and then the subject was dropped. Somewhere in their minds, all three of them knew I had lied. And naturally, because I had lied, at that moment I stepped off Sibyl's chair. Although I had the sight to be a Sibyl, I hadn't the detachment to vocalize what I knew without getting swept up in it somehow. A shield of shy tension blocked the easy flow of the truth and I gave the lie as a defense, tossed my Sibyl's scepter into the trash, and stepped down out of the spotlight to see if I could vanish into the crowd.

We all have it, I know we do. We are all Sibyls. I see people acting on such knowledge all around me. Oh, it's not just when a person will die, that's a very dramatic question. Of course there are many others just as dramatic: "What's happening to my marriage ... to my health? ... to my teenage daughter?" I hear people all around me saying repeatedly, "I don't know the future and I don't want to know it." I hear it so often that it's obvious to me that it's people denying such knowledge as they have, their reasons being refusal of responsibility, or respect for others' wishes for ignorance. Or perhaps there are other reasons.

Yuseph died seven years later. And Ellen died fifteen years later. These numbers might have been changeable but they didn't change. I don't think that what is foreseen is inevitable. I think a person sometimes comes to a choice that can change his or her destiny. And I think that we make such a choice with knowledge of the results.

I believe that this occasion was such a case for me. Typically, it was the sort of occasion that one forgets within minutes or at least by the next day. I didn't forget it because I had deliberately dishonored myself and was disturbed and confused about it. If I had had more social graces at the time, I could, perhaps, after making sure that Yuseph really wanted to know, have given him the number privately.But we are not, in this culture, trained to such politenesses, at least I never was. In this culture, we have traditional fears carefully passed on from generation to generation of such things as are called witchcraft. My fear of inadvertently becoming harmful to Yuseph, of hurting him through my knowledge of his future, caused me to lie to him. But I believe now that if I had then had more respect for myself, and more respect also for Yuseph, i.e., recognition of him as a real person and also a brave one, it might have done him good to know what number had come to my mind.

I think it would have done me good to have found a way to tell him. At that time, in spite of these recognitions, I was aware of people more as forces or figures of authority than as living, worrying creatures like myself. I lied to Yuseph because I felt my position was untenable. I felt as though I was being ganged up on and teased. I was too much what's called "self-conscious" and I felt the need to develop my perceptions in the privacy of my own mind. If I had had the grace and maturity to answer truthfully at that time, it would have been a statement, a proclamation that I held the reins and that my childhood was over.

If I had had the grace and maturity to answer truthfully at that time, I wonder, what and where would I be now?

GOODBYE TO BARBARA

We were just pulling out of our parking place when the girls saw Elfriede coming down the street. I had a vain hope that she wouldn't see us. Only because I had one more errand to do and fifteen minutes before the stores closed. But the errand had to wait.

Elfriede spotted us and waved urgently. Have you ever considered how much can be conveyed with a wave? One could make a study of waves. A wave is really a blatant revelation of the state of mind of the waver. And a wave is an order. There are waves which say: "Let's get together soon," and those that say: "Don't bother me. Don't come a step closer," and then the ones that say: "I'm feeling fragile. If you speak to me, be gentle." Or how about the one that says, "Let's have a party!" or "I'm drunk!" or "Come and embrace me!" And the whole set of goodbye waves. "No problem; we'll see each other soon." "Thank God that's over." "It's been a real pleasure." "You're leaving me here alone." "Bless you." "Now you know me!" "This is the end!" As I think about it, the list is endless. And strangely, we all do read these waves and know them and their meanings.

Elfriede waved at me urgently. It was a wave that couldn't be denied. I was, as I said, pulling out of the parking place and looking at the traffic, but the power of her wave was such that I had to succumb. It was very intense. She crouched, formed her mouth in an 0, looked at me, waving fast and furious, level with her head. What could I do? My mind raced thinking what it was that she had to say. With a flash, I remembered.

Forrest had told us that Barbara was dying. We had gotten the impression that she was past visiting. She had, according to rumor, gone to the doctor with a stomach ache and he had said terminal cancer. She had then put all her affairs in perfect order, had lain down and gone promptly into a coma. The only thing to do was to wait for the funeral.

Dear Barbara. She was a real lady. We hadn't seen her for years. And if we had seen her, would we have thought of things to say? Or do? What was our relationship with Barbara? A year buried in the past. But that that is buried always affects the landscape.

I opened the car door for Elfriede. "It's Barbara. She's dead," I blurted, uncool as usual.

"No," said Elfriede. "Not yet. I think she would like to see you. She's remembering old times."

"I had heard that she was unavailable, in a coma or something," I stammered. "Here, come in and sit down for bit." I turned off the engine. It was cold out but the car was warm.

Elfriede sat. She said that Barbara chose to die in her own bed. "She's not the hospital type," Elfriede explained apologetically. It was not the sort of thing Elfriede would say, but it felt as if she had said it many times. "I've gotten another person to replace me in my work and I'm just taking care of Barbara. I've been doing nothing else. No Christmas presents, no pastries either, just taking

care of Barbara. Nobody's even offered me a cookie."
There was a cookie left in a bag on the seat of the
car. I offered it to her. She wolfed it hungrily and
went on. "Just this morning, I thought of your
family. She's been remembering, living over the
past, and I had a sudden feeling that she would very
much like to see you all."

I was touched. That such a tender sophisticate
like Barbara would really like to see us on her
deathbed excited me -- frightened me. But I resolved
then and there that we would go. On our way to
Barbara's, I picked up Stan. When he learned where
we were going, he was angry, mean, glowering. He was
in no mood to be kind or gracious to anyone. But I
held firm. We were going.

It had been the four of us then, Barbara and
George, Stan and me. '61 it was. George had wanted
Stan to make a film about his biology book. The
foolish idea had been that we would make a big
success in the educational film field, make a series
of films from all of George's books, and thus solve
the quite desperate problem of buying groceries.

George and Barbara, of course, had no such
problem.

The books were selling well. George used to
like to show people all the translations of them.
The University was proud to have him on the faculty
of the Physics Department. George's son Igor and
Igor's new bride Elfriede were also prized members
of the University.

In spite of the fact that some people called
George a drunk for the amazing amount of vodka he
consumed, he commanded respect, even awe, in the

campus and the town. He was a presence and an intelligence, a mine of information, a bursting vitality in spite of his red-lined face and his vast paunch. In his younger pictures he was quite slim, but when we knew him he was carrying an impressive bulk on his long lean legs.

In those days, Barbara had fluttered pleasantly about him. Elegant and sophisticated with a real sense of taste, she had made a soothing and gracious environment around George. Their apartment, and later the house they bought, was simple and warm, his flamboyance contained in her modesty.

Barbara had worked in the publishing house where George's books were produced. She was always very involved in literature. Their romance began with little rhymed notes in manuscripts and amiable postscripts at the bottom of business letters, also rhymed. An ancient courtship tradition. Lady Murasaki tells of it in the courts of Japan in the 11th Century. They were both good at that sort of thing: quick, witty, and sharp with words. Though Barbara would never say anything that would hurt. Her forte was whimsy. Light and feathery.

It had been strange to meet George after reading his books because he maintained a very thick Russian accent. "Beeg Cheorge," I liked to call him. And he had a very high voice. Barbara's voice, characteristically, was low and warm, musical. I'll never forget her warm chuckle. She really knew how to chuckle. A quiet, modest sound from deep down, an audible embrace, it sent warm chills up the back. Not many people know how to chuckle these days. She was a master at it.

It was strange, now, to look at an apartment house and know there was a lady dying in there. Frightening then to deliberately push the button by her name, to jump at the sound of the buzzer. It buzzed repeatedly as we trooped through the entrance and up the carpeted stairs to her door at the end of a long hallway. George had died years before.

Elfriede had said that Barbara would like to see the children in spite of the fact that more than a dozen years had passed and they were all teenagers. "What'll we do?" they asked me. "Just smile," I said. "She knew you very well when you were little, so it would be nice for her to see you for a minute."

Could this little old face on the pillow be Barbara? A white face in a sea of white sheets? It was clearly the face of someone dying and so it must be Barbara. It's amazing how important hair is in one's memory of a person. Barbara's hair never called attention to itself, being brown and fine with some gray mixed in, neatly arranged on her head, modestly accentuating her terrific cheekbones. She was one of those beauties of whom it is always said, "She has bones." Always slim and willowy, very difficult to tell their age, they drift through the world, insulated by an aura of grandeur.

Yes, there were her bones, cheekbones that anyone might envy. A shame to be taking such bones to the grave. But of hair there was very little, a few gray wisps just touching the pillow, and her face was left there in this sea of white without support or decoration. Not much in the way of wrinkles either. Not even on her forehead. But I remembered wrinkles on her forehead before. It may be that in the past few years, or maybe just in her dying, she changed her attitude somehow -- stopped raising her eyebrows. There are several ways of raising eyebrows, too, one being a challenging question. Of course she didn't do that. Ever. But there's another way, raising just the insides of the eye brows, holding the outside down, that widens the eyes and gives an expression of kindly open sympathy and understanding. It was for this expression that she did get a few shallow wrinkles on her forehead. These wrinkles had been reassuring to me in the old days. I took from them the kindly feeling that if I were my usual bumbling self she would be patient and try to understand.

But now on her deathbed they were gone. It may be that in the act of dying she had relaxed her face, quit being a gracious hostess, so that she could concentrate on her own feelings for a change.

What were her feelings? She was very weak. I didn't think that head, so pale, could raise itself. We all thundered into the room, a white bedroom with a dresser holding a few vanities from happier times, a jewel box, some medicine bottles, a pleasant picture on the wall, no mirror. No mirror at all. She must have removed it just before she went to bed. Could it be that she never had a mirror? She always had that quiet beauty. It would be vanity or shame that would actually remove a mirror. Almost an act of violence.

Barbara was in pain. There was no doubt of it. It's always amazed me, the different responses to the different levels of pain. When you bang your

shin or scratch your finger, you jump about
hollering, contorting your face. Very impressive.
But when the pain is real and deep, a relaxation
seems to take over. The voice becomes muted, the
face clears. A few quiet moans and a look of
internal concentration replaces the intensity of the
surface response.

It was hard to see beyond the shock of her
condition to her actual feelings. I think she was
bewildered. All those big children. What were they
doing there? Who were they? But then, with
Elfriede's help, she realized who they were, what we
all were. The weakness in her face shifted to
recognition and then a wan smile of gentle delight.
"What a panorama!" she sighed.

The five children all stood in a row around
Barbara's deathbed and smiled. Stan entered the room
last with a shy grin on his face. We all seemed
somewhat embarrassed at the mass of the children,
how they had grown.

Soon Elfriede and the children filed out of the
room and left Stan and me with the dying woman. He
took her hand and talked gently and pleasantly of
old times. How could he do it? He had just been grim
and gruff, weighted down and uncomfortable. How
could he rise to an occasion like that and achieve
gentleness and warmth? I sat and looked at Barbara
as they murmured together.

Stan was sitting on the side of the bed, I at
the foot. He was leaning toward her with courtly
grace, holding her hand. They talked of old friends,
of James and Frank, and, of course, of George. They
remembered old times. She opened up with the

131

slightest lean of her head toward him and I saw her eyes opening to him like an infant nursing. Eyes of pure clarity without the need to get anything across, without the need even to see, with only the swirling, contained fire of life.

Once I saw eyes like that in a bum on the streets of Denver. He was staggering along clutching a bottle with a little bit left in it, clutching it to his heart. I was amused at first, but I looked at him again. He was shambling, his eyes -- of necessity -- on the sidewalk. He came abreast of the car I was sitting in and stopped, raised his head and peered around, and for a brief instant I saw in his face the burning maskless, unspecific passion, the helpless, placeless, flaming affirmation of life found perhaps in any eyes, but accentuated beyond measure in those who know they are dying.

Her eyes were breathtakingly full of life. They were gray volcanoes, they were wild, swirling storms at sea. "I'm so accustomed to having nothing in my hand," she murmured. My first thought was that she was babbling in her extremity, but suddenly with a shock, I understood. Her hands, then, were to her not tools, not part of her form or her image, but her own living self, moving over the sheets, clutching her side when a stab of pain racked her body, lying still sometimes like trees on a windless day. And now Stan's hand was in one of them and she must have felt it as amazing and wonderful.

Her arms were startlingly thin with great prominent veins, but her body under the sheets seemed swollen and shapeless. "Ouch," she said quietly, then apologized. "Please excuse me if I say 'ouch' and 'oh.' I'm not very brave." The pain of terminal cancer. There we were, hale and strong and as helpless as she to do anything for her.

"Elfriede says you're being heroic," I offered. She had said the doctor had informed them that Barbara had been in very intense pain for several months, but hadn't expressed it anyone. Stoic. Like the Spartan child who put a wolf cub in his shirt and didn't let on when it started eating his insides.

A couple of times as she and Stan talked quietly of other people, she chuckled. I hadn't dared to hope to hear that chuckle again. Very soft and weak, but it was the real thing. When I heard that, I knew it was right to visit her. She was enjoying it.

Stan bent and kissed her hand, then she took my hand.

I couldn't think of a thing to say. The old smile was still stuck to my face and I couldn't get it off. I held her hand and stroked it and soaked up those eyes in silence for a couple of minutes. She didn't say anything either. Then I wrenched myself away, stopped at the door to look back. She waved weakly. I did, too. "Oh, well," the wave said. "Goodbye."

CHOREOGRAPHY WITH WILDLIFE

We four humans stood on the path at the top of the talus, a big one, a steep slope of boulders upon boulders above timberline, home and haven for marmots and pikas. Three marmots had run across the path before us, the middle one small and young, between two adults. It was late July and the young one was squirrel-size. Obedient to his parents, he went into a barrier of rock open to the South. It looked to me as though he had been there many times before. He knew what to do. He hid from us behind the barrier; the big male marmot in front of him vanished somewhere into the many interstices in the boulders. The mother stood between her offspring and us, her gloriously auburn back to us, neck craned around to look at us sideways, one black eye checking us out for movement or sign of aggression. And although we chattered among ourselves, we made no such sign.

Her dark brown body was bulky, her fur bushy. We were arrested by the expressive intelligence in her eye. She was used to people on the path, even to seeing them stop and look at her and her offspring. Marmots have about five babies early in the Spring, but I saw no others in her care. Soon the young one crept out and stood on his hindquarters to look around. Pikas bubbled up from caves under the boulders and dibbled about. One came quite close to us, looking at us, chittering in what seemed possibly a friendly or

134

begging tone. I pulled a peanut out of a pocket and was bending with it when, from across the talus, I heard a pika's shrill whistle quickly repeated, a sound with the obvious urgency of a siren or an alarm bell.

I looked across the talus at the sound, and saw the pika who had given the alarm disappear into the maze below her. Then I saw at the far side of the talus a tiny dainty form, innocent face alertly attentive, round ears standing out, long slim body, deep gold with white chest, black-tipped tail: a weasel on the hunt. She stood briefly on the rock, her eyes going to the young marmot, to his mother, and back. Then she started off toward the young one.

But the mother marmot saw her, saw her thoughts, and leaving us four now wildly chattering hikers on the path as the lesser evil, she ran toward the weasel, her fur standing on end.

The weasel flickered this way and that among the boulders, superior to the marmot in speed and agility. But the mother marmot, her last baby to defend and ten times the weasel's size, showed herself a determined and formidable antagonist. I heard no sound from either of them but we humans were so noisy, perhaps I missed it. Mother marmot was amazingly quick. She had tremendous surety on the rocks, showed power and force, and her rage was immense.

The weasel, after a few seconds, gave up the hope of young marmot for that meal but now had the problem of a great angry creature after her.

Finally, she ran toward us. Some inches in front of us was a flattish rock, two or three feet across, with a small passageway underneath. The weasel ran to the rock, the mother marmot took a shortcut to it and was close, very close, when the weasel shot through to our side of the rock. The marmot, too big to follow, was stopped. The weasel dashed then across a few inches in front of our feet toward where the pika had been, the one I had thought to offer a peanut to. Mother marmot went no further from her young one huddled out of sight. The weasel slowed her pace and danced lightly away, her golden pelt flashing in sunlight, seeming not to touch the ground, across a luminous bit of greensward and vanished over a ridge of rock.

We looked around the talus. There were no pikas in sight. Mother marmot returned to her post between her hidden young and us. After a few seconds the pikas came out again; the baby marmot peered out from behind his rock; another mature marmot rose up from below and looked around. A pika across the way whistled the long call, "All clear!" throwing her body forward as she whistled with all she had, like a bugler. We four hikers, suddenly remembering our desire to reach the top, stood a few seconds longer in reverence of lives we saw were full of solid intensity. Then we headed on up the path.

BIOGRAPHY OF A HEN

I was not present at her hatching, nor did I
have the pleasure of her chickhood. But one
evening, Neowyn brought a miserable red hen in from
the chickenhouse with some of her feathers gone and
a pronounced limp, plus bloody spots on her head
and wings. She had gotten her foot stuck between
the floorboards. The other chickens had been
gathered around her, tearing her slowly to bits.
She had been lying on her side waiting for death.
Neowyn put her in the bathroom in a tipped-over box
with some straw in it and a little dish of
chickenfeed and one of water and -- with more hope
than irony -- named her Sunshine.

Sunshine sat gloomy and frightened for several
days, producing huge splats of droppings in
profusion all over the bathroom floor. Finally Stan
and I agreed that it was time to put her out. But
then it seemed obvious that she couldn't go back to
the chicken yard, so Neowyn set up a box on the
front porch for Sunshine to sleep in.

Her wounds were nearly healed. The feathers,
of course, were in quite as miserable a state as
they had been, and her limp appeared to be
permanent. But she was eating well and seemed
cheerful enough.

That first winter, Sunshine spent most of her
time in her box, coming out only on warm days. It
was during the next Summer that she opened up some
and showed us her character. When the snow melted

and the sun was warm and the wind no longer howled across the porch, we took to coming out and sitting there, drinking tea, eating, talking, listening to music through the screen door. Sunshine, having understandably developed a dread of chickens yet being a gregarious creature, naturally gravitated to the company of humans.

It began with the sunflower seeds, I think. Stan and I were sitting on the porch one day, and I was giving sunflower seeds to the chickadees. Sunshine was pecking around under the table, and Chopin was on the record player. The chickadees hit a lull in their activities, and I started eating the sunflower seeds myself, giving complete attention to one seed at a time, cracking a hull between my teeth and dropping it down onto the porch floor while I concentrated on eating the seed. Sunshine expressed interest in what I was doing, racing to each hull expectantly, picking at it, then dropping it in disappointment. Then she took to looking at my hands with her head tilted to one side. Obediently, I held out one of the hulled seeds and she pecked it from my fingers with that quick, forceful hammer-blow characteristic of chickens. It was an act of courage on my part to keep from pulling my hand back and dropping the seed but her eye was completely accurate. Gulping it into her crop, she'd look up at me for more. Keeping an eye out for chickadees, I went on with this entertainment till I thought it might be too rich for her digestion, but the ritual was repeated many times. It was months before I realized that she liked them just as well with the hulls on.

There were other favorites, too. She had an inordinate fondness for blue cheese and I once watched with horror as several dollars' worth of it vanished down her gullet. Her favorite food of all was a delicious vitamin-packed cake, good fare for dieters because one piece would do for a meal and the cake kept well. She ate it with glassy-eyed enthusiasm. When visitors put down cups of wine or beer, Sunshine would rush over to plunge her beak into it and after a few beakfuls her walk, tricky at best, became hilariously difficult.

I should mention Alice, the little female raccoon that Neowyn got for her birthday two years before, and had raised with infinite care and tenderness to adulthood. In that Summer when Sunshine began to open herself to us, Alice became impatient with the confines of her cage and we felt it was necessary to release her, at least for the summer. We left food in the cage but she wouldn't eat it because she feared a trap. Instead, she went to Sunshine's box on the porch and tried to open it, so we took to leaving food on the porch for Alice night after night: dog food, granola, bananas, eggs, meat. The price of keeping Alice out of Sunshine's box was enormous.

But that October, Alice came to the porch with a coon's ravenous Autumn hunger, managed at last to open the latch of Sunshine's bed-box, grabbed her and hauled her squawking wildly out of the box. I leaped up out of a sound sleep, crashed down the hall, banged the door, and saw Sunshine standing alone on the driveway with blood dripping off her wing, but not too much battered. I propped a chair against the door of her box and later the children made a more solid latch. Anyway, Alice was caught and locked up for the winter, when she mostly slept.

Peace returned to the porch as the Winter came on, the wind blew, and Sunshine preferred most days to stay near her box.

The next Summer, Sunshine really got involved with the classical music that Stan was playing on the record player. He would pick out a Beethoven Quartet, and he and Sunshine would sit together reveling in sun and music. When the record came to a stop, Sunshine would get up and hunt for food while Stan turned the record over.

Then in the Summer, when Alice's energy made her clamor for freedom, we again found it prudent to let her out, but what with the new latch and putting out food every night, we felt Sunshine should be fairly safe.

Toward the end of that summer, Sunshine became quite shameless in her passion for music, and as her love of music emerged, she revealed her preferences. She didn't like Glenn Gould's performances at all or, for that matter, any solo instruments except the organ. Her all-out favorites were Bach and Beethoven orchestral works with Tchaikovsky, Rimsky-Korsakov, Shostakovich and Rachmaninoff as lesser delights. But give her Beethoven's Seventh, and she would squat beside the screen door, lean her head against it, close her eyes, then lie on her side with her feet dangling limply, her wings sprawled out, and her beak sagging open. At first seeing her this way gave us quite a fright, but then we all got used to it and respected it. We always checked on Sunshine when we wanted to go out while the music was on, to be sure not to disturb her musical ecstasies. Whenever a record would come to an end, she would jump up to get out of Stan's way before he went in to turn the record over. Clucking quietly, she would peck around under the table waiting for the glory to continue.

By this time her feathers had more or less grown back, except for the long wing feathers, and she looked quite splendid, glistening auburn rainbows in the sun. Her walk, however, had not improved. I felt that her leg was dislocated and that a good pull in the right direction might pull it straight. But that is the kind of thing one puts off. She was happy. Why cause her the excruciating pain that would come from such an operation—and a chancy one at that? But she did always step on her left foot with her right and then had to pull the left foot out from under. And with no long wing feathers, she couldn't fly at all, so she only clucked and chattered around the porch, going from sunlight to shade, joining the people and gathering tidbits with a professional air, and of course – her greatest joy of all – listening to classical music. Stan said she was the most intense and truly interested music appreciator he had ever come across.

The other chickens were grown now and had a complex social scene in the backyard. Sometimes the two roosters who, contrary to the natural tendency in roosters were the best of friends, would come around to the front porch to visit Sunshine much against her will. She would protest and one of us would go out and chase the roosters away. Their visits were clearly a disturbing trauma and sometimes we would find her huddled in a ruffled and discomfited ball in a corner of the porch. It seemed that, although she had many happy things in her life, she was neurotic if not psychotic about chickens and about sex in particular. In the years she lived on the porch, she never laid an egg.

That fall, Alice struck again and very much the same thing happened. Sunshine squawked, I came out, scared Alice away, and found Sunshine bloody, but well enough, in the driveway. Again we locked Alice up for the winter and settled down for a time of peace.

It was about this time that by chance we acquired a male fantail pigeon, and after he'd been in the house for a few days I took him out to the porch to sit in the sun. Very quickly, he and Sunshine formed a relationship. Fanny, the pigeon, was dominant but benevolent and a fifth Sunshine's size. Sunshine's problem in the chicken house had been a fatalistic humility. Fanny never took advantage of this, having no desire to peck at her, though he always pecked at everyone else. And so, over the weeks, the relationship of the two disparate birds went from curiosity through fascination to delighted companionable friendship. They went together from sun to shade and back again, Sunshine chattering away in her amiable tongue, Fanny cooing and burbling back at her, chest thrown out in an accentuated strut which hid his head completely from a front view and brought him up on his toes. Yet he was much more agile than she and he would prance circles around her in this position. At times, they would nap together in the shade of the table, facing opposite directions, tail feathers touching, eyelids drooping and rising, drooping and rising. At night, we'd bring Fanny in the house to perch on his high shelf and put Sunshine back in her old box.

The following summer was lush and gluttonous for Alice, partly from the attentions of a friendly neighbor and partly from our own continued ministrations on the porch — and the rest I don't know. I hate to think of the robbed birds' nests and whatnot other tragedies she caused in the woods around. In any case, when we brought her in that fall, she was incredibly fat, but with the colder weather coming on, she lost her appetite, as coons do in the Winter, and mostly slept. By Christmas she had lost weight and found it at last possible to slip outside through a small hole high up in a corner of her cage. This she achieved one sunny day in the Christmas vacation. Of course, we worried about her finding a good place to sleep and getting enough to eat in the long Winter ahead and of course we began putting out her usual dish of goodies. We also fortified Sunshine's box, which was a stout wooden one with the door made of chickenwire screen. The top and sides were covered with burlap bags and she had a bed of hay on the bottom. At night, she would go in there and the kids would close the chickenwire door, drape an old blanket over it, latch the hook, wrap a rope around the box, tie it to the porch railing, and jam some logs up against the door for good measure.

The months went by and Alice never came. I assumed—nay, hoped for Sunshine's sake—that her untimely escape had led to hard times for her and she had died, so that In April when I heard little scrabbling sounds on the porch for three nights running, I attributed them to a cat we had seen in the neighborhood. But on the fourth night, a strangled squawk shot me out of bed, down the hall, banging the door, looking down the driveway—but this time it was different. Alice was in the box and Sunshine's body was still, her head held firmly under Alice's little delicate hand. Alice looked up at me with her sweet mischievous face as I yelled at her, started to grab at the loose skin on the back of her neck, remembered a couple of severe bites she had given me in the past, pulled my hand back and yelled some more. Alice dragged the unprotesting hen by the head down the steps and under the cars, then disappeared around the side of the house as I stood wailing in the snow.

I went in and wept for the death of the lovely personage who had graced our lives. Eventually, I calmed down and dressed, sleep being beyond my capabilities and went around the house, looking at shadows. One shadow by the back door attracted my eye. A dark lump not lying down but standing. Sunshine, or whatever Alice had left us of her. I stood for a moment straining my eyes into the night trying to fathom why Alice would break into Sunshine's box, hurt her, drag her off, and then leave her mangled but on her feet by the back door. I felt that if I could understand Alice's action, it would open my mind to understanding the actions of other creatures.

We never saw Alice again, though we heard she was living down by the lake.

I think she must have heard something in my cries of caring about this particular hen. And as she cared about and respected me, she lost her appetite, dropped her prey, and left. She felt bad, knowing she had damaged Sunshine beyond repair. Raccoons are sensitive creatures. She knew that now we would feel differently about her, and so she moved to the lake and never returned to us. So that was why Alice finally reverted, as they call it, to the wild.

Sunshine took three weeks to die. We hovered around and medicated her, played music and offered her wine and beer. Fanny the pigeon came and cooed his best but nothing was able to reconnect what Alice had cut. And then one morning Sunshine was dead, and we buried her in the yard.

It was some time after that, after the grieving was over, I found myself saying to someone, "We once had a chicken who loved Beethoven." But I heard some wrong note. She was much more than that, she was a complex personality.

And Alice was, too. Alice, playing the villain from the viewpoint of Sunshine's will to live, nonetheless was no villain at all if one looked into her actual mentality. I can't fault Alice for liking the taste of chicken, nor for coming to us for food when she was hungry. Both creatures opened themselves for me to see into their minds by doing things that were not direct or practical. Neurotic things, like people do.

145

CASWÁLLON AND THE ROMANS

It was Caswállon himself who was the first
to see the Roman ships come across the channel for
the second time. He was young then: young, tall,
gray-eyed, slim, and so fast he could outrun any
man or even any pony on the Island of the Mighty.
He saw the Roman ships and he spread his men along
the top of the bluff and watched as a small boat
came to shore pulling behind it a swimming horse.
When it came out of the water, Caswállon could see
that the horse was nothing like the stubby brown
ponies of Britain. It was twice their height, it
was slender and lithe and gray. Spirit flamed from
its eyes. A man got on its back and it ran faster
than the wind, faster than anything imaginable,
its gray mane and tail held high and flowing out
behind it. And Caswállon wanted that horse more
than he had wanted anything else before.

Then the man slid off the horse's back and
walked toward Caswállon, leading the horse. He
bowed before Caswállon and by sign and gesture
said he could have the horse, if only the ships
could land on the beach.

And Caswállon took the horse to the ring of
huts behind a rock wall that he called home and he
named the horse Meinlas. And thus began the second
invasion of Julius Caesar on the Island of
Britain.

This exchange was called one of the Three
Terrible Mistakes in the history of the Island of

146

the Mighty.

It didn't take Caswállon more than a day or two to realize that he had been deceived and he got really angry. But his tribe, the Catuvellani, weren't called the Fighting Experts for nothing. Before a week was out, the men in all the Catuvellani villages were sharpening their iron knives and their javelins, fitting up their covinni, their war-chariots, with iron blades on the axles, shaving with their daggers every hair off of their bodies, every hair, except for their moustaches and the long hair on their heads, which they stiffened to fierce, raucous peaks with lime-wash, and dyeing their bodies and their faces blue with the extract of the woad plant. Then they gathered a few Roman heads from sentries and food-gatherers at the edges of the Roman camp, and they brought the heads home so that the Druid shamans could glean secrets out of them and thus weaken the Roman troops with haunting and confusion.

The spirit of a man was in his head and the Catuvellani Celts collected heads and brought them to their Druids. The Druids performed magic rites with them to weaken the enemy and strengthen the tribe, to appease the gods and keep everything on the right track. For there to be harmony and fruitfulness in the tribe and in the land, there always had to be fresh heads for the Druids. Some heads were special, and a man, especially a chief as Caswállon was, could embalm the head of an enemy chief or of his father or grandfather or a favorite uncle, embalm it in cedar oil and keep it in a cedar chest. It would keep that way for years and years. The man could at any time open the cedar chest and talk to the head and be in touch with the spirit of the man whose head it had been. Thus he could gain strength from it or get inspiration or good advice. Heads could be placed in a row to guard a fortress. Or a single head of a truly great man could be buried in a powerful location and, by the power of the spirit contained in it, ward off invasion for so long as the head was undisturbed, even to hundreds of years.

Caswállon's cousin, Bendigeid Vran, a giant who was at that very time conquering and killing everyone in the island called Eire (except five pregnant women in a cave), would soon receive a poison dart in the foot and then say to his men as he lay dying: "Take my head and carry it with you wherever you go, and for eighty-seven years my head will be uncorrupted. All that time, my head will be as pleasant a companion as when it was on my body. When the eighty-seven years are over, bury it at the White Mount in London facing Gaul. For as long as it is buried there, there will be no invasion in all of the Island of the Mighty." His men would do exactly as he told them to do. For eighty-seven years, they would live in a happy dream that would be called The Entertaining of the Noble Head. After the eighty-seven years were over, they would bury the head in the White Mount facing Gaul. By the time that head of Bendigeid Vran was buried, Rome would have all but conquered the Island of the Mighty. For over four hundred years there would be no further invasion.

That would be called the Third Goodly Concealment.

After the four hundred years, King Arthur would come and dig up the head of Bendigeid Vran, saying that he would guard the Island of the Mighty himself. In less than a year from that act, which would be called the Third Ill-Fated Disclosure, Cerdic the Saxon would invade and fight with Arthur and settle his people in the Island. And a quarter-century later, the Vikings would invade from the north and kill King Arthur.

By that time there would have been no headhunting for centuries. None would shave their pubic hairs or cover with blue woad or use lime-wash to make their hair stand on end. No Druids would dance and chant rites or pull secrets out of enemy heads. Cedar boxes came to be used to hold jewelry.

But the Druids were strong when Caswállon accepted the Roman horse. And as the Druids were performing magic with the Roman heads, Caswállon and all the warriors of his tribe decked themselves in woad and lime, in gold and silver torcs and armbands, with oval leather shields, spears, javelins, daggers and swords, with two-wheeled, two-pony covinni, some with scythes attached to their axles. Then, naked, bluer than death, hair in white, fierce spikes, Caswállon and his men would ride out from behind a hill or a rock or a clump of trees into the armored marching troops of the Romans, zigzag in short blinding dashes, hurl javelins and then spears, rush through the stumbling weighted Roman warriors, their swords lopping heads as the scythed covinni cut through legs of any man or horse that came near. Then, in a flash, they'd turn their ponies, still at a gallop, and zigzag away, the belated weapons of the Romans missing them (most of them) as they galloped, dangling Roman heads in the air, whooping and shouting their victory, home to hang the heads over the doors of their huts or let the heads join the family at dinner, as centerpieces.

Four thousand covinni Caswállon had, eight thousand ponies galloping, eight thousand scythes on axles, uncountable javelins and spears and sword thrusts — and then the covinni would dash away before a Roman sword could barely be unsheathed. And they went back again the next day and the next. Any enemy the Catuvellani had ever encountered would have broken up and vanished under such treatment. But the disciplined troops of Rome held firm, closed their gaps, marched on. Sometimes a group of Roman soldiers would follow the covinni on their big horses, and then the fleeing Catuvellani would lead them like the mother grouse leads the predator with the pretense of a broken wing, lead them into ambush, take their heads and their horses, and call it another battle won. Still the Roman troops marched on.

Caswállon, respect and fear whipping him to superhuman energy, rode the fleet-footed gift-horse Meinlas to one circle of huts after another, ordered his neighbors to help him stake the river, to hide their cattle, burn their crops. He threatened them, bullied them, then rode madly on to the next place and the next, then back to his

warriors to ride Meinlas before them into the
Roman mass and to gallop out again a few moments
later, sometimes with as many as half a dozen
Roman heads more to his credit.

Then he'd ride, tireless, forward to the
river to see how the staking was going on at the
ford. He had high hopes for this project, heavy
staves buried deep in rock in the depths of the
ford. Their bases, encased in lead and thick as a
man's thigh, would still be visible under the
water eight hundred years later. The main part of
his own tribe's lands were on the other side of
this great river. If only he could keep the Romans
from crossing, if he could head them back at the
ford, maybe they'd go home.

He gathered his warriors on the other side
of the river. Thousands of new javelins were made.
When the Romans came to the ford, Caswállon would
be ready.

The Romans came to the ford and they started
across. Caswállon's men threw javelins and with
the stakes impaling the Roman horses and the
javelins impaling the soldiers, the river ran
blood and floated corpses, but somehow many many
of them crossed. The Roman army moved across the
river and up the bank on the other side.

The Catuvellani could bear no more of it.
Blue-dyed men fled in all directions and made
their separate ways back, slinking, hiding,
through marshes and hills, avoiding the Roman army
and avoiding Caswállon, too, back to their huts
where they spoke of the god-like inexorable might
of the Romans and of Caswállon's raging threats

and bullying. They whispered that the Romans would sometimes actually pay for the cattle they fed on, pay with little plates of gold or silver called coins that had pictures on them, whereas Caswállon simply took what was his due.

Caswállon still had some of his best warriors but many of those men who had been fighting and working at his side were now working against him, spying for the Romans, feeding them.

Some covinni still dashed into the troops and out again with heads. Other men kept busy riding ahead to chase off cattle so that even if the Romans did offer people coins for them, the cattle wouldn't be there to sell. But the spies were showing the Romans the way to Caswállon's own fort, his headquarters, a rock-walled fortress, with a stream inside it, and cattle and goats and horses, women and children, stored food, possessions, riches of gold and silver, Druids and heads and icons and places of worship, everything that a great tribe needed.

He sent as many warriors as he could to fill the fortress, but the massed and armored Romans took the fortress. Caswállon got away, and some of the warriors with him, and now there was only one thing left for Caswállon to do.

He took what he had left of his men all the way back across the land to the beach where he had gotten the great horse Meinlas. There were the ships, strongly guarded by fresh Roman soldiers. Caswállon attacked as he could, using the lightness and quickness of his naked blue savage men dashing in, then fleeing, then dashing in

152

again to cut the Roman guards with quick slashes. Caswállon was so very fast that he has gone down in history to this day as being invisible in battle. Only his sword could be seen, flashing and slashing in the sunlight. He and his men rode in and out and in again, sometimes jumping off their covinni to fight together on foot then leaping on again between the ponies, who were trained to circle back.

He and his men fought well but more Romans came out of the ships to replace those who had died, and Caswállon had no more men. And the Romans stood their ground and could not be defeated.

Caswállon and his men became exhausted and had to quit. And when Julius Caesar then asked him for parley, he said he would parley. He could think of nothing else he could do.

Julius Caesar prepared for the parley a feast. He served every kind of meat and great vats of Italian wine. Caswállon sat beside Julius Caesar, and on the other side of Caesar sat the most beautiful woman in the world. Caswállon could see that Caesar loved her. But he could also see that she didn't love Caesar but loved him, Caswállon, instead. Her name was Flur.

Caesar said that he would take his legions and leave the Island of the Mighty if Caswállon would agree to two minor concessions, which were these. The first was that Caswállon would not mistreat those tribes that had helped the Romans. And the second was that the sons of Caswállon's tribe and of every other tribe on the Island of

the Mighty, including most specifically
Caswállon's own sons and sons of other chiefs,
would come to Rome for four years of their early
youth to learn how to be Roman soldiers and to
fight as the Roman troops had fought.

Caswállon looked about him at the soldiers
who had so amazed him for their discipline, their
unity and their loyalty. As he looked at them, his
eyes in passing caressed the eyes of Flur, which
were shining at him, and he thought there could be
nothing better than that his sons, by her, be
raised to be stalwart like the soldiers of the
Roman army which went through the Island of the
Mighty like a tide and never once broke or ran
away, no matter how much blood was shed. Caswállon
smiled at Flur and said he would do as Julius
Caesar said, though everyone knew he wouldn't be
any more kind to his neighboring tribes than he
had ever been.

It was at that moment that Bendigeid Vran
received the poisoned dart in his foot just as he
had totally destroyed all the people of Eire
except five pregnant women in a cave. That night,
just as Bendigeid Vran was foretelling the future
to his men, Caswállon managed to get a private
interview with Flur, and although they couldn't
speak each other's language, they understood each
other very well. The next day, Julius Caesar
sailed away and took Flur with him and also every
soldier of his troops left alive. Bendigeid Vran
breathed his last and his men cut off his head and
placed it in a vat of cedar oil mixed with herbs
and thus began the eight-seven years called the

Entertaining of the Noble Head.

Then Caswállon called together all the Catuvellani and all the neighboring tribes, friend and foe alike, to a great feast that went on month after month, and there were always many kinds of meat available and wheaten loaves baked in honey, there were milk and cheese and roots and greens and there was cask after cask of mead and ale. There were servants ready to serve everyone with the richest fare at any time for months. This was called one of the Three Extravagant Feasts, and at this feast Caswállon made sure of his power in the land. Also at this feast he gathered three hosts of boys, sixty-three thousand boys, and decked them all with silver torcs so that they were called the Silver Host. When the feast ended, he took those sixty-three thousand boys across the water to Julius Caesar to be trained as Roman soldiers. Then he went in search of Flur and after a long wandering of a number of years he found her and all that time he never looked at another woman, for which he was called one of the Three Faithful Lovers of the Island of the Mighty. But when he did find her, she was so well guarded that he had to disguise himself as a shoemaker before he could speak with her, for which he was called one of the Three Gold Shoemakers.

By that time, he had learned the Latin language and how to make coins and helmets and other useful things. The boys of the Silver Host had grown up. They had all sold their silver torcs and some of them didn't want to go home. But Caswállon got together as many as he could. He

took Flur as his wife and they all went back to
the Island of the Mighty. And there, because of
the training of the boys who had now become men,
and because of the things Caswállon had learned,
began the great Roman Age of Britain.

And by the time the head of Bendigeid Vran
was buried, Rome had all but conquered the Island
of the Mighty except for a small but very fierce
and fiery band of heroes led by Caswállon and
Flur's great-grandson, the mythical and much-loved
Caradoc. But of Caradoc, I will tell another time.

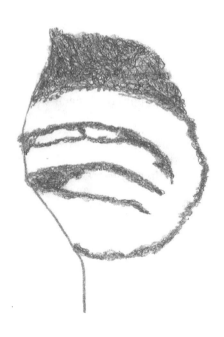

WYOMING WILLIE

"My third grade teacher felt it was time I learned to read. She got me to come in to school a half-hour early, stay a half hour late, she couldn't do anything. My fourth grade teacher asked me, 'Why don't you learn to read?' I said, 'My horse don't care if l know how to read.' Now, my dad was running the general store back there in Fremont County and she knew I didn't have a horse but she said, 'There are a lot of books about horses. If you want to learn how to take good care of your horse, you will want to be able to read those books.' So I learned to read in fourth grade.

"Then my rich grandpa died and by the time I was a senior in high school, I had eighty acres, a hundred fifty head of cattle and my dad and I were in partnership buying and selling high quality bulls. Got us another eighty acres, another hundred forty head, then we thought we'd go into cows. Things went bad then. I was in college studying animal husbandry and Dad was in charge. Then my mother died and six months later Dad and I went bankrupt. We'd been real close up till then but there was forty thousand bucks missing and he never told me why. He ruined himself and me is what he did, too, but I come out smelling like a rose, yessir, I come out smelling like a rose. He threw away half my life's work but I can forgive him now. I don't hate him; I just don't have a whole lot to say to him.

157

"His new wife, she thinks the world and all of him and they're happy as larks. She tries to tell me what a swell guy he is but she don't know him like I do. It couldn't have been gambling. He's real straight-laced and never gambled in his life except the cattle, of course. Must've been blackmail, some thing like that.

"I used to be as prejudiced as they come, cowboys tend to be prejudiced, especially against hippies. I had a lot of fun back in college fighting with the hippies. That was great.

"But there was one hippy changed all that. I got my tire in a hole in a parking lot and I couldn't get out. It was undignified. I was working away at it, getting nowhere, and I saw this hippy walking over toward me. I tensed up, almost got out of the car to fight him right there but he waved and went to the back of the car and pushed me out. I looked around to see what he'd do then. He'd got mud on him from pushing me but he smiled and waved and walked off. That hippy has saved about a thousand hippies from me. From that moment I don't pigeonhole people; I think of each one as individuals.

"Well, I come out of being bankrupted smelling like a rose but I couldn't afford to go back to college so I got drafted into Nam.

"I went and saw this movie a while ago. Everyone said it was close to the real thing, how it really was in Nam and it sure was, though we were armored so it wasn't like the movie in that way. But one part, they were going down this canal, the gooks shot everyone up. That happened to me

158

too. It's rough when guys you've been living with
for a year and count as friends suddenly blow up in
your face, guts flying around, arms, legs, a head.
When I went in I was a good shot and as it happened
I was the first guy in our outfit to kill a gook.
Boy, I couldn't wait to go down there and cut off
his ears. Time I got out though I wasn't near a
good shot, end up just throwing lots of lead into
the jungle. Never have been a good shot since then.

"Wasn't long into that movie, my stomach was
in a godawful knot and I had an imaginary machine
gun I was mowing them down with. Shaking, teeth
chattering. I'm all over it now but for a couple of
weeks after that I was having nightmares every
night. I drove the tank mostly over there and
whenever we got a prisoner the thing to do was lay
him on the ground and drive up the tank to his
head. Then if he says he won't talk, drive up
another inch or so. I never did have to run over
any heads but I sure got close a few times. I
didn't like it at all but I think I would have done
it if I'd got the order. I really think I'd have
done it. I'm not sure but I think I would have.

"Prettiest thing I've ever seen was a fire
fight across the way. It's an awful thing to live
through or die in but beautiful to watch different
colors of flames dancing about all across the
mountain. I'm glad it was guys I didn't know over
there.

"There was one time when I and one gook were
in an area and we couldn't both leave, just one of
us. I didn't like it much. The problem was, of
course, the first one to be spotted by the other

159

one dies. Sort of like a game, win or lose all. I wouldn't want to be in that position again. Finally after a godawful long time I realized he had to be in a certain area. I'd been thinking gun or even bayonet but then I pulled out a grenade and threw it in there and that was that. I didn't go in to look.

"We had to run every morning after doing our daily dozen. You're supposed to do these dozen calisthenics a dozen times each, well we did them a hundred. We got in such good shape we'd run everywhere we went, the airborne run, little short steps, really go fast, and endurance! I was smoking two packs a day and never felt near as good before or since as I did then. We'd run everywhere, messages, reveille, didn't think nothing of going ten miles to town.

"You couldn't trust any of those gooks, even on our side. There was one gook bitch we called Aunt Fanny, she ran the girls in town; Everyone knew her well, of course. She come into camp one day, a guy come up to her to see what she wanted or whatever, she pulled out a knife and slashed him across the middle. He jumped back in time, only got a cut across the stomach; one of the sentries mowed her down with his machine gun. Nobody ever figured out what her complaint was.

"I was the first one of my outfit to get home alive, it was because I broke my back. But it wasn't right at all because it wasn't a war wound. It was a road accident. I wasn't driving, this other guy was driving too fast and hit a rock, rolled the jeep, and I flew out and landed on a stump. There wasn't a gook for miles. If it had been a war wound I might have felt okay about it but it wasn't. I felt terribly that those guys needed me and I had up and left them. It was awful. I tried six times to go back in but they never would let me go. Six times I tried, but they wouldn't let me go.

"Well, so I got out of there and decided to finish up college.

"I got a good high-paying indoor job after I graduated but I can't stand being cooped up, air conditioning in the Summer, heated in the Winter, I was going crazy. That's when I got the job in Sweetwater County. Boy, that job couldn't be beat. Lived in a mansion, all the meat we wanted free, beautiful country, fine cattle, and practically my own boss. It was wonderful country, top of the world.

"I think my best friend in Sweetwater County was a hippy named Tim. He and I worked together for a couple years. He was a good man even though he was a hippy, worked as hard as any cowboy did. When my back would give me trouble, he'd fix it in a few seconds. Lived in a little place out back and was always having women visitors, sometimes as many as three and four at a time. Never saw anything like it. He had a sense of humor that was amazing. Great guy, he was a great guy. He finally went off to Canada to start a commune. He talked with me a lot about it before he went. Not one of those places with a common kitchen and all that, just neighbors, good neighbors. I've always wanted to go up there but there's no money in living in a commune. I need money, as much as I can get.

"That job in Sweetwater County was the kind of life I wanted to lead. Lots of space, the finest cattle you could find for hundreds of miles, streams and plenty of wildlife to chase around. I got into trapping there. I tell you that is fun, battling wits with badgers and beavers, cover my scent with calves blood and grease, sweep over my tracks with branches, use the foot of yesterday's kill to make tracks over the trap.

"Some of the funnest times I ever had were with my friend Jerry, roping coyotes. Coyotes are smart all right but we'd chase that little bugger down then we'd both rope it and then pull it apart. That was before we learned how much a pelt is worth. After that we did it different. I'd rope the coyote then run my horse over by a tree and whap! Snap it on the tree. Man, that is fun! And no holes in the pelt.

"One time me and my friend Tim were driving along the road and I saw a roadkill whiz by and after a bit I said to Tim, 'wasn't that a fox?' 'Well,' he said, 'I was just thinking it was a fox,' So I stopped and backed up and it sure was, smashed and tore up, took me an hour to skin out, more time to sew it up. I didn't think it was hardly worth it but I took it down and showed the guy, showed him my stitching, told him it was a road kill and all. I didn't know what he'd say but I didn't expect what he did say, 'Seventy-five dollars!' I just stood there for a second. Then I said, 'That's fine.'

"Another time Jerry and I smoked out a den of
fox kits. We did it right, blew kerosene smoke in
one hole, out the other hole come the mother,
sneezing and coughing and glaring at us. Boy, she
was mad! Whapped a gunny sack over the hole and in
it jumped the kits, six of them. There was a big
stink in the paper. 'FOX KILLERS SLAY SIX.' All the
town dudes had been coming out to see the mother
promenade her cute little babies every afternoon so
the whole town hated us. Didn't say in the paper
who did it though. We sold them kits to the
Sheriff's deputy for fifty bucks apiece. That's
three hundred for about half-hour's work. The
deputy raised them for a couple months, skinned
them out and probably got over a thousand for them.
Real nice for everyone. Even the mother got away.
    "One time I got a tape of dying rabbit, twenty
minutes of continuously dying rabbit. You know how
they sound when they're dying, sort of like a baby
crying. Well, I got up about two in the morning,
packed up my tape recorder and a little speaker and
my gun and headed out to a place I knew where I'd
seen coyote tracks, a big meadow with a little
rise, nice big tree on it. Built me a blind up
against that tree in the dark, put the speaker
about twenty feet away with the tape recorder
beside me in the blind then leaned back and smoked
my pipe until dawn. Soon as it started to light up,
I turned on the tape, didn't take five minutes
there was a coyote circling around me. He paced and
circled and doubled back and I waited. Seemed like
that coyote knew what the range of my gun was and
he was keeping out of it. Soon as the tape run out,

that little feller pointed, nose forward, and tail straight out behind, one forefoot raised under his chest. I never saw anything that good in pointing outside of a purebred pointing dog. It was a perfect point.

"Well, I rewound that tape as fast as I could, him pointing the whole time, then I turned it on again. When I did that, the coyote crouched down in the grass and started to crawl toward me on his belly. By this time there was half a dozen ravens had gathered and they were circling around above me. I raised my rifle real slow as the coyote crawled into my range and I slid it through one of the slits in the blind. The ravens must have seen the glint of it in the sun even though I had it stuck out all of about an inch but they set up an awful squawking and flew away fast. The coyote sprung up I swear five feet in the air turning as he jumped, I never saw anything like it, and he landed running like hellfire across the meadow.

"Calving was real hard. Those old cows would drop their calves in the oddest places, on a rock or into a puddle or a thicket a coon couldn't get into to lick it off. I didn't like it when they died, didn't like it at all. It wasn't because I cared about them, nothing personal, it was my reputation. Honor. I wanted to do a good job, be the best, and bring in a lot of money.

"Calving time I'd ride out constantly checking up on the cows. Seems like we'd get some bad weather, snow, wind, blinding sleet and there they'd be bellowing in every field, especially at night. Nobody sleeps calving time if they want to make money off of cows. One time I went out, real nice little bull calf out of our best cow, it was wind and sleet but that little bugger was sucking good so I thought I'd check on this other cow further off that was due. Cold night, like to froze. This other cow, she'd dropped her calf and it was thrashing around, couldn't get up, so I put it across my saddle and headed back to take them to the barn, went past the other cow with the handsome little bull calf to pick them up. When they've sucked, supposed to be they'll be all right. I hadn't been gone more than half hour, looked over, there he was lying on the ground dead and stiff as a doornail, froze to the ground. Bothered me a lot that kind of thing. That's where getting into cows is such a big gamble, If the weather's bad, that's when they're going to drop 'em and then they die and your year's money's gone. A cattleman can be ruined by one good blizzard at the right time.

"We had lots of trouble with dogs too. Any dog I see on the property I shoot it, even if it isn't paying attention to the cattle, matter of principle, no dogs allowed, that's all. And any dog I see wandering around at night, no matter where, I shoot him. I don't sanction packs. Packs are the worst thing about dogs. And it's at night they pack up most.

"One neighbor, I liked him a lot, still do, but his dog come over once and was chasing the horses around the corral. So I caught him and took him over there and told my neighbor he'd better tie up his dog because it was chasing my horses and if I saw that dog again on my property I'd shoot it.

And he said he understood and he sure would tie up
his dog. Next afternoon there was that dog again in
my corral and I shot it, tossed it in the back of
the truck and took it to him, ready for a fight.
But he took one look at it, said, 'Daggone, I
forgot to tie him up!' and that was that. We're
still friends.

   "There was one time I didn't tell anyone
though. This other neighbor had bought a five
hundred dollar coon dog and wasn't anyone prouder
than that man was of that hound. Well, he took him
out first time hunting coon and that four-star coon
dog got lost. They looked and hollered all night
long for that thing. Early in the morning I saw him
out in the pasture barking at the cattle so I shot
him. That guy looked and looked for weeks for that
dog but I wasn't about to admit to killing no five
hundred dollar dog.

   "I've got a little dog now, Spot, he's a
devil. He's part pit bull. All I have to do is I say,
'Go get'm, Dog,' and off he goes like a bullet. He
can beat any dog around. Except there was one time he
lost. That was a big Malamute-police dog mix that
came on our property when I was at work. My neighbor
went out and hit the big dog over the head with a
shovel and sent him out of there but Spot was about
dead, all tore up, lot of blood all over the ground.
Took him two weeks to recover. I didn't take him to
the vet for that one, nossir. I'd take him if I'd
have sicked him on that other dog but if the dog
decides to do some thing on his own he's got to pay
for it on his own. That's only fair. Two weeks later
Spot went back to that other dog and killed him;

didn't get a scratch.

"If I had my choice, I'd be a mountain man back before the settlers came. I don't like a lot of people around, I like space. I'd as soon never go to town again. Towns make me nervous, people irritate me; I can't even find my way around in a town. I get up early every day and work past dark, I don't like to sit around, don't like to be indoors.

"There are three things a cowboy can't take, one is if you insult his wife, another is if you insult his horse and the third is if you touch his hat. One time I put my hat down on a fence for a minute and my brother picked it up and put it on his head. I couldn't help it; I got this rage in my gut. I didn't fight him, I didn't, but I don't want anyone to touch my hat. This hat fits me, fits my head, and if anybody puts it on they mess up the shape of it. If they touch it they put their fingerprints on it. It's not the same thing with my boots. My brother's wore my boots several times, didn't bother me a bit. It's just the hat; I don't want anyone to touch my hat.

WHY GRACIE TURNED OUT LIKE SHE DID

Gracie was born on a farm in Iowa in about 1910. It was a nice farm with dairy cows and a few sheep, some pigs and chickens and ducks, oats in the barn and three dogs. And one of those dogs was hers. His name was Georgie and Georgie and Gracie roamed the woods and fields together whenever Gracie could get away from chores and school. She'd get through what she was supposed to do, call Georgie and go. That was her life and her joy. Roaming with Georgie she saw things, hawks and weasels and deer and the way the clouds roil, how the shadows move across the land, and how the magpies build their nests.

Then one day Gracie's father ran over Georgie with the tractor and he died. She knew it wasn't her father's fault and when he said, "I'm sorry, honey," she told him it was okay. But now she didn't know how to act. She couldn't somehow roam without Georgie so now when she finished her chores and her schoolwork, she just stood around in the farmyard and stared at the animals and sometimes she'd reach out and pet them. She quite liked the old sow named Hattie and the striped rooster and they weren't afraid of her. The striped rooster would stand near her companionably after he'd filled his crop and they would watch the hens together. Chickens talk a lot to each other. They cluck and growl while they eat and when a hen lays an egg she goes into a huge song of glory so Gracie got good at finding where they were hiding their eggs. And sometimes the whole flock would sing together for the joy of it and it was closer to God than singing hymns in church.

Hattie, the old sow, was, like all pigs, a hedonist and Gracie went often to pet her. When Gracie scratched her on the cheek in a certain way Hattie would close her eyes and slowly sink to the ground then Gracie would crouch beside her and scratch her till her skin wiggled.

Hattie farrowed late in the Spring with eleven piglets and Gracie's father was going to kill the runt but Gracie begged hard and said how she needed a pet real bad and her father felt guilty still about Georgie. The whole family and all the neighbors told her how impossible it was to raise a piglet and the more they told her, the more she knew how to do it.

He was a tiny little thing, she could hold him in one hand, and she nursed him first with a rag then taught him to drink from a bowl. He followed her wherever she went and she had to feed him all the time. When he could drink out of a bowl it was a lot easier and then she started mixing bread and scraps in the milk.

She named him Georgie, of course, and his greatest delight was to lie in her lap and she'd pet him and look at the animals and she felt a lot better. When he got a little bigger she'd take him on walks with her. Georgie the pig didn't look around like Georgie the dog had and find squirrels and rabbits but he followed her closer and talked to her and her alone. As Spring went to Summer he

found things to eat, showed her where a strawberry
patch was that she'd never found before and an
otter's slide, taught her which mushrooms were
good and which to avoid. He told her when it was
going to rain and warned her away from a pack of
dogs that was roaming that Summer.

But the sweetest thing was to sit with him
in her lap and scratch his head and neck and he'd
nestle and close his eyes and they were very
close, closer than anything.

Georgie grew very fast indeed and pretty
soon he was too big to hold and could only put his
head in her lap. In spite of being a runt and born
half size, he grew to be bigger than any of the
piglets in the litter and Gracie was very proud
and her family and the neighbors were impressed
though they thought it was more than a little
disgusting how she was so close to a hog and sat
and cuddled him all the time.

Then school started and when she got off the
bus he'd be there to greet her and she'd put down
her books and hug him and he'd escort her home. On
nice days she'd try to do her homework outside so
he could lay his chin on her foot. It was getting
now to where even just his head was heavy for her.

He weighed nearly four hundred pounds and
although he wasn't quite a prize pig, he was a
very big fat pig and one day when she came home
from school he wasn't there to greet her, her
father had butchered him and Georgie was hanging
in the shed, the dogs and the chickens had eaten
up most of his innards, her mother had scraped the
meat from his head for head cheese and his bare

skull was half-buried in the compost pile.

This time her father didn't say "I'm sorry, honey" like he did before and even if he had it wouldn't have worked. He said, "It was a pig and it was time to butcher it." That's all he'd say but she knew that beyond that was everyone being disgusted that she had cared, truly cared about a pig. They never took the trouble to know of the intelligence of pigs, the sensibility of them, their stalwart affection, only they fed them up and then butchered them.

It was at this point that Gracie's head turned. There were any number of ways she could have gone from this and perhaps one of the others would have been nicer but the way she went was she froze the warm feelings she had for her family and for church and everything respectable. During the next months she ate ham and bacon and pork saying to herself, "This is the body of my Christ." She even ate some of the head cheese. Whereever she went, she looked for the dirty and the low and she ran with them. When I met her, she was living in sin right in the middle of the town of Rollinsville with Johnny C_____ after he had left his family. She and Johnny drank together every night at the Stage Stop till Johnny busted a gut and died. After Johnny C_____ died, Gracie moved away and nobody knows where she is now.

171

HENRY NICCUM

The thing that's maddening about looking for gold is how well it's hidden. Always the next blast of dynamite could bring millions and the worst of it was that once in a blue moon it did and the stories went around and people got the gold fever. And once a man had the gold fever there was little he could do besides grub in the dirt for the rest of his days. There were many like that here, there are still some rummaging around, old guys setting off dynamite on the weekends. It's the Fourth of July up here all summer long.

Henry Niccum had the gold fever worse than most. He was a delicate little fellow not much over five feet tall, with a long nose, close-set eyes, a forehead full of fine wrinkles, a wide friendly-sad mouth like a clown's and a habit of screwing on his cap clockwise. He didn't own any mining claims, he was waiting until he struck gold before he made his claim and he never did strike gold. What he'd do, he'd wander through the Gulch and now and again he'd get a bug in his ear and he'd dig. He used to run to Joey C__ or some other good miner with a few pieces of rock he'd found and Joey would look at it, Henry's eyes sparkling with excitement. "Nothing," Joey would say, then Henry would be hurt and depressed and he'd wander back off into the hills.

Sometimes he'd get excited about a spot where he was digging and he'd set off dynamite there. Nobody knew where he got the money to buy dynamite, he didn't seem to have any money for food. Henry liked dynamite a lot. One time he got some dynamite and stored it in the stove in the little cabin he was living in. Across the years, he moved from one cabin to another all over the Gulch and this one was a tiny place. No one remembered then who had built it. But it had a stove with a fire box and an oven and Henry, who never cooked, hid the dynamite in the oven and for several weeks that summer he went with his shovel looking for a place to set it off.

One morning he woke shivering, the summer seemed to be over so he started a fire in the stove and went out to get more wood. Good thing he did, because while he was out cutting wood, the place blew sky-high.

It was then that he moved to the shaft-house of the Alice. The Alice had been a good mine in the seventies and then it played out. A horizontal adit for fifty yards into the hillside, a fair-sized dump glittering lifeless but tantalizing in front of it and at the portal of the mine, smack up against the hole, a cabin, sixteen-inch thick logs, a little window on each side, a gaping hole at the back straight into the mine and a wide door in front for when the ore carts would come out on their tracks in the old days when it was working. The tracks were still there but Henry took them out of the cabin because he kept tripping over them. Alice is actually at the top of Colorado Creek on the ridge between Lump and Ellsworth so that when he came down, he'd walk down Colorado into upper Lump around the bend under Molly Ball's house there west of the peat bog they have now turned into a fishing lake.

As it happened, Henry ran out of food about the time it started snowing and it came down thick for the rest of that day and all the next. So that when the third day dawned blue, Henry was mighty hungry and although the snow was over two feet deep, he set out to go visit Jim Murray because there was no future staying at the Alice with no food.

Molly Ball saw him from her house up well above as he was coming around the big curve and she watched him from her front porch as he slogged along, head bent and knees going up, arms swinging hard to twist his back around so the next leg could kick through the snow for the next step. It's a lot of work to walk through two feet of snow.

Molly didn't know he'd been through two days without food but she did know something he didn't know and that was that some several yards behind him a mountain lion was mincing down his track. Even if Henry hadn't been deaf, there would have been little use for Molly to call out to him because he couldn't have gone any faster, there wasn't anything there for him to escape up or into and so Molly watched as Henry plodded laboriously along the long slow curve that circled around the peat bog and the mountain lion kept the same distance behind him and eventually many minutes later they both went out of sight around the next bend. It wasn't until days later she learned that he hadn't been killed, hadn't even known there was a lion behind him until she told him.

One drawback to gold mining was that the dynamite made most of the miners go deaf and Henry was an excellent example. As soon as he'd see somebody, he'd put his hand up to his ear and shake it and keep shaking it. He always shouted at the top of his lungs so he could hear himself. One afternoon, he came to the Merchant's one-room cabin looking for Harry. He knocked on the door and Maureen answered. "Harry's out back," she shouted. The only reason really that Maureen didn't like to see Henry was that she wasn't good at shouting. Henry stood in the door, little and ragged, the mad gleam of the gold fever lighting his eyes, his hair askew, his cap respectfully in one hand and his other hand shaking and shaking at his ear.

"Harry's in bed?"

"He's out back," she shouted again.

"In bed, is he?" Henry shrieked. "Wall, I'll come by another day." And he screwed his cap back on clockwise and wandered off.

I don't know when he moved up here and got the fever. When Laura Mae was a child it seemed he'd been here forever. And Laura Mae was born here in 1893. But he had all the signs of a very bad case of the fever: deaf, talking to himself, eyes dreamy then jerking wildly into sharp focus, shabby, dirty, and poor.

Henry had no money of his own so he was often out of food and despite his having a serious case of the fever with all the trimmings, he was a

friendly little cuss and he'd visit people
mealtimes and have a bite to eat and a little
shouted conversation, then be on his way. He was
always gentle and kindly and as good to the kids
as he could be. He used to visit them when they
were sick and the kids liked him a lot. But Mother
C__ shook her head. "Wait till Henry gets sick
himself," she'd say, "Nobody'll even notice he's
not around." Probably she saved his life more than
once by saying that because when he got sick,
people remembered what she said and went to help.

Whether it was patriotism or general
madness or a kink to his gold fever nobody knows,
but the fact is he went all out for the Fourth of
July in the strangest way. Not far above the
Alice, at about ten thousand feet, a meadow lies
draped across the top of Ellsworth Gulch, over the
hogback to the spring which is the beginning of
Colorado Creek and down for a good view of Lump
Gulch. Here Henry composed his biggest dreams. He
called the place Velvet Valley and painted a sign
on the tin cabin at the east end of it. "Velvet
Valley," it says, " Ent." It was at the top of
Ellsworth that he did most of his Fourth of July
projects, the picnic table that would hold fifty
people in a semicircle with a heavy iron stove in
the middle, the pigeon-holed box tacked to a tree.
And on the day of The Fourth, he'd haul lots of
whitewash up there and whitewash all the aspen
trees. Then, all alone, he'd celebrate. Nobody
knows how he celebrated it because he could never
get anyone to come up and join him. I imagine him
dancing among the whitewashed trees, putting

candles around on the picnic table, getting a fire going in the stove, writing messages to put in the box then opening it later and reading the messages and, at the end, setting off some dynamite. It was clear to everyone that he set off dynamite and that he whitewashed the aspen trees. Some of the neighbors go up there on the Fourth now for a picnic lunch though they don't whitewash the aspens or set off dynamite or anything like Henry did when he was alive.

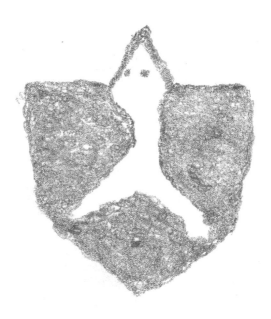

ABOUT THE BEAR

About the bear, there's very little to say. I never even saw him. I came very close to seeing him, but I didn't.

I went out to get water at the spring and I had to take the shovel. I'd been away and the snow had piled up, so I had to shovel down to the spring. I was glad to see that the chickadees had survived without me feeding them but they were glad to see me and they were gathered around and I'd have to stop shoveling and hold out my hand full of sunflower seeds and when they'd land on my hand to take a seed – ah, those little feet on my hand – I was glad to be home.

Then, as I was going back to the cabin and stopped with my load of bottles full of water and I was feeding the chickadees again in my hand, I smelled a smell and I thought, "That smells like a bear." And then I said to myself severely, "How do you know what a bear smells like? Maybe it's a porcupine. Maybe it's a weasel or a deer."

"It's not a deer," I said, and I looked around through the trees but I didn't see anything. The breeze was light but it wasn't steady so the smell would come and go and I saw that the chickadees smelled it too and it disturbed them, they were jumpy and scared.

The next day it started to snow and when I went down to the outhouse there were maybe three inches of new snow on top of the old. But I could

see the tracks and I looked at them with
astonishment. They looked like human tracks except
the person didn't walk right, didn't act right,
and besides nobody could even be there without
skis or snow-shoes.

As I say, there were three inches of new
snow so what I was seeing was merely indentations
and there was no hope of finding any detail.
However, the indentations didn't make human sense.

My first thought was that two people had
come up to the steep bank below the spring side by
side, eight feet apart, and dived into the deep
snow at the bottom of the bank and then turned
around and wandered out again, putting their new
tracks carefully in between their previous tracks.
Each trail had too many footprints and the
footprints were too close together for a human.
And then they hadn't done anything human, they had
meandered in and dived into the bank and backed
out, making double prints. And the prints did
seem, even with three inches of snow on them, to
be different sizes and shapes, so that one pair
seemed quite human but the other pair in between
was roundish or smaller ... or maybe the person
was walking tiptoe?

The worst of it was that, for various
reasons, the main one being that I never
acknowledged the possibility of these being bear
tracks, I didn't study them, so I can only tell
what I noticed.

So many people come up around here to play
or to be alone with nature or with themselves and
I really don't want to concern myself with their

actions unless those actions impinge on me somehow. So I only looked to see that the tracks went back out and away and then I got back into the cabin out of the snow.

And it snowed well over a foot so then the tracks were gone. Only two slight dimples in the bank brought the tracks back to my mind as a puzzle so that it was two days later or maybe three that I finally did put the two incidents together and realized that if those had been bear tracks, they'd make lots of sense. If those had been bear tracks, the bear had meandered up to the bank having, in the second week in April, recently emerged from his winter's sleep, then had plunged headfirst into the bank, perhaps had even napped there safe and quiet for hours some hundred yards from me in my little den, then, nose foremost, had emerged from the bank some eight feet more or less from where he had entered and had meandered away again. If it had been a bear, it made perfect sense.

BOBO

Bobo was a smiling dog. He would curl his
body tightly around to bring his wagging tail
beside his big glorious smile, his head tipped
back. Some people were taken aback.

Bobo always walked slowly with his head
down. He was not dejected. I often wondered at the
way he walked and I studied it. The way a dog or
anyone carries himself tells all. He did have a
big heavy head. That wasn't to be discounted and
as it affected his posture, so it would affect his
personality, his attitudes, and his places in the
various social situations he found himself in. He
looked pretty much like an Australian Sheepdog,
although he could, I suppose, have been a cross
between a husky and a field spaniel. He had
freckles on his nose, very thick wavy hair with a
heavy undercoat, each hair a different color from
light blond to black so that one was hard pressed
to say what color he was, usually settling on
brown. His tail was not bobbed but it was quite
short and feathered, going down and then pointing
straight upward. His ears were neither up nor down
but the sort of crumpled type ears that show
emotion well. His eyes were a rich dark brown, set
wide apart. He moved his eyes a lot. Maybe it was
because of his head being so big and his neck so
thick. He moved his eyes while he walked with his
nose close to the ground. It is valuable, of
course, for a dog to keep his nose close to the

ground if the information to be found there fascinates him. He loved smells always. Of course, he could smell it all in the air but with his nose to the ground, he could get such a wealth of detail - every nuance, every hesitation or moment of emotion in the track or the collection of tracks there on the ground. To an animal who can smell, walking along the ground can be a lesson in biology or psychology. A dog with a good nose could really follow a train of thought right there where it happened. Sometimes he would slowly follow a track for hours, absorbing whole stories laid out in the dirt - tales of adventure, tender or passionate love scenes, suspense, mystery, the daily lives of all who lived in the gulch.

I wish humans had the gift of smell like that. I would give a lot to know what he knew. Of course, most dogs are more pragmatic and self-centered than he was, so that, like most humans, actually, if they scented a rabbit, they would immediately leap to the joy of the chase. The response would clank down with the finality of a wall of iron, blocking the mind from exploration. Bobo, although his responses were quick enough in times of need, was not at the mercy of them. He was a dog with an active and thoughtful mind.

He was always looking at everything as he moseyed, giving the superficial appearance of being lost in a dream but if one noticed the smile of knowledge in his eyes, the quiet recognition of everything, one had to hail him as an active intelligence.

BOBO

The slow walk and the low head was actually a tremendous advantage socially. Nobody can be afraid of a dog who holds his head low. People were inclined to think, "What a nice old fellow," and give him a treat. And similarly with dogs. He had no chip on his shoulder. It was a wonderful device for cutting down on dog fights. As he ambled by a dog's house, the other dog would come out, barking or not as fitted his personality. There would be the usual smelling and pissing, all attended to with respectful care and interest, and utmost politeness on Bobo's part. When the time came for him to amble on, every dog he met knew it had met with someone out of the ordinary. Many of them followed him so that we would sometimes see him with a train of two or three courtiers. He loved company. When the other dogs pranced around him, he would encourage them, opening his mouth wide, waving his short plumed tail slowly and delightedly while they leaped and cavorted about him. Sometimes he would even chase rabbits and squirrels with them, reveling in the other dogs' adoring energy.

It was thus that Bobo was the lord of Lump Gulch among the dogs. And in those days, all dogs ran free. In all social animals, there seem to be leaders. It's a very natural thing. Some struggle for the position out of ambition, others are born to it, attracting followers to them without seeming to try. Bobo was one of the latter and may well be the most perfect example of it I've ever observed. He seemed to glow with benign majesty.

Well, perhaps more like Mahatma Gandhi.

Bobo was the Hoffman's dog. Mary Hoffman never let him into the house. He didn't mind. He would sit on the patch of cement in front of their door for hours some days, smelling the news and watching the cars go by with a benignant look. Once a day, she would dump a pile of dog food and scraps onto the cement and he would eat it gratefully with slow sensuality. Earl Hoffman kicked him when he was drunk. Never responding with fear or anger, Bobo learned quickly to recognize the symptoms and simply and with quiet dignity melt around the corner of the house, listening with sad concern to Earl and Mary yelling at each other inside.

There were several children in the family but little Cindy was his special concern. He adored her; he enjoyed her; he gave himself gladly to her. Whenever she had Bobo along, she was safe.

I used to see him there on the cement as I walked with Durin past the Hoffman house to ramble in the woods. Durin had growled and pissed a line around our property so that Bobo never came to visit us as he did other people in the gulch, but when I saw him sitting there, I recognized him as royalty and as an understanding mind. How does anyone recognize those whom they meet? How did I recognize Bobo? He was simply sitting, not moving much but his eyes and his ears. Carriage, perhaps, the slight movements of eyes and ears, slight gestures in relation to me or to the rest of the world. He watched us out of the corner of his eye as we walked past his house. He would be sitting in a settled-in way, and by the way his eyes

184

moved, lids half down, watching us surreptitiously, I could see that he found us interesting and he felt friendly toward us but realized that Durin wouldn't accept friendly advances so he chose to keep still. He didn't even have to try us out once to know. When he was sitting, he carried his head high and looked proud and alert and benign. We simply looked at each other and we were friends. Later on, I would nod discreetly and he would reply by twitching his ears, then he would turn his head away. Sometimes he wouldn't be there for days at a time and sometimes I would see him miles from home hanging around a bitch in heat or visiting distant friends.

The Hoffmans didn't take care of him at all, except to feed him. He took very good care of himself. But one Spring, I saw the long hair under his neck weighed down with a huge mat of shedding fur. It bothered me as I saw it bothered him. Couldn't they cut it off? Days went by and the thing grew until it dragged on the ground. He was miserable. I worried about him. The thought rose in my mind that if it wasn't attended to, he might kill himself. Then one day, I went out with Durin through a field near Bobo's house. I was amazed to see Bobo coming obliquely after us. He followed us at an angle, keeping a good distance away so that Durin, although he became very tense, couldn't actually accuse him of being with us. Bobo caught my eye, circled ahead of us and stopped directly in our path, hung his head dejectedly with that horrible mat displayed to best advantage, and looked pleadingly at me.

Naturally, I stopped. Durin leaned trembling against my leg, and for the first time ever, I spoke to Bobo aloud.

"This evening," I said, "when I put him away, you may come to our house and I'll cut it off for you." I simply spoke in English. I knew Durin couldn't understand what I was saying or if he did, because I spoke conversationally, he wouldn't feel that it concerned him. But I also knew that Bobo was intensely interested in what I said. When I had spoken my piece, he beamed hopefully, raised his head as best he could and trotted home again to wait for nightfall. It was mid-morning and a long wait. We finished our walk and I put a pair of scissors on the windowsill by the front door.

It was a dark and moonless night when we called Durin in. He was upset because Bobo was standing waiting at the property line on our road. I could see his eyes gleaming orange. I grabbed the scissors and went out. There was a little light close to the house through the windows. I stood silently in one of these dim patches of light. He approached me, although he had never done so before, and I must have been a frightful sight with my scissors gleaming in the darkness. He came up to me, lay down and rolled over onto his back. I stooped down, groped in the dark for the mat on his neck, cut it off carefully and quickly. When he felt the weight of it come away from his neck, he rose and vanished into the night.

Some time not long after that, Cindy got a new puppy named Tuffy. Tuffy was a sore trial to Bobo. If there was one thing he couldn't sanction, it was puppies. They had no respect, no protocol, no sensitivity. They leap without warning and playfully bite portions of one's anatomy that are never bitten; they chew up and deface things that should be respectfully guarded; they piss without consideration or preamble. Bobo had many occasions to growl and yelp and walk away in disgust. Tuffy, as his name implies, was a spunky little fellow. Undaunted or perhaps even attracted by Bobo's unresponsive behavior, Tuffy took Bobo for his master. Oh, he liked Cindy well enough but he followed Bobo everywhere. This was rough on Bobo at first and he would find ways to escape but as time went on, Tuffy learned the proprieties and became a lively and cheerful companion.

While Tuffy was growing up, Durin died. The coyotes have a quaint way of catching a bite to eat sometimes that smacks of cannibalism. Sometimes, when a coyote bitch comes into heat, the pack will come near the homes of men and dogs. A dog will answer the call of that smell and walk into an ambush, providing a goodly supper for several of them. This, at least is the story that many folks around here tell. Whether it's true I don't know, but the form of Durin's death led me to invent the story and when I asked around, the people who had lived here for decades and involved themselves with the animals all without exception told it to me again.

Durin had, of course, succumbed many times
to the voiceless call of a bitch in heat. I knew
the signs and we tried to keep him home at such
times as he was an indifferent fighter but inept
at avoiding fights. So when again the pacing
whimpering desperation took over his manner, we
kept him in. But there was a difference this time,
a difference which raised the hackles on my neck,
for he pleaded with terror in his eyes. "He's
fallen in love with Death," I said to myself. He
was a terrible presence in the house. If somebody
leaned back in their chair, he would place his paw
where they would smash it when they came down. And
he would scream. If somebody walked across a room,
he would block their way, looking accusingly up at
them. If a door opened, his tail would be in it as
it closed. And he would scream. If, in
exasperation, we locked him in the bathroom, he
spent the time furiously digging at the base of
the door. The only time he was still was when I
sat with my hand on his back and for three days I
did little else.

On the fourth day, company came and I was
forced to leave my post. With the added stimulus
of company, he increased his overwhelming
behavior, interrupting every budding conversation,
whining, yelping, being locked in the bathroom and
scrabbling at the door, frightening our guests and
exasperating us all beyond measure.

At last, in a moment of rage, I said to him
silently in my mind, "Well, if that's really what
you want, then go and die." - and I flung open the
kitchen door. Without a glance at me or anyone, he

leaped out the door and was gone.

I went through minimal motions of minding the company in misery and self-disgust. At last, in a couple of hours, the guests left and Stan asked me, "Where's Durin?"

"Dead," I groaned miserably and sagged down onto the couch.

Stan was shocked. The children started to cry. "How do you know?" he asked.

I had seen it all in Durin's eyes, the coyotes coming on him from all directions, tearing him apart. Why hadn't I simply tied him to a tree? I think he would have gnashed and torn his way out of any such fetters. He had chosen the form of his death. It had been a passionate death.

"You'll see," I mumbled. "He won't come back." It was all I could say. I didn't feel I could tell the images in my mind. I had no proof. I still have no proof. Heaven knows, maybe he fell down a mine hole, got into someone else's car, was shot for target practice.

Not long after that, our friend Charlie brought over a puppy, a bright little black collie mongrel bitch he brought back from an Indian reservation. Somehow the fact of her coming from the Indians gave her a magic and a depth. He showed us a picture of her father, a proud and wise-looking collie with a ruff like a golden halo. Stan named her Timbre.

Timbre was smart and playful, patient with the children. She grew to be an incredibly beautiful dog, proud, graceful, elegant, alert, her coat thick and gleaming in the sun, her head high, her eyes warm and knowing. After she got out of the puppy stage, Bobo and Tuffy visited us often. We would be sitting on the porch and they would come up the road, Bobo walking at his lordly pace, Tuffy skipping about him. Timbre would see them and run gloriously down to greet Bobo. She adored him as did everyone. He would come up to us and pull back his lips in a big smile, curling his body, moving his behind in a wagging greeting to us humans that would win any heart, especially mine. He would sit with us awhile enjoying Timbre's attentions and then he would be on his way, Tuffy following.

When Timbre came into her second heat, we let her out, hoping that we could get puppies from Bobo. It was the sweetest scene of sex I've ever seen in dogdom. For days, Bobo and Tuffy lived in our yard, going down the hill to the Hoffman's. house when we brought her in at night, coming back in the morning, waiting graciously for her to be let out. It was like a Nineteenth Century love scene with Bobo. Tuffy was obviously turned on but Bobo seemed deeply stirred. And Timbre, in character, patiently put up with Tuffy and went to Bobo.

Big Red was a young, clumsy cow-eyed, overgrown golden retriever. He would come as far as the swing set and gaze longingly at her. The only attention he got was little Tuffy chasing him away.

After her heat, Bobo didn't desert her, he simply came less often. Big Red too came by every morning at ten o'clock and sat for a while adoringly by the swing set.

We set up a spacious box in the corner of the kids' room. One day, Timbre and Crystal were sitting together on Crystal's bed and Crystal felt something wet in her hand. Startled, she looked and saw a puppy. Timbre started licking it. Crystal watched in amazement as the little creature squealed and sneezed, then Crystal called us all in. By the time we got there, there were two. I moved them to the box, the kids all gathered around and we watched Timbre bear six more puppies of assorted colors. She was a good mother, cautious, constant, and full of milk. We had no trouble giving them away. Charlie got the pick of the litter, a stout little fellow who looked like Bobo. We were never sure about the paternity of the others. We finally decided that most of them were from Tuffy and maybe two or three from Bobo.

Less than a year later, Timbre was killed by the school bus. Bobo and Tuffy mourned on their bit of cement in front of the Hoffman's door for several days.

Big Red came by on schedule the day after she was killed and sat on the little knoll by the swing set. He knew something was wrong but he wasn't sure what. I went out to him although I had never approached him before, sat with my arm around him and told him, "I'm sorry, dear. She's dead." I whispered, with tears dripping down onto his strawberry-colored ears. He licked me and we leaned against each other in sorrowing communion for a few minutes. I never saw him again.

It was about this time that the great Hoffman scandal came into full blossom, a scandal so scandalous that the folks around here snicker about it to this day. In spite of being a popular County Commissioner of Gilpin County, Earl Hoffman ran off with his son's wife. Mary took the kids of course. The son went to California in embarrassment, disgust and hatred. It was early Summer. Earl left his horses running loose in the gulch. Mary and the kids took Tuffy with them to a suburb of Denver. They all drove away. Bobo sat on the slab of cement, guarding the empty house, catching the smells, watching the cars go by, waiting for their return. After a couple days he wandered up to our house. I gave him some dog food and sat with him while he ate it. Then he went back to his vigil. Weeks went by this way. He would come up the hill for food then go back to the duty he had set for himself. He was the best dog I've ever met.

He had started going on walks with us after Durin died and I took him on many walks that Summer with the goats. One walk in particular stays in my mind. It was a wild and windy day. The other dogs in the neighborhood wouldn't stop yapping and howling. We walked away from it as best we could but on the way back, the goats became skittish with the wind and terrified as we came closer and closer to that increased and now-frantic yammering of the neighbors' dogs. Goats are terribly jumpy in the wind anyway. I guess we all are. They were running in all directions. I was afraid they'd bolt and I'd have to go find

them. In general, goats are very good on a walk,
staying close by my side, closer than a dog.
Goats, it must be remembered, are herding animals
whereas dogs run in loose packs. So Bobo followed
by scent and sound, sometimes out of sight for
half an hour at a time. With the goats, the magic
word is proximity, so that although they would
come to my call, the main thing is an invisible
connection which is weakened by distance and by
wind and frightening noises and smells. They
weren't all that used to Bobo either, yet. He
could see what my problem was. I heard him
frolicking up behind me, though. I looked at the
goats and knew that if he frolicked into them,
they'd run for sure.

"Maybe," I said quietly without turning
around, "if you would just stay behind me until we
get to our road."

Bobo had never been trained at all but for
that last mile, he walked perfectly to heel,
spreading an aura of reassurance to the goats so
that they immediately calmed down and we walked
the rest of the way in peace and dignity as though
there were no wild wind ratcheting around us and
no maniacally yapping and yowling neighbor dogs.

It was a real challenge to get Bobo into the
house. For all those years, he had never
considered entering a house. We hooked both doors
open and I sat on the floor and coaxed him until
at last respectfully he crawled across the
threshold on his belly. We gathered around him and
patted and praised him and told him that our house
was his house from now on. But we left the doors

open so he wouldn't feel trapped. He left after a few minutes.

The next day, he came back and I let him in. He walked with slow embarrassed assurance across the threshold. The day after that when he scratched to be admitted, I knew the long effort was won. Still, though, he sat for hours every day at the Hoffman's house, sleeker and healthier than ever before and with an assurance of security but if they had come back, he was ready to follow them to the ends of the earth, even to Denver.

In the Fall, Earl phoned Jim Steele, a tough, mean man who shoots everything that moves - dogs, coyotes, beavers, anything – without, seemingly, a moment's thought. "Jim," said Earl, "if you go over to Lump Gulch and gather up those horses, I'll pay you for pasturing them over the Winter. Oh, and by the way, while you're over there, why don't you just shoot that old dog."

So Jim Steele came up to Lump Gulch and there was noise and excitement as he and a couple other men gathered up Earl's little herd of horses and ponies. I don't know what Bobo did. I only know that he didn't get shot. I heard about the phone call a week later from Jim himself at the post office. I told him we'd been taking care of Bobo. I was afraid he might come back to finish the job.

"Oh, I wouldn't shoot that dog," he told me.

"Why not?" I asked. "Did you know we were taking care of him?"

"Naw," he said, stalking out the Post Office door, "I wouldn't shoot THAT dog if you paid me to."

  These hills are full like the hills of the South with mountain men - rough, self-centered, lonely, unkempt, lawless and trigger-happy. They all seemed to love and respect Bobo. Back in the woods there are camps where such men come and live when they can, panning and blasting and digging for the gold that still runs in the creeks.

  Bobo knew when they came and often visited them. Maybe he recognized their trucks going by or maybe he heard their kind of noise. He had extremely sensitive hearing as well as smell. "Hello, old feller!" they would greet him. He would curve his body, wag his tail and his whole back end, pull his lips back into a huge and startling smile.

  I really like to see a smile on a dog. Smiling dogs are a rare and marvelous phenomenon. I remember the first time I received a smile from a dog. It frightened me. I must have been in high school. In my perambulations through Boulder, I always looked for dogs. One can expect a straightforward response from a strange dog if one approaches it, whereas approaching strange humans tends to result in cold rebuff or even more disconcerting expectations or schemes of one's possible usefulness. Dogs tend to be more civilized than humans in the main. And smiling dogs the most civilized of all. But that first smile from a dog was startling. All of his gestures were friendly, the tail wagging, the muscles loose and relaxed, the head respectfully down with the ears lightly back on the head. A sure winner. Then I saw that his teeth were bared. I backed away slowly. He was too polite to press the point and let me go. I remember I went home and asked -- I think it was my parents -- and they told me there were grinning dogs who learned to smile from people. That was a real twist because I had for years been trying to learn their gesture language and here were dogs gesturing in ours.

In the Fall when the Habercorns moved into the Hoffman's house, Bobo gave up his vigil and lived with us. I never felt that he was "ours" as he seemed to have belonged to the Hoffmans. I felt, though, a great honor at his second choice of habitation. His presence in our family was a powerful source of warmth and wisdom. He always thought about everything and his thoughts were clearly readable. Often I would find myself glancing at him to see what he thought of whatever was going on.

I have always enjoyed conversing with dogs. For years in my childhood and early teens, I spent hours every day studying their slightest gestures. Many of them are quite subtle and hard to describe. Maybe someday, I will write that dog dictionary that's fading out of my consciousness. One set of gestures is easy to describe and a pleasure to use. A slight licking of the lips, that is placing the tongue even with the lips, then withdrawing it back into the mouth with as much noise as such a small gesture can make - not much. One lick means affirmative, two negative. This doesn't necessarily or even usually occur as an ANSWER, but very often is an opening to a conversation. I.e., beginning a conversation with "Yes" suggests that things seem more or less right. Or it could be a question, "Does it seem right to you?"

Opening a conversation with "No" is a statement of discontent or a request for some correction or reassurance. A dog will lick his lips twice when a member of the household is out, when he is uncomfortable, when the weather is not to his liking.

Three licks means "You and I are friends." And four is an expression of quiet, blissful joy - "I like it here with you!"

Bobo slept on the floor beside our bed. He always enjoyed talking with us as we were going to sleep. We would turn out the light, look out the window at the night, and hear Bobo say, "Yes." When Stan first tried to converse with Bobo in these late night talks, he would answer Bobo's "Yes" with "I like it here with you." Bobo would heave a huge groan and refuse to answer, maybe stirring uneasily, sometimes even leaving the room. I had to admonish Stan for quite a while until he got the rhythm of this set of gestures right. You can't leap up and answer enthusiastically with this particular set of expressions. Because they're for resting. There has to be a moment, at the very least two or three seconds, for Bobo's affirmative feeling to sink in and an honest response formulated. "Tell him the truth," I would whisper. "He won't believe you if you gush four right away. These things have to be worked up to. Besides, you haven't built up a good

197

enough feeling yet to deserve a four."

"Three!" Stan would say and wait breathlessly for an answer.

"Yes," Bobo would reply, then there would be a long silence. "Yes," I would say, feeling amiable.

"We're friends," Bobo would say after a goodly pause.

"We ARE friends," Stan would say.

For a while, there would be a silence, then Bobo would say, "We are friends," and sigh a peaceful sleepy sigh. It was a fine ritual for going to sleep with a sense of security.

Stan struggled always to get a "Four!" out of Bobo and often he would succeed. Sometimes these conversations went on and on like kids in a slumber party, with a complex of sighs mixed in for depth and detail. It was amazing how much could be said, how there were no repetitions, how fascinating it could be and how blissfully an aura of peace and friendliness and all being well could build up in the room, giving us relaxed and pleasant sleep.

Bobo thought little of barriers. He could always go in or out of anyplace. He had quickly learned to open the screen door in the Summer by slowly pushing his nose around a corner of it and carefully sliding more and more of himself through. One day in the Autumn, I was in bed with the flu and the wooden door was closed. When Bobo scratched at the door, I just didn't have the energy to get up to let him in. As I lay there, I heard the spring on the screen door slowly creaking as he pushed himself into it. "What are you going to do now?" I thought, amused. For a long time, there were little sounds through the door. My flu forgotten, I lay there listening in fascination. After a long time, the doorknob slowly turned as the hackles rose on my back. For a long time it moved. Finally, he turned it far enough in the right direction and the door creaked open. He entered very slowly, apologetically. He was not one to dwell on triumph.

Of course, there were problems with this, among the neighbors for instance. Jim and Carol Healy had a little white dancing rat-terrier bitch who, when she came into heat, was locked up in the garage. Bobo found a weak spot in the plywood door and ripped a hole in it, getting the little dog pregnant with dispatch and efficiency. The Healys were very angry. Jim said he'd shoot Bobo if he ever came on their property again. We pacified them by saying we'd give away the puppies when they got to be six weeks old. Stan offered to pay for the fixing of the door too, but Jim, impressed with our helpfulness and our support of Bobo, mumbled that he had some plywood to fix it and it would be no problem.

When the puppies were weaned, I went to get them. There were five of them, all males. The Healys, after being very gruff about it, had said they had fallen in love with one of them and decided to keep him, though the last thing they needed was another dog. They were raising Australian Sheepdogs in kennels. They called their puppy Scamp. Not long after that, they gave him to another neighbor, the Klines. Three of the other four puppies we found homes for and one we kept. We named him Pete.

Bobo had a lot to put up with then as Pete grew up. A dainty, dancing little dog like his mother, Pete soon showed himself to be very sensitive and an eager student of Bobo. Mollified, Bobo soon doted on Pete and taught him everything he could and it was a pleasure to see them going around together, the heavy old dog with the wise eyes and the doting young dog attentive but circling and sniffing around him. Pete learned to smile too.

I have no idea how old Bobo was when his killer came, a huge Malamute/Akita cross, who just picked him up by the neck and shook him until his neck broke and this great and wonderful dog was dead. I do know that people I didn't know for miles around grieved at Bobo's death and also that those people with the Malemute/Akita suddenly moved away a week later. I would be surprised if the killer dog had survived that week. Bobo had a lot of friends.

GROUND LIFE

In a warm week in April the boys filled the compost box with goat manure and straw bedding and it really stank until I raked it and spread the old hay on it. After a few days, I put my hand in there and it was warm. The day was cold, there was ice in the buckets, snow was spitting around me, and that stuff was warming my hands. It was less time than I'd expected when I saw that the heap had cooled enough so that grass was growing up in it, growing fast. I decided to put in a few squash and cucumbers right then even though I knew there'd be more snow. I figured the compost would keep them warm. I pulled aside the hay and buried the seeds in the compost, then covered them over with hay. I was going along well, had put in the cucumbers and was starting on some melon seeds. I measured to the next spot, pulled aside the hay, and there was more hay. I pulled that up and there was more hay. Well, I'd thought I'd raked it smooth but here was a good-sized hole. I pulled up another hunk and suddenly, coming from under the hay, there was a yelping squeak as loud and as anguished as a frightened puppy. I looked in the hole; there was nothing to see but more hay. I replaced all the hay I'd removed and the yelping quieted down. So I skipped that spot and I finished planting and the next day some friends came by and I was telling them about it.

201

They wanted to see so we trooped out there and with some trepidation I carefully pulled aside the hay till I found a nest-roof like a cocoon of fur and pulled aside a hunk of it that was attached to the hay and there were two baby voles, eyes closed, pink skin starting to fuzz out with fur, and they squeaked and hopped up again and again, like mammalian popcorn. We carefully covered them over again, replaced the hay, and left them.

A couple of days later was the big snow. It was a grand snow, big flakes, two feet deep, drooping the tree branches. When it was over, I thought I'd check the nest. I went out there, the snow was shallow and slushy on the compost, and above the voles' nest there was a hole in the snow. I peered in and saw the fur-added nest. I supposed it must have gotten soggy in there with the snow melting into the compost and the mother vole had moved them to a drier place in the middle of the storm. There were no tracks.

THE CLIMBING TREE

It was long ago that this happened, and in a place I seldom go but I've been back there twice since and looked across that gully at that tree. It's a very popular place; people walk up that path constantly and none of them -- well, at least I haven't heard of such a thing being seen there at any other time.

It was simply this. I was walking up that path, the one that goes up Flagstaff Mountain, and early on I felt like sitting down. I always feel a bit guilty when I do that but this time I had no goal to achieve, only some time to myself. I settled myself nicely in a tiny flat place below the path where I could see the hillside across the gully. I noted immediately an easy climbing tree and a game trail going by it. The sun was bright, the sky blue, and a breeze blowing in my face. It must have been Autumn. I was enjoying the day.

Then emerged from the game trail across the way into the clearing around the climbing tree a mother coyote and four cubs tumbling after her. And like a good disciplinarian, she sent them all up that tree. Two clambered up as though it were a daily routine; one took a bit of a nudge and the fourth had to be helped up but soon they were all four in the tree. Mother stayed down below peering up the trail one way and then the other, pacing around, sniffing here and there, very like a dog who wasn't finding much of interest to sniff at but it was something to do while she was guarding.

I sat as still as stone, hoping that no one else would come up that path. The cubs nosed carefully about on the branches. They were keeping pretty still, two on a big level branch and one each on smaller higher branches. It was a tableau I have never forgotten and a lesson in stillness, in balance, and in the beauty of discipline.

Then I heard a sound of voices coming up my path, turned my head to look. And when I looked back, there were no coyotes in sight.

TREE'S LAST GIFT

Tree was a goat. We named her Tree because of the white tree emblazoned on her head and the horns reaching up from it like branches. She was very picky about her friends. Some goats she liked and others not. There was a donkey she was very fond of. She let him pick her up with his teeth holding the top of her shoulder, as a mother cat picks up a kitten, till she went bald there. She very much enjoyed the company of a pair of geese. I was the only human she loved. She's the only one-human animal I've ever had. She trusted me and told me everything. She was very expressive and I could understand her very well.

She helped me too. At my side she danced a love of life that feared no knowledge. Death, pain, loss, cruelty, greed, illness, decay, foul smells, ghastly noises, waste, confusion; she saw them all, felt them, acknowledged them, suffered from them, accepted them with clear eyes. So she gave me the courage to do that too. That was a great gift.

I got her and her sister when they were a month old, and a few days later they got into the birdseed and her sister died of bloat. Goats are so involved with each other, I feared that Tree would die of grief. I could see in her expression even then how she could imagine no happiness with her sister gone. That evening, I put her in the chair by my bed, pulled her attention to me. "Give me a chance," I said. And she did.

I must make it clear here that Tree was not a saintly personality. She was an extraordinarily mean and nasty goat. She attacked humans particularly, her favorite spot to attack being the crotch. From the time we built the fence to the day she died, she claimed and fought for dominance of that yard and never lost that dominance, even when other goats were twice her strength. She had intelligence and leadership and was always ready to fight.

The inevitable Winter came when Tree and I both knew she would not see Spring. She could feel it and I could see it. I'll spare you the details. She was eighteen years old and it was way past time for a goat to die.

I recognized the final day when I went out one morning. It was a cold day, harshly cold, but the sun was shining. Tree stood alone, hunched, her lower lip hanging. It must have been a stroke. She stood all day, moving from one spot of sun to the next. The temperature remained very cold and from her lower lip grew an icicle. I had always childishly wished she had a beard and now, in her dying, she indulged my whim. I watched her through the window, went out a few times but she sent me away again. Her concentration was inward. I was only bothering her. The beard was becoming quite big. "On a human," I thought, "this would look ghastly, but on her it looks great."

In the evening when the sun had shone on her for the last time, she went into the old drafty abandoned lean-to instead of joining Godot in their cozy place. The temperature had fallen to twenty below. I put Godot in with the other goats. They all knew what was happening and they kept quiet. But I could see their faces peering through the window. When the chores were done, I crawled into the old lean-to.

Tree was lying curled in her favorite position, her chin on her shoulder. Her ice beard was now massive and splayed out down her shoulder, several icicles now, like a pharaoh's beard. Her whiskers were each frosted with her breath. Yes, she was breathing, her eyes half-closed, seemingly asleep. Her tongue was hanging now out the side of her mouth. I thought of bringing her into the house but it would possibly prolong her death and I could see no value in it.

As it happened, we had company that evening and I felt obliged to be running into the house, cooking and such, then out to her, in again to preside at the table, out again. I couldn't take that cold for long anyway. I took the flashlight out and lay it in the straw to reflect off the ceiling onto her. The next time I went out, she was bellowing. She had lost her voice some five or six years before but now she was bellowing. Her message changed when I entered the shed. Then she cried precisely like a tape I had just heard a few days before, the slowed-down cry of a human infant. For a moment, I thought to call a friend to come and shoot her but that thought also I dismissed. I had promised her years ago that I would let her live out her life in her own way. It was she who had taught me that pain is life too.

Her tongue where it hung out was turning pale, freezing. l told myself it was all right. She didn't need it any more. I tried to pet her. She'd never much gone in for being petted. We had often sat together, her chin on my shoulder. And many, many times we had butted heads. She butted goats' heads hard but mine always gently. Perhaps she was sensitive to the comparative thinness of my skull. It was a butt that was a kiss really, a recognition of our equality.

I was honored to be the only living creature given equality in her mind. When she was a kid, I was her mother, fed her with a bottle, held her in my lap. When she grew up, I was her sister. We worked things out together. At the same time though, I milked her and was, thus, her daughter. For the last years of her life, she was too old to walk far or to have babies, so I left her in the yard as the queen of it, the old, old queen, and as she was so old she was like a grandmother or a great-grandmother in her ways, an ancestor, and, in very old age, almost a goddess.

I knelt in the straw at her side, the flashlight shining obliquely onto her as on an icon, and I sobbed wildly over her, over her pain, her coming death. The cats came to my cries and crawled over me, worried, consoling. I ignored them. But Tree rose to the occasion. Though her face was partially paralyzed, her icicle beard in the way, her body hardly functioning, she managed to move her head enough that she and I, for the last time, butted heads. "Don't feel bad, dear friend," the gesture said, "it's just something I have to do."

I stopped crying on the spot. She had had babies in this shed, and this was like that -- the straining, the weakness, the intense feelings, the bellowing, the infant cry.

I stopped crying and looked at her face and there it was. Her face, the expression, seemed to contain all of life, birth and death, dance and decay, flying and crawling. But it went beyond life. It was light and darkness. It was time relentless and the caught and savored instant. It held the idea of the lightest speck of dust at the top of the atmosphere and the heaviest jewel melted in magnum at the center of the earth. She seemed to be observing all of this with joyous fascination and passing it on to me effortlessly by simply allowing her face to reflect what she observed. What she showed me was life unseparated from death, from earth, life as energy, energy as the natural essence of being matter. She seemed to be observing all at once the whole universe, every speck, in some way or another bursting with this energy. Her death was only the end of one story.

I gasped and stared at her. She closed her eyes then. The eternal instant had been conveyed and I was sent away again to warm up in the house.

"She's probably dying this instant," I said to Crystal on the phone. Crystal started to cry. "But it's all right," I said, "she told me it was just something she has to do. Like having babies, you know."

"She told you that?" Crystal knows I converse with animals.

"So don't feel bad," I said. I talked briefly with the guests, then went out again. Tree was dead. She was lying on her side as she had been when I left her, her feet stretched out a little further. That was the only change. That, and the fact that she wasn't breathing, that her body was already, in this deep cold, hardening. Her head was still up, so that when I pulled her by a back leg out of the shed and through the yard, conscious of watching goat eyes through the windows, her head stayed up off the ground. I couldn't go into the house and face the concern or sympathy of others. Although it was twenty below, I got out the toboggan and pulled Tree's body a quartermile through glittering moonlit snow to a mine hole. All this had been in her face too, moonlight, snow, cold, the depths of the earth. As well as sunshine, flowers, heat, and clouds looking like lambs and castles and old friends. I undid my jacket as I pulled her. It seemed so warm out. She fell off the toboggan several times. Her horn dragged in the snow. Or her foot did. The ice beard broke off piece by piece until, when I slid her over the edge, there was nothing of it left.

I slid her over the edge but she didn't go down.

She was too big, too stiff to bend. Well, I could do no more that night. When it warmed up, I'd move her somewhere else.

This was a sticky problem. There was no way I could dig a hole in the frozen ground, but she had to be moved and the sooner the better. Obviously. Then finally, after two weeks, the

temperature rose above freezing and I knew I'd
better move her right away.

I called Crystal and we took the car to the
mine hole and hauled Tree's body out of the hole
and into the car. Her head was still up. There was
little change in her appearance except her eyes
had sunk in and the tip of her tongue had been
eaten where it had hung out so that it didn't show
any more. The expression on her face was still
close to what it had been. Her last gift, that
deep love of life she had, that included her own
death as naturally as any birth or any rock or
tree, any old bone lying around in the woods.

That was the only possible thing to do, lay
her out on top of the ground, far enough away from
any human habitation that the smell in the Spring
wouldn't be a problem. We drove as far up the road
as we could. There had been very little snow that
year but there was a drift too big to drive
through. We had brought the toboggan though, and
some ropes, so we tied Tree onto the toboggan. It
was a toddler's toboggan, bright orange plastic,
but she fit on it.

It was just the sort of occasion she would
have enjoyed to the fullest -- sunlight on snow, a
walk up a mountain through trees and scrub, a
piece of work to accomplish, good cheer, teamwork.
Tree seemed to beam from that face, to beam happy
encouragement. We trundled through snow and trees,
always steeply upward. Tree kept falling off the
toboggan and we'd have to tie her back on again.
It was goat-like behavior, finding ways to get out
of some constriction, testing our rope-tying and

finding the flaw. And she had always been very good at such mischief. "Now, she can't get out of that!" we'd say, but a horn or a hoof would bump into a fallen log or a tree trunk or she would slowly sag. She looked as though she was enjoying the ride, keeping her head up to see the view. And the more difficult it was, the more we liked it. The harder we worked, the more delightful the occasion. The more tired we became, the more we were somehow fed by sun and snow, by the old dead goat-queen in state on the orange plastic toboggan, and by the magic of the mountain itself.

Finally in exhaustion we stopped, untied the ropes and pulled and pushed Tree's body into place, uphill of three small trees, forefeet on one side of one of the trees and hind feet on the other side so she wouldn't slide downhill. In such a position her raised head could gaze, as long as it could stay standing up, through the forest, across the valley, to a glimpse of the mountain across the way. She seemed to be settled comfortably as if she were just waking from sleep and about to get up.

We sat beside her then a while in the shallow snow and rested, but not for long. A great joy filled us and we danced down the mountain, leaped and cavorted like young goats, ecstatically surefooted, never stumbling, our minds and eyes going much faster than needed by our dancing feet, laughing, whooping, sliding down where we had trudged up, sliding down on the toboggan.

Oh, if only I could draw. That face. The face of all of life, which included everything that is -- the face, perhaps of the great old god Pan? Pan, of course, meaning "All." Everything. I had just been given a camera and so, one afternoon a week later, I took the camera and went back. She hadn't changed much. Only her lower jaw had gone aslant. I took the picture, I took a dozen or so. And again I danced and cavorted surefooted down. What was it about this corpse of a dear old friend that pleased me so, pleased Crystal too? We tried to tell people about it, about what a lovely funeral it had been. "Gross," they'd say. "Ghastly." "Grotesque!" It was, of course, that we were leaving out in our telling what was delighting us so, which was Tree's last gift, most of which is beyond telling or showing in any way, not a thing or a phrase or an image, but a feeling, a feeling for life and death as a single thing and as part of the vivacious whole of earth and sky.

I went back up there again months later, Autumn leaves rattling in a cool, gusty wind. As I started up the hill, sharp beautiful flute-like tones resounded through the woods. I went to investigate. A tall thin dead tree had fallen onto a live tree and was resting on a branch and, when the wind blew, the live tree swayed and the rubbing of the dead tree on the live one caused the music. I went on up. There were the three trees where we had placed her but she was gone. Not a bone nor a hank of hair. I suppose the coyotes got her in the Spring.

FOLLOWING FROGS

I used to have a plastic frog on the
dashboard with his mouth open and I always kept
ten dimes in his mouth so that I'd never be broke;
but then one day not long ago someone said you
weren't supposed to use dimes, it was supposed to
be a silver dollar and I had one of those gold-
colored dollars so I took out the dimes and put
that in his mouth and wouldn't you know it he then
commenced to move about; he'd look off out to the
left, then I'd go round a bend and he'd've shifted
to look over my shoulder and the dollar skewed his
mouth around so that he'd look seriously worried
about what was behind me but then when his mouth
commenced to tear and expose the dollar I finally
put the coin in my pocket and threw the frog away.
It had served me for many years and was definitely
past its prime.

Now I want to stress the fact that I do not
have a thing about frogs but there was another
frog on the dashboard; it was a Hmong frog and
quite attractive in a way although there was no
place to put dimes and no need either since it was
heavy with the sand it was stuffed with. I did
consider cutting a small slit in the top and
slipping in a few dimes but then I worried about
sand getting into the works of the windshield
defroster and decided especially after the fiasco
of the other frog that I'd better let well alone.

FOLLOWING FROGS

When I got to Los Gatos I asked Anna about all the frogs. "My mother likes frogs," she explained and it was stunning. In a nice clean well-ordered house there were frog lamps and frogs made of china, frogs of glass and frogs of seashells and it brought the thought of frogs back into my mind.

So that when I visited Linda in San Anselmo just after Anna and she had god statues from everywhere and I sifted through them, looking for I knew not what. But then I saw it — an ancient perhaps Egyptian frog-headed god and I was more than happy. It seemed that The Frog was with me and all was well.

Driving back east after the two really delightful visits, I searched for a place to park my van and knew I'd found it when I heard the frogs tuning up. They sang me to sleep in the evening and then they blessed me on my way in the morning.

When Linda read this story, she looked through all her god statues and said there were no frogs, however I must have found the crocodile god, Sobek, the god of nature and transformation.

THE ANT JOURNAL

Day 1 - I arrive in the desert and set up camp. The ground is wet but the surface dirt dry so that, although the sand is loose, many spring plants are starting up.

Day 2 - Walking back and forth between my camp and the Visitors Center, I notice a double anthill on the edge of the dirt road. Middlesized black ants run about busily.

Day 4 - The ants are working on a new hole further into the road. I shall have to either straddle the three holes or else go out into the soft sand whenever I drive by. The ants are very busy and energetic.

Day 5 - Over behind the green trailer there's a wide road (maybe four inches wide) with ants going back and forth between two holes about thirty feet apart. Everyone looks gloriously happy and full of hope.

Day 8 - Coming home from the museum in the dark, I think I ran over the third anthill. I'll see in the morning.

Day 9 - I can't believe it. There's no action at all. And there for all to see is my tire track across the third anthill. Did I kill them all?

Day 10 - As I was passing the anthill, I saw black specks all around it. I bent to look and they were dead ants. Dozens, maybe two hundred dead ants had been carried out and placed at a distance of about fourteen inches from the anthill. In the second hill, nearer the road, a great wad of maybe fifteen dead ants lay in the entryway.

Day 11 - Like in the great plagues of the Middle Ages, the village must have all died but the sexton who laboriously buried them all. Or in the case of these ants, unburied them.

Day 12 - I thought I saw a few tiny brown ants carrying things into the first anthill but I haven't seen them again.

Day 14 -The way I'm situated now, I have to back out the road and the other morning I ran over both anthills at once with front and back tires, that is I ran over the other two anthills. When I saw how the tracks dipped in at that point, I realized that I had crushed what had been, to their size, great caverns and underground corridors. But with none left to inhabit them, there seems no point in mourning their ruin.

Day 15 - The other anthills behind the green trailer have had some horrible setback, too. One of the hills has been deserted and the road is untraveled. I see two horny toads camouflaged in sparse vegetation.

Day 16 - Great day in the morning! A new anthill has emerged a foot away from the original three in the road up against a rock which I don't suppose will protect them but there's still another rock below and lots and lots of ants! Were they working underground all this time?

Day 17 - Anthills are opening up all around where I park my car. One of them is open like an atrium and I watch ants each carry a pebble of sand to place on the hill.

Day 19 - Behind the green trailer both anthills seem to be dead. I swear I have done nothing, nothing, to make this happen.

Day 20 - When I rode up the road with Dee in her truck to her trailer, I knew she had run over the new anthill by the rock. "Leave the lights on," I said, and jumped out to see the tire track smooth across the new hole. "Are they out running around?" she asked. I bent to look. Yes. They were. It must have been that the wider tires of her truck made less havoc than the narrow tires of my economy car.

Day 21- Dee has joined my concern for the ants with everything she's got, is wondering what barrier to erect to save the ants from the party next month. She tells me that horny toads eat little else besides ants.

Day 24 - Well, I'm heading out. Had a wonderful time. Refreshing anyway. The ants will be glad I'm gone. I left some moldy bread by where I parked and watched the ants there go to work to carry it into the hole. Won't it mold more? Maybe they like the mold. I think next time I'll come in the winter, then I won't be bothered with these emotional concerns.

DESERT LION

In the desert, three things are hard to avoid: bare ground, the sun, and obsession.

Lion Lake gleams and you can see it for miles. Even with no water in it, it gleams. I spent forty days and forty nights there one time. Oh, it wasn't pure at all. At the very start, I used a ten-foot pole to string up my ham radio antenna and I was gabbing in Morse code every evening. Also, I was trying to learn to draw stone artifacts accurately, and so was going into town weekly to my teacher. Once or twice I even went to the museum in San Bernardino to work in the basement with the museum crew, sorting and studying stone artifacts. But that's another story, and I hope I can tell it one day. Then I would return home to Lion Lake with water in bottles and food to last the week.

At first I parked down near the lake in what I smilingly called "the beach." It had a totally different surface from that of the lake, and for a week or two I lived there on the lee side of a low ridge of rock. I had a little fire pit for cooking, and a big flat rock where I could do my drawing. I had a big hat to keep the sun off and I could put the passenger seat back and sleep in the car, the stars and moon shining in and the windows open a crack for air. Some time during the day I would take a little walk.

The Mojave Desert has very little sand. The ground surface on "the beach" took tracks well and held them for months. Although the wind howled endlessly, it only softened the details of the tracks, so that I could tell the age of a track by its edges and its detail.

There were truck and jeep tracks, some quite fresh. Each weekend maybe three or four vehicles would come through, but none would stop near me, so there were very few human footprints besides mine. There were coyote tracks, roadrunner tracks and the tracks of other birds, kangaroo mouse and snake and lizard and lots of jackrabbit. But the track that caught my eye was nearly five inches across, a good-sized lion. And there were a lot of these lion tracks.

At the south end of Lion Lake, the map showed a well. And there, as I looked through binoculars at the south end nearly a mile away, was a tree. It was the only tree in sight. It was a mesquite tree, twenty or thirty feet tall, and I got the notion that if I could get my car over there, that mesquite tree would be a better antenna mount than my ten-foot pole.

So one day I walked over toward that tree. It was at the top of a little gully and as I approached, I saw that there was a little barbwire enclosure maybe ten feet square, and I figured that must be the well, so I headed for that enclosure.

The closer I got to the tree, the more of those five-inch mountain lion tracks there were, until I yearned to have the barbwire fence around me, so that I could get in there and think.

There was no gate. The barbwire was sturdy and difficult to enter. This was all to the good. I slithered under the bottom strand and stood panting, looking down ten feet or so into the hole at old jackrabbit bones, no water at all.

The mesquite tree was perhaps thirty feet away. And in those intervening thirty feet, the lion tracks left little space between them. Around the mesquite tree's trunk was a great clump of dark shrubbery. I glanced at it very briefly and then after that, I only looked at it peripherally. This was because although I couldn't actually see cat eyes in there, I could feel them looking at me, watching every move I made. Of course, that's just the kind of thing one makes up. But I've been right with those things too often to ignore. And besides, there were those tracks packed around that tree like cobblestones.

I am very aware of the way that a predator will bring out the flight response in its prey and then when the prey runs, the predator can run after. And catch it and eat it. I've seen it. The prey mustn't fall down, jump or even gasp or twitch. What my feelings were, I felt obliged not to assess. What I had to do was to act convincingly in a manner that would keep the cat in his lair while I walked the mile back to the car.

I didn't want to slither under the barbwire again. I decided that what I should do was to climb over it, to keep tall.

I should climb over the barbwire and walk the distance to my car more slowly than I usually walk. I am not a good runner. Besides, I was aware that no human could outrun a mountain lion. I decided to emanate a calm and studious boredom and, who knows,

I may have achieved something of the kind. I know that I walked quite slowly, turning my head to the side to see out of the corner of my eye if the big lion was perhaps quietly stalking me, but he was not. I reassured myself that to get that big, a mountain lion must have lived several years, and would probably have attacked someone else by now if he were going to attack a human.

I sauntered endlessly across that desolation of lion tracks, my car slowly changing from a tiny speck to a toy car to some distance away to closer. By this time I felt fairly secure that he would not come after me, but I maintained my calm and casual attitude the whole way. It was somewhat like one of those dreams of struggling endlessly through molasses to get somewhere and not making progress.

That evening I rolled up my windows to within an inch of the top. I did manage to get to sleep. I'm very sorry I was asleep when the lion came and walked slowly across, thirty feet in front of my windshield.

Finding those new tracks in the morning, it seemed to me that I had gotten the lion's attention more than I wanted to. I had not come to the desert to harass a lion. I decided to move out of the territory of the lion and up to a nearby hillside lacking in lion tracks, but thick with coyote tracks. From there, I had a fine view of the lake and of the mesquite tree. But although I watched for the lion often by moonlight, I never saw him.

MRS. SCHUSTER AND THE PORCUPINE

There was an old woman lived up Travis in a little log cabin all by herself, Mrs. Schuster. Her husband had died in a cave-in and she got a little money, enough to go on living in the cabin. She chopped her own wood and hauled her own water and once in awhile someone would come to visit, but not very often.

One evening after supper she was at the creek getting a couple of buckets of water to wash up with. It was in the Fall. She always left the door open a bit so she wouldn't have to put the buckets down to open it because the knob was difficult and it took two hands to open. So she got back, it couldn't have been more than five or ten minutes, and pushed open the door and there was a porcupine on the table eating up the rest of her supper. Well, Mrs. Schuster went into quite a tizzy trying to shoo that porcupine out of there but porcupines don't normally shoo very easily. They have their defenses so well set up that they don't think to run away when someone comes up to them. They rather tend to want to get in a corner, curl up, and let whoever it is take a bite of quills if they want to.

Mrs. Schuster got the porcupine off the table all right but then he went under the bed, and poke as she would with the broom, she couldn't get him to budge out of there. She left the door open then, lit her lamp as it was now dark and went to wash

223

her dishes at the other end of the cabin. The cabin was just one room, table in the middle, bed at one end and stove at the other, so she couldn't go very far away from the bed without leaving the cabin. But she did up her dishes and banked the fire in the stove. She went out to the outhouse and came back and looked under the bed but the porcupine hadn't budged. She poked at him again with the broom but he didn't even wiggle. She stood awhile by the stove and wondered what to do but there seemed to be nothing else she could do. So she carefully got into bed, left the door open and tried to sleep.

Mrs. Schuster didn't sleep well that night and in the morning she got out of bed very carefully as soon as it was light and the first thing she did was look under the bed and by golly that porcupine was still there. She brought in some wood and fixed herself breakfast, all the time leaving the door open though the sky was clouding up and it was pretty cold.

When she'd eaten most of her breakfast she noticed that it was probably going to snow so she went out to stack some wood she'd cut the day before and when she got back in the cabin, there was the porcupine on the table again. He'd finished her pancakes, had spilled the salt shaker and was licking up the salt he'd spilled. He looked at her briefly, then went back to licking the salt. She realized with a start that she was glad to see that he was still there and making himself comfortable. She left the door open though because he was a wild creature after all, cleaned off the griddle, set the fire and sat down to knit awhile on a sweater she was making for herself.

Pretty soon the porcupine climbed skillfully down the table leg and trundled under the bed again and some time later she saw that it was snowing and closed the door.

By the next day, he was eating out of her hand, everything she ate except meat, though he did like to gnaw on bones. She could scratch him on the face in a few days and it wasn't too long till he climbed into her lap. He'd go out of the house twice a day usually and often would rummage in the woodpile but soon he'd be back in the cabin again. He never hurt her with his quills, keeping them tightly attached, and she learned she could stroke his back and rub his tummy. He stayed with her all that Winter and into the Spring but in June when the flowers were blooming, he wandered off and she never saw him again.

She often said afterwards that it was the happiest time in her life since her and Mr. Schuster's honeymoon.

GAITS AND THE CANYON

Learning Gait

Gait is something I have thought about all my life. I remember my father's great springing stride, his back arched to stretch the back leg behind him to increase the distance of each footstep from the previous footstep, his hair bouncing. It was an amazing mile-eater, that stride. He had raced as a youth and had not forgotten the wild joy of going fast.

Naturally my brother and I learned as early on as we could to walk fast too. My brother, being five years older, had the stride down pat when I came clamoring along -- "Wait up! Wait up!" And I recall Daddy teaching me The Walk. He was a truly great teacher. He took teaching seriously and often he would be inspired. I remember him showing me how to push the old foot back, grab forward with the new heel, swing the arms, chin up, eyes up, be attentive peripherally. And as soon as my legs were long enough, I was there. I could fly along with them -- they had to slow down for me only a little bit.

City Gait

At nineteen I took that stride to New York City -- arms swinging, passing New Yorkers as if they were going backwards. But I got a lot of unwanted attention for it and within four months I had given it up for the slum shuffle -- elbows in, cling to your purse, sidle along hunched, eyes low and darting, short steps. I lost half an inch in height in those four months and it took half a year in the Colorado mountains to get it back. It was well worth it, though, because I learned to be aware of the environment. Not every sidewalk is in a gentle suburb.

Gait and Place

Gait states status. Gait is one's relationship with the place one's walking in. Gait is one's connection to Earth as one moves around on it. Naturally, the gait changes to match different situations, different kinds of terrain.

That great springing stride was a gait for suburban sidewalks or for country roads. It had a physical flaw though, and that was that in that stride one would tip the pelvis forward so that that back leg could stretch all the way back. This encouraged all three of us with our long torsos into a swayback, which was not, in the end, a good carriage, not a good well-balanced posture. In his seventies, my father had a lot of arthritis in his low back and finally had those vertebrae fused. I still use a modified version of that stride if I'm in a hurry on a flat and manicured road, keeping my tail tucked under, thus shortening the step. However, I think my hair still bounces whenever I use that springing gait.

But when we moved to the mountains of Colorado, with very few sidewalks, new gaits had to be worked up. Naturally, since we weren't thinking about it, these took years to develop. I was just eleven years old.

Walking in the Canyon

Always, always I have loved to walk. As an adolescent living in the foothills, I walked up and down the hills. And the springing stride was not suitable. I had to work up other gaits -- and in the end, there developed a set of them -- different gaits for different situations, even for different footgear. Almost like a tool chest, I chose my gait.

Going up is one thing and coming down is something else entirely. And going across the mountain is something else again.

Walking up a steep mountain, I learned to go in a kind of a crouch, to lean in to the mountain. I'd get a foothold that wasn't too high up and then I could shift my weight to balance onto that foothold and find another. Very soon I got into using two sticks so that I could shift my balance quadrupedally. I found this a much better system than climbing uphill bipedally and realized that our ancestors must have learned to walk on two feet in a more or less flat territory.

Using two sticks to climb, I discovered that I could go more smoothly by making smaller shifts in my weight. I could create a tripod out of the two sticks and one foot that would hold me steady while I hunted a foothold with the other foot. Using two sticks, I could easily climb the steep, steep gravelly scree just below the saddle between Klondike Mountain and Baldy.

Routes Up

Between the cabin and the saddle, one can go numerous ways. There is the route up the crumbling treeless slope of Klondike and across the scree. This has a certain charm in the Winter because between the afternoon sun and the wind and plain gravity, very little snow manages to stay on that slope. However it is very crumbly for one thing and as to climbing it in the Winter, I have had the infuriating problem of trying to cross a patch of snow in a small gully or a protected hole. Only a very few steps across that snow and if I didn't go to the trouble of putting on my snowshoes, I would find myself floundering waist-deep in the snow, groping for a bottom I couldn't feel.

The sanest route up in the Summer is to zig via the deer trail angling up the open patch, then zag up the old Crackerjack Mine trail. But my favorite route is fairly straight, up through trees to the bottom of the rock avalanche, around that and up the steep gravel part. Elk have made trails up through the gravel and those trails really help.

At the top you can see that the Fourth of July Canyon is a mere knife-slash, a gouge in a sweet rolling meadowland that slopes gently up and up to the Arapahoe peaks.

This spot can be reached on foot or by four-wheel drive by going up Caribou Road from Nederland and then four-wheeling or walking up road 505A which angles northwestward from the townsite of Caribou. Road 505A is very nice on skis. As a road, it leaves much to be desired. I hope it stays that

way always. There is a junction or two along the
way. One road goes down to the right to a quiet
little private mine with an old cabin. One road
cuts left to the clump of houses called Eldora. And
the other takes you to that place up the steep hill
above my cabin. Look for the saddle between
Klondike Mountain and Baldy. You can't, like they
say, miss it. From there, you can walk along the
edge of the cliff that forms the northeast side of
the Fourth of July Canyon with the updraft blasting
in your face. Or, more sensibly, take the trail
through trees and up out of sight of the cliff's
edge for maybe a mile until the trees are gone.

Tundra

     And there the tundra begins, the exquisite,
the precious and the dreadfully fragile tundra. To
take this walk from the saddle above my cabin to
the tundra, the gait should be a modified crouch --
only slightly bent to carry water and lunch in a
fanny-pack and walk always upward. One is torn
between tearing up the trail in an ecstasy of one's
own being or skittering about trying to recognize
and understand everything one encounters. In the
former case, the crouch is very slight, the head
high, eyes up. In the latter case, the neck is
flexible, eyes angled every which way -- up to see
birds and weather, down for tracks, flowers. But
mainly, walking along a trail, one must go with
bent knees, raise the knees high and keep them bent
because here we are not dealing with a level road.
Here, each step is a different height, therefore a
different act, and with bent knees, one can adapt

to the differences.

Some places tundra spreads for miles, or so I am told, and tundra used to be the ecology of much more land than it is now and all that's left at this latitude is in that strip of land between the tree line and, if the mountain is tall enough, that barren section at the top.

Forget-me-nots

If there were only one trip to the tundra allowed in a year, I would choose June when the forget-me-nots are in bloom. When they open up and one of us mountain people goes up there and sees them, we send out the message -- "The forget-me-nots are in bloom! " Stop the car, interrupt anything, call long distance or get on the ham radio -- "The forget-me-nots are in bloom!"

The reply is always "Ohhhh" and the eyes drift upward to the mountaintops where huge deep snowdrifts still predominate. It isn't the glorious shade of blue around the white nor the perfect shape nor the microscopic cavern of yellow pistils of pollen. It's the vibes; that's the amazing thing about them. It's the vibes. Those crazy tiny guys, maybe fifty or a hundred to a cushion, pump out all this love of life and it's palpable. And then in the dark of Winter, one can remember them and make it through.

On the tundra, the flora comes in cushions. There's the intensely blue sky and massive rock and huge snow drifts in June and at ones' feet, tiny florets in cushions. Moss campion, chickweed, forget-me-not, stonecrop, tiny rock primrose and kings and queens crowns, tiny paintbrush, bistort, wallflower, the amazing alpine sunflower, its petals touching the ground, and all the rest of the miniscule flora and fauna of the tundra come in cushions, little clumps; many of the cushions are hundreds or even thousands of years old. One can easily smash and destroy any one of them with a hiking boot -- please don't. It won't come back in your lifetime, not a chance. If you get off a trail, walk softly. Walk delicately. If you're careful of them, they may survive your visit.

Walking out of the trees into tundra, one can feel that the history of humanity was under the trees. No matter how many times I go to the tundra, I feel that. In the tundra, the ways are different. The laws of the land come up from the rocky ground and touch down from the air. I go to the tundra to visit the gods.

Krumholtz

Patches and streaks of krumholtz are common as moss campion on the lower tundra -- groups of ancient trees, dwarfed and twisted, wondrous places to get out of the wind in, protecting worlds of small birds and mammals, bushes, flowers, and beds where elk have slept and will sleep again.

And at the top of the krumholtz is inexplicably a ten-foot tree, long dead and marked as a corner-marker of the Gold Medal Lode. Another patch, looking very like one tall tree from any distance, turns out close-up to be twenty-four trees all growing under the protection of one fallen tree thirty feet long, held off the ground by its own branches. A tiny spring emerges into this clump and spends itself in watering it.

Close to this clump I have watched respectfully, quite still, for a full quarter hour as a marmot stood on a rock whistling up an echo that threw back his whistle a half-second later. When I at last moved (I believe I raised my hand to scratch my nose), he stopped and fled.

Pika

Pikas live here too. Marmots are large rodents; pikas are small lagomorphs, related to rabbits. Pikas live in villages, gather hay across the Summer and pile it carefully in front of the entry to their dens. The village is almost always under a tumble of rocks. I have watched a weasel trying to catch a pika who was doing sentry duty for the village. The pika watched the weasel, whistled his warning to all his neighbors, kept his place partly as decoy until the last moment, then dashed just ahead of the weasel who then tore around the little rock pile village looking for possible stragglers before he ran off, discouraged.

Bald eagles glide above the ridge. The steep hillside down a thousand feet into the Fourth of July Canyon very often presents an updraft. I first met the eagles upon awakening from a nap on the ground partway down the side of the ridge. When I awoke, I didn't move at all, merely snapped open my eyes and saw three bald eagles rise quickly from a place in the air very near to me indeed. Two of them had the full white head and tail, the third was all brown, the baby, and the two parents were

233

solicitous and watched his flying with concern. He did fine. I watched too. It takes bald eagles four years to get the full display of white head and tail.

Some years later I watched as a young bald eagle practiced his dives into that updraft. He would sail out over the canyon, then close his wings, tip over sideways, and fall until then he would whap open his wings and rise back up and do it again. And again and again. It made me realize that birds are afraid of falling too. Then he may have noticed me, I don't know. But he was suddenly above the divide and gone.

Fountain Creek commences in dozens of places, tiny springs, and so there, in a gently sloping tundra meadow, the bushes grow up tall -- so tall that one day I counted seventy elk going toward that meadow. And then when I looked away and back again, they had all vanished behind those bushes. One of the spring sources is a snowfield, which generally stays all Summer. However, one Autumn I found it gone and there where it had been were four short skis with old-fashioned sneakers bolted on to them. I turned each one over to shake out toe-bones but there weren't any.

The Scree

The scree above my cabin, that sloping boulder field, is thought-provoking. I've been there, walked across it this way and that. There is a tantalizing, very straight shelf across this sloping scree which I first thought may have been a road for the miners. That the miners had not made the shelf I finally had to concede after a few years of exploring it. There is another such shelf on the other side of the canyon on the same level. And they are neither one the least bit comfortable to walk on. What they are is side moraine for the glacier which has scraped and stirred and dumped rock rubble around, has smoothed huge boulders and left them high on the ridge, has made the sides of the canyon steep and steeper as one goes up.

Walking on scree, don't trust anything. Shift your weight carefully to the next rock, ready always to return to the steady one you just left. Many of these rocks wiggle and wobble and some even roll. Others won't move for anything. The worst are the ones that seem steady until they've got you.

When I'm feeling weak, I use poles. Then I have three points, all potentially wobbly, but with the law of averages on my side, while I move the next foot forward. Other times I skim across, stepping surefooted as a goat from one rock to the next and if a rock wobbles, I've already left it before it endangers me. Not that I'm going that all-fired fast, but that the center of balance is in motion. This takes a great deal of attention to the rocks and to the placement of the feet. I have found after crossing a boulder field in that manner that although no part of me is worn out, what's amazingly tired is the mind -- estimating, noting shape against shape, moving on to the next rock, a safe rock? Then which way? Etc. All that noticing and estimating, exhausting.

Fountain Creek goes down beyond the scree over two waterfalls and deep into the trees. On either side of it, inexplicably, are two shoulders -- War Eagle and Golden Fleece are the names of the lodes that inhabit them, each one at the same level down a few hundred feet from the top of the ridge. War Eagle however is away from the main stream of Fountain and forms the well-timbered edge of the treeless scree. Golden Fleece is below the Fountain Creek waterfall and is an open meadow full of flowers. In the mountains, whenever I find an open meadow, I wonder why the trees haven't moved in. I seldom find an answer.

Down close to Fountain Creek, the hillside soon becomes very steep. "If you fall down," I told my grandson, "don't indulge in flying at all. Just dig in. Grab the ground and scrape to a stop."

In my youth I would leap and bound down hillsides, crashing from one foothold to another, whooping. I'm not sure what made the change. I think it was my knees. Leaping downhill, stiff-legged, one hammers horribly on the knees and at some time in one's life, whether from a fall or the eyes going bad or simply painful knees, the change occurs. With me it was the knees seeming to slip out of place, causing excruciating pain. The chiropractor helped a lot -- and told me to be much more kind to my knees.

It was at that point that a conscious awareness of gait re-entered my life. I had to learn how to walk downhill, my knees always bent now to keep them from "slipping out" so painfully. I found this new downhill gait (especially with two walking sticks) a much nicer system, allowing me to enjoy flowers and birds, to stop and watch insects,

236

to admire the view -- all these things had been barred from me in the exuberant leap. Now I found woodpecker holes, deer standing like statues, wondrous passageways, grouse dancing their courtship dance, squirrels burying fresh cones in the detritus from generations of squirrel mulch.

Squirrel Mulch

Let me explain. One tree in a clump of trees has a branch that is just right for the squirrel to take pine cones to and keep an eye out while she peels each flake off the cone and drops it to eat the seed beneath and soon there develops quite a heap of broken up cones there below that branch.

In a few years, the heap of flakes has layers -- the older flakes from previous years are darkening and crumbling to a fluffy black flaky dirt and new flakes on top form a cover, which are then covered in turn. As the tree grows, the branch grows too, maintaining its good location as combination lookout/eating platform. The children's children's children of the original squirrel can now use that heap of flakes to bury the Autumn's store of cones and mushrooms and other treats for Winter. The mulch protects the tree's roots, holds in water, keeping that tree wetter and thus healthier than its neighbors, discouraging undergrowth.

Rocky Mountain Trees

People who come from wetter climates marvel that one can see into the woods, that generally, the trees are far enough apart and the undergrowth

237

is sparse and low. Pine and spruce are on the acidic side and that keeps the growth of bushes down. If you find a tall bush, you can jump to the conclusion that there's an underground spring.

The aspen groves are a different situation entirely. Under the dappled shade of the aspens where their non-acidic leaves fall every year is where you find a lot of the flowers. The aspens come first where fire has cleared the pines. Aspens bloom quickly before they leaf out in the Spring -- long hanging catkins show their relationship to the willow family.

The Life of Aspen Trees

But what you should realize is that aspens walk.

Let me explain.

The redwood was thought to be the oldest living thing. One could count the yearly rings back a few thousand years. Then people discovered the bristlecone pine, found that some section of an old pine will have been alive some thousands of years ago. Then it was discovered that perhaps one could make a case for the most longevity in the creosote bush which enlarges in a circular shape, the central bush dying back but the suckers in a circle around it doing well, then they dying back too, replaced by their suckers further out. I have found circles of creosote bushes many yards in diameter in the Mojave Desert.

Then along comes the aspen tree, a short-lived little tree, but it puts out suckers in an opportunistic manner, shooting up another sprout here and another there, trying out places and directions. Aspens go so much by suckers that calling a single trunk a single tree is almost always, in the wild at least, not encompassing the whole truth.

Imagine that the root sends up the trees to feed and enlarge itself and also to stretch -- to reach out and go in a direction. Reaching, stretching, going after sun and water and chemicals and microorganisms in the soil, the aspens can move a few feet or even a few yards in a year. In a century, an aspen root system could travel a thousand feet -- in a thousand years, that same root system may have encircled a mountain or moved to the next mountain.

Sometimes in an aspen grove you'll see a clump of aspens that seem different from the others. Probably they are a different root system -- a different individual.

It is said that the largest living organism is an aspen grove in the Wasatch Mountains of Utah.

Getting a Hand Up

When you climb the steep crumbly hill and want to grab something stable, I would recommend you grab something that's alive. Even a dead tree or bush could fail you and pull out but at least a live plant will cling to its place with everything it's got. A live tiny aspen a finger-width in diameter clings to the ground with a suppleness that its dead sister beside it ten times that size won't have. Aspens seem to rot out at the soil-top level or close under. Bushes seem to let go when they die. The tiny rootlets separate from the main root and the mass of the dead bush will pull right out.

Grab the live one but do not yank it. Let it help you up the slope -- as though it were alive. Thank it. And if you hurt it, apologize. Weep a little. What's the use of thinking you're all alone when in fact you're surrounded by life?

The Filled-in Pond

The Fourth of July Canyon goes from Eldora in the southeast to Arapahoe Pass in the northwest -- about a seven-mile gash, fairly straight, although the Fourth of July road curves sharply and often. One place in that road, about two miles up, the road goes through the last remnant of an old pond.

You can always tell how much water there is in the soil by how straight and thick and tall the aspens are. Here, they're huge and glorious. And between them, very fast, are growing the spruce trees that will soon crowd them out.

There was such a pond I used to know in Lump Gulch which was in an earlier stage. When I first visited it I called it The Frog Pond and I swam in it in those earlier years.

Across the twenty-three years that we lived there, I watched the pond turn to marsh, watched the aspens closing in a bit so that eventually it wasn't a good enough year any year to swim in the pond and I changed the name to The Magic Circle.

Avalanche Scars

The angle of the Fourth of July Canyon, keeping one side in the sun most of the day and the other mostly in the shade, forces the two sides of the canyon to have very different flora. The sunny side is, however, more steep and rocky. It may be that it burns more often. Whatever the reason it has large bare areas and large aspen groves whereas the shady side is very thick in trees, and almost all are the dark green pines, spruces and douglas fir. Except for a few places where springs come up out of the ground, where avalanche has cleared the trees down.

One old avalanche site starts about halfway up the side of the ridge, a narrow inverted V-shape of young trees among a hillside of older trees, the V of young trees widening downward to the heap of dead trees at the bottom, rotting.

There was one I heard -- thunder in February -- and the word "avalanche" came to my mind. But I didn't see it until the following June when I went up the trail at the top of the road. Coming around the bend in the trail, I saw it -- saw sunlight where before there had been shade, stout trees bent and broken as though they were twigs, all at the same level -- about four feet -- and there at the bottom a huge tangle of dead trees, a man with a chain saw and a truck clearing it away.

I was interested in the four-foot level of it. No doubt there were creatures who lived under the avalanche, there beneath that four-foot crust, whose lives perhaps were not that affected by it.

241

There must have been an amazingly sturdy crust that held the avalanche up as it roared by.

Snow Crust

Each storm leaves behind its own layer of snow as the Winter progresses and so across a Winter there will develop a set of strata in the snow that can be seen and felt and may have to be dealt with. Sun and wind and temperature changes after a storm will make the crust on the top. If the sun of a comparatively warm day melts the top surface of the snow, it makes a layer of slush above soft snow. And if that is followed by a hard cold spell, the slush freezes to a good crust. And if that cold snap is accompanied by wind, that wind will polish the crust until it is smooth and slick.

Most avalanches happen in the Spring when water runs down between snow and dirt, lubricating the snow until it starts sliding down in a sheet. But this avalanche happened in February and the bottom surface wasn't the ground but a crust. The day was warm and windy, with new snow coming down and a heavy overcast. The hillside was very steep indeed, steep and smooth. The people looked, but there was no dead creature amongst the rubble who would have started the avalanche. Perhaps that creature escaped, or maybe it was only that heavy new snow coming down and the warm wind that set off the slide.

In the Winter, on snowshoes or skis, one has to be careful of cornices and of steep smooth slopes. One Spring day, I was walking across the steep canyon side near the top of the road and came

242

to a stretch of snow before me that looked soft and deep and steep and smooth. I had the feeling it was kind of quavery, just a bit unstable, and so although it caused me to go a long and tiring detour, I decided to go around it. And so I have no riding-the-avalanche tale to tell here. I lost a friend once in an avalanche. They move fast. He had been a superb and careful mountaineer, but had set up camp in a bad place.

Once I found a dead cow elk who had slipped on the edge of the top of the ridge, had fallen down across the scree and then had tumbled into the trees below. Even with four legs, one can lose footing.

Snowshoeing

One Summer I badly sprained my ankle and the following Winter I couldn't face the strain I would have to subject my ankle to skiing and so I went to snowshoes. And although I miss the sweet sailing dance of the step-and-glide, I find snowshoeing a great deal easier than skiing and so now I seldom ski but only wear snowshoes. With snowshoes, when I walk, I can keep on top of the snow and think of other things, can go straight up a hill and down too without worrying about technique.

Walking on snowshoes, one tends to take longer steps, to put the one snowshoe ahead of the wide part of the other snowshoe. And thus a fairly fast lolloping gait develops if the route is smooth and easy. Knees bent, of course, pick up the one foot, tipping it so the snow slides off as you pick it up and use the bounce from the previous step to give

243

impetus to swing the next step forward to its place. Skiing, one tends to hold the legs together and snowshoeing one keeps them apart, although with the new styles of snowshoes, that is not so emphasized.

Climbing up a steep slope with snowshoes is best done in a zigzag. There will be differences in relation to what kind of cleats are on the bottom of the snowshoes. My first five years of snowshoeing was on rawhide bear-paws with no cleats at all. But the rawhide mesh had a way of digging in if it was level enough. And it is very useful to kick or mash out little fairly level shelves for each footprint. If you're walking on a slanted crust, this can be hard work and it's then that those cleats can be useful, on slanted crust and on ice.

Winter

Fourth of July Canyon is closed to automobile traffic for about half the year. When snow and wind make drifts big enough to thwart the four-wheelers, the wild birds dance and shout with joy and gather around me fearlessly for handouts. When vehicular traffic stops, the tone of the canyon changes radically and overnight to serene grandeur.

Into the Wind

Looking at a map, one can see that the Continental Divide goes along fairly straight north to south except for a five-mile jog at Arapahoe Pass where it goes east and west. This bit of a jog corrals the common prevailing western winds in Winter and sends them tumbling into the Fourth of

July Canyon. The steep narrowness of the canyon funnels the wind and actually speeds it up by compressing it. So, in Winter I can very nearly estimate the speed of the wind because I can see the snow it carries (even under a blue sky) roaring by horizontally very like traffic on a road. This increase of speed via funneling is called the Ventura Effect.

Walking upwind is like walking uphill. You should zigzag, or, as they say in sail boating, tack. Tacking, of course, is a different thing, but still there is all that force and I feel strongly that natural force should not be opposed. It should be worked with. It's amazingly different to tack up a fifty-mph wind rather than try to hammer one's way straight into it. Before I thought of tacking, there were times when I either turned back or actually crawled.

The problem with crawling is of course the cold. Going that slowly, you can lose the warmth-by-exertion effect. Snowshoeing up the road, I like to wear head-to-toe breathable wind protection over not much more than another head-to-toe of breathable and flexible high-tech long underwear. Then get into a slow steady stride I can keep myself moving with. In other words: dress light (carry more layers in your pack) and don't stop. Don't stop to catch your breath; keep going slowly enough to keep your breathing steady and workable.

Snow Depth

I send my weather in to the National Weather Service via ham radio. Naturally, in different

245

places in the canyon, the snow is different depths. Every year at about two miles up from Eldora, the depth of the snow increases. The tracks of wildlife change at that point also. Below, you'll find cottontail rabbit, red fox, bobcat, mule deer and red-tail hawk; above are snowshoe hare, coyote, mountain lion, elk, and bald eagle. Actually, the elk and mountain lion move down even lower in the fall -- together of course -- to be where green food can be dug down to through the snow.

Here, where that wind corral catches and tumbles the lower snow-bearing clouds, the snow is deeper, averaging perhaps three to five feet for a few months, although there are places blown bare by the wind and other places where twelve- to fifteen-foot drifts always pile up. At the top of the ridge, the updraft piles the snow up twenty feet or more and packs it hard.

One could say that Spring commences in April with deep snows. We mountain people love our three-footers with the luminous green-blue depths -- the mysterious black jumping snow-fleas congregating quickly in footprints, big lacy flakes. In such April snows, one should have a small piece of black velvet and a magnifying glass to look at each flake. It is said that the pattern of each snowflake is unique -- I suppose as each person is.

I wouldn't go on the shady side in the Spring. The whole ridge is very steep indeed and very deep in snow. And in the Spring, the snow changes in texture as the temperature rises. At first only the surface is affected by the warmth but as soon as the temperature stays in the 30s overnight, the snow starts to lose all solidity. The snow, instead of being layers of crust, turns to a formless mass of slick pebbles of ice with no form. Even old footprints or well-worn tracks cannot be trusted at this time. Eventually, even the snowshoes go to the bottom because the crusts become ruined. But even before that, the danger is too much and so I only look at the shady side so deep in snow and walk either on the level or where sun and wind have thinned the snow.

Springs

There are places on the shady side where a Spring of snowmelt will bubble out from the middle of a steep place and run down into a small flatter area where the stream runs noisily underneath boulders and some fertile soil may have managed to develop. In such places, the huckleberries will likely produce a fine crop of tiny but luscious berries in late Summer. In some of these moist places I have been mystified by a seeming aberration of the light. Somehow the light in such places seems to shimmer as though something utterly magical could easily happen. No such thing in my experience has happened, however such places are cheering spots to visit, a guaranteed mood-improver.

Chittenden

The ridge on the shady side has a stream running along the top of it commencing at a stone-lined fifty-foot dish above timberline made by several springs that gather in that one spot. Just at timberline is a marshy pool and below that a

straight strip of marshland, sloping downward,
bordered with tall old trees well-spaced and a
faint trail, called Chittenden Valley, although it
is not a valley. The Chittenden Trail starts at a
sharp bend in the Fourth of July Road, crosses the
creek on a couple of logs laid across the creek,
goes up steeply along a small but noisy torrent of
water for about a mile. Walking west up Chittenden
Valley, you get a great sense of space. A smooth
round treeless hill is framed by tall trees above
the top of the valley and if there is any
possibility of wind, it will be blowing on that
round treeless hill. The trees along the long
narrow marsh are tall and thick, well-watered by
the plentiful water alongside the marsh.

Partway up, that hill is crossed by the trail
from Diamond Lake on the Fourth of July side to
Jasper Lake on the Hessie side. And I want to tell
you right now for size and different recreational
possibilities and for multiplicity of places to go
and things to discover, Hessie beats the Fourth of
July on all counts.

On the Hessie side, there are several routes,
numerous directions and places. From Hessie, you
can go to the two Storm Lakes, wild and well above
timberline; you can take the Woodland Trail up to
Skyscraper Lake and Bob and Betty Lakes on
Skyscraper Mountain. You can walk up and along the
top of the Continental Divide to where the old
Corona Pass railroad route crossed the divide,
where trestles still stand and the road is still
open on the west side. Or if you don't want to walk
far, still there is lovely Lost Lake, sweet old

mining cabins, and tailings piles, there's a beautiful waterfall that slides across the rock and then falls. One year I saw a water ouzel dash through the waterfall again and again to feed a family safe in a nest behind those falls.

The Water Ouzel

The water ouzel is an amazing creature. It is a small bird, not much bigger than a sparrow, gray and round with a narrow tail that points up. Sometimes they are called "dippers" because they all do a little bow often as they stand on a rock midstream. I do not understand why they dip -- it looks like a nervous twitch. But if you watch one on a rock for long enough, you'll see her dive into the water -- and if the water is clear enough, you can see her swimming with her wings, hunting bugs and minnows. Then she'll hop back up onto the rock and dip for a while. Perhaps it's to shake off the water from the feathers, although she never looks wet. This one had little time for dipping. She would hunt and then fly through the waterfall, then fly back out through the waterfall to dive into the stream and hunt again.

The Ancient Ones

There is one area on the Hessie side I have become acquainted with, and that is in the Devil's Thumb Circ. Three times I have spent a few days there, each time helping archeologists as a crew member.

In spite of the cold and the altitude and the rough terrain, people have been here in the brief and beautiful Summers off and on since the Ice Age cleared back, about nine thousand years. Nine thousand years ago, the glaciers receded enough that life moved back in -- not tiny and slow, but big and very energetic. And the people came, and other predators too, to hunt for the big game – elk, deer, bighorn sheep, mountain goat. The people lined up stones to accentuate rough edges, to guide the game on green trails that led beside blinds where hunters would be crouching. And then there would be much meat. Sometimes many years would go by before they would return -- sometimes centuries. But then when they did return, there would be those stones lined up and ready, those blinds still there.

There's something about a trail that becomes a sort of magnet. I have made trails near my cabin and then found elk and bear, rabbit and martin using them, claiming them as their own, leaving scat to show their claim. The Diamond and Jasper Lakes Trail shows tracks of elk and deer more than of humans.

There is an Upper Diamond Lake, stark and rocky, above Diamond and that trail that crosses Chittenden goes from Chittenden first down past Upper Diamond, then to Diamond Lake, then down across the canyon and up again to the main Arapahoe trail.

I remember one time decades before I bought land in the canyon, trying to shortcut to Diamond Lake with my brother, getting outrageously lost, discovering a little group of a half-dozen or so abandoned cabins at timberline, all low-roofed, maybe five feet high, to keep hunkered under the wind and to make less space to heat. We found a

half-empty bottle of whiskey in one of them, gone
to vinegar. I can't imagine where those cabins
were. They're probably crumbled and blown away by
now. There was a lot of mining here in the old
days, even in the Thirties, Depression years.

Mining

Fourth of July Canyon was not one of the great
mining districts. It was a side pocket. The biggest
mine in the canyon was the Fourth of July Mine at
the top. The blasting must have echoed painfully in
this narrow place but there was no comparison to the
energetic mining or to the gold and silver taken out
to the bustling town of Caribou just over Klondike
Mountain or to Eldora at the bottom of the canyon.

Caribou was high on the hill above Nederland
and the train which served it (The Switzerland
Trail, which was a loop route) had to stop lower
down, at the town of Cardinal and then a steep
wagon road took freight and passengers the rest of
the way. Cardinal is in a narrow little cleft so
that the train had to nose into the cleft, then
switch tracks and back two or three miles around
the hill to Eldora at the foot of the Fourth of
July. Then it had to switch again at Eldora so as
to go down Boulder Canyon engine-foremost.

One of the weaknesses of the mining in Boulder
County was that more than likely what you got was
90% silver. And silver was a very good thing, except
that the same amount of gold was ten times as
valuable. Further down, below Nederland, there was
tungsten, an alloy used in the making of steel. In
the Fourth of July they found garnets and so some of

251

the lodes have names like Ruby King and Rosebud.
The Arapahoe Trail

So many people now on the trails keep to the
trail. I find it a miracle -- it brings tears to my
eyes -- that literally thousands of people can come
and park and walk these trails among all the
glorious show of flowers and not trample them and
pick them to destruction. In several places along
the trail you find yourself in fields of thousands
of various wild flowers and often on the trail
there will be people with their flower guides,
trying to decipher them all.

Going up from the Fourth of July Trailhead,
now called Buckingham Campground, the first sure
wonder is the long waterfall coming out of Diamond
Lake across the way. Then, the very interesting
site of the February of 1997 avalanche. There are a
number of creeks to cross, and sharp turns of the
trail. Then the Diamond Lake turnoff. After that,
one gets up to timberline, where a big mining
operation at the turn of the century has left ruins
and heaps of tailings.

It's at this point that more choices have to
be made. One trail zigzags on up to the South
Arapahoe saddle from which you can look down on
Arapahoe Glacier, which was the water source for
Boulder. You can easily climb from there to the
peak of South Arapahoe and from there some intrepid
people cross the narrow ridge that goes sheer-sided
to North Arapahoe Peak. These peaks are not
"Fourteeners," only thirteen hundred feet high or
so. But Arapahoe is a fine mountain for all that,
massive and smooth and noticeable for miles.

The other trail goes over the pass. You can see it from the road, miles below. It's a straight shelf trail at maybe a ten percent grade. It's when you get to the pass that you finally understand why a road hasn't been made up it. Standing on the pass, Middle Park is all there. Byers Peak, Winter Park, mountains and valleys, lakes and streams, for miles and miles. The jet-stream rises up the steep west side of the pass, in an updraft, disconcertingly up your nose and the trail is disconcertingly steep, zigzagging down the other side. With the steepness and the updraft, I felt a yearning for a well-seated rope to go down with. I'm sure however that it's not as bad as it looks. Go on a clear day. Bring binoculars.

A few minutes away, on the side of Mount Neva, is Lake Dorothy, cold and rocky with a steep snowfield feeding it. Strange thing about a lake. People will walk and struggle for miles to get to a lake. Partly it's simply a point of reference -- something to aim for. But also then on achieving it, there is an inexplicable delight at gazing on a body of water, especially if it's in an obscure and difficult place.

Just below the divide on the east side, south of Mount Neva are two little lakes, really quite tiny and less than a couple of hundred yards apart. However, in September, the upper lake is in a world of endless Winter, frozen at least partly -- usually frozen solid -- with great lumpy snow. The lower lake, only yards away, is sparkling clear with no speck of snow or ice around it, only rock.

Below those two lakes the germ of the glacier lurks, covered with rock and rubble and mud from the last glacial age, slowly moving downhill. Often, when I come upon a snowfield or a great smooth boulder which has obviously been tumbled in a glacier and dumped in an incongruous spot, I look at the Fourth of July Canyon as a place only temporarily denuded of its glacier. There are so many signs of glacier everywhere -- in the shape of it, the steep sides and the deep rubble of rock at the bottom, in the erratic boulders perched anywhere and in the terminal moraine down at the high school three miles below Eldora. But just the fact of that glacier moraine seems to be the clincher.

The glacier still lives. And it's waiting.

MY FLOCK

The wind was howling and flailing the trees madly against each other that day, years ago. I was standing on the porch watching it when a woodpecker whapped against the porch railing just beside me and broke his wing. He grabbed at the vertical post and clung there. And quicker than thought, I reached over and took him in my hands.

I'm an animal nut from way back. My world is peopled with dogs, goats, rabbits, geese, pigeons, chickadees, jays, donkeys, ants, beetles, and sometimes an occasional human. I feel strongly that this is the true and proper perspective for life on earth. Not forgetting the plants, too.

And so naturally my family was not surprised when I brought in this woodpecker with a broken wing, put him on the rustic post in the back room, and started feeding him meat and peanut butter in suet.

I kept thinking I'd better get some Terramycin to fight infection but there was a lot going on just then and I didn't get around to it.

And In a couple of weeks the woodpecker, who seemed to be doing very well, developed an infection and he died. And I felt guilty because I hadn't medicated him.

Years later, then, I was living alone in the woods. I had no pets but I had been feeding the wild birds by hand and they were wonderful company, yelling at me for food, landing on my hand to get

255

sunflower seeds or dog food. The dog food was for the jays and the Clarks nutcrackers and the sunflower seeds brought in the chickadees.

And then one day in the early Spring, the wind was howling in just that same way as it had so many years before. I was watching the trees flailing outside my window and then my mind was suddenly swept up with a feeling of need to have some Terramycin in the cabin, just in case. I kept looking around but I saw no casualties. Nonetheless, you can imagine I felt a strong need to go to town and buy Terramycin.

I didn't go to town much but the next time I went to the mountain town seven miles down and I saw the feed store there, I thought I'd go in and see if I could get some Terramycin, so I did. I went in there and expected to see that old guy from the plains with the cowboy hat and the dusty Levis. Country people always waved at each other when we'd meet on the roads and he knew exactly how to wave when he met you on the road -- using the left hand, the forefinger up and a slow check mark in the air, a slight nod of the head, just a little bit of a smile. I might have been able to talk to him about having Terramycin in the cabin just in case.

But he wasn't there. Instead, it was a young man with long straight fine hair and a vest with bangles on it and tight pants and he was wearing sunglasses indoors. And instead of the welcoming smile of the old guy, he had a predatory gleam. You could see at a glance that any animal would flee on sight of him, and I wanted to but didn't.

I pulled my eyes away from him and was looking along the walls for a small container of Terramycin but I knew that young man wouldn't leave me in peace.

"What can I do you fer today?" he said, and he clumped out from behind the counter in his brightly-colored high-heeled cowboy boots that I would bet had never seen a horse. He was doing quite a job of it to be friendly, even with people he would otherwise ignore, which I would have much preferred because when people who wouldn't normally talk to me do so, I tend to get very shy and fall all over my feet.

But I tried not to be shy this time. "I can just act normal," I thought.

"I'm looking for some Terramycin," I said, cool and collected.

And he did it again. He stomped across the room towards the tackle department and he said, "What's it for, a horse?"

No," I said, somewhat crushed. "It's for a bird."

He turned in mid-stride and stomped then in the direction of the dog food. "What kind of a bird you got?" he said.

It was in response to that question that I lost touch with myself. I'm usually an exhaustively honest person, feeling that each move and each word spoken contributes to an interweave of clear animal logic amongst all present that I find fascinating and dynamic.

The thought of trying to explain to this particular young man all about the woodpecker and the chickadees made me shudder. Telling him that actually I had no animals at all and that I wanted some Terramycin just in case seemed like madness. "What can I say? How can I answer this?" I thought. Then I jumped to the sly defensive mode -- the liar's mode --"What does he want to hear?" All this taking less than a second, and the answer was obvious.

"It's a chicken," I blurted out then, feeling that I had pulled off a social coup.

"Oh, a chicken!" he said. "What kind of chickens ya got?"

Well, I felt it was important to shrink my chicken to somewhat approach the size of the woodpecker or the chickadees so I said, "Well, I have Bantys."

And he said, "How many Bantys do you have?"

I was totally swept up now in this hypocrisy. When an honest person falls, she tends to fall hard. I realized that I had inadvertently saddled myself with a flock of chickens. Images came to my mind of a chicken house, feed bins, Winter watering problems, trying to fight off the foxes and weasels with whom up till then I had developed a good and neighborly relationship. It seemed horribly complicated. However, I saw nothing else to do but to go on with it.

"I have seven chickens," I said.

"What's wrong with yer chicken?" he asked.

I tried to think of a reasonable wound or illness for a chicken, finally blurted, "I think she has a broken leg."

"Well, is she layin'?"

But I just couldn't bear to think of a chicken with a broken leg who'd be trying to lay eggs, so I said, "No, she's not laying."

And then he said, "Then why don't ya have her for supper?"

My head swam. Perhaps some tattered rag of my actual present life entered my mind, or perhaps it was a memory of having had chickens and never eating them. I don't know. I knew that these were the ways of agriculture throughout history and so again I took the defensive course. "When you name your chickens, it's hard to have them for supper," I said, and I knew for a flashing instant that by that statement, I was saying that I didn't have real chickens, they were pet chickens. And to defend their pet status, I was prepared to invent a barnyard full of weird animals if the need arose.

At this point, it came to my mind to say, "Look, I don't have any chickens; I made them all up. It was a woodpecker but he's been dead for years."

I wonder where that would have got me.

However, the young man missed his chance for that. He was still trying to encompass my chicken yard. "Are any of your chickens laying?" he asked.

"Laying," I thought. "What is all this fuss over laying?" Then I realized that it was early Spring and Easter was just around the corner and I knew that at Easter time all the chickens should be laying eggs, so I said, "Oh yes, the others are laying."

Then another thought came to the young man. "Did ya get your Bantys from Ol' Alfred up Big

Springs way?"

And I thought, "No, I mustn't let this young man ask Alfred about me – they'd call me a liar!" I could see the whole conversation. It was appalling. But I could get out of it.

"Oh, no," I said, "I got them Down Below." That's the Great Plains, the breadbasket of North America. We mountain people call it "Down Below" with a smirk.

I could see that I had, by that stroke, separated the young man from my chickens so much that he was at last speechless.

"Do you have any Terramycin?" I asked, remembering why I was there.

"I guess not," he said, and waved his hand in the direction of the shelves, where giant bottles of Blue Lotion and Hoof Joy resided. "But we have this great deal on chicken scratch right now." He waved in the direction of a bin where a few bags of yellow grain were stacked. "Five pounds for a dollar!" he said. "Organic!" And he snickered.

"Organic?" Well, I knew that if it was organic, it was good. I felt that stores should be encouraged to sell organic stuff. So I bought a five-pound bag of organic scratch and paid for it beside a small bin of what looked like pig hooves. "What are those?" I asked.

"Those are pig hooves," he said. "Chew toys. The dogs love 'em."

As I drove away with the five-pound bag of scratch on the seat beside me, I wondered how the conversation would have gone if I had said I had pigeons?

THE PALM TREE

The tractor was actually there in the vacant lot in Riverside, CA. I felt there was no reason not to take whatever plants I could. I slipped off to a hardware store and bought a trowel then back with plastic bags. I had to bear in mind the limitations of air travel. I had no notion if I'd be allowed to take plants back to Colorado.

Palm trees seemed such a miracle to me then, great puffs on long poles or stumpy ones like pineapples or tight bouquets.

Dates and coconuts. I craned my neck looking for coconuts then heard very early on that they didn't grow coconuts in the city because they were capable of killing folks when they fell. This saddened me.

I looked over the vacant lot in amazement. I'd known vacant lots in Illinois and in Colorado, grasses and thistles and maybe an old lilac and a place where there were concrete blocks and cement, a baseball diamond worn down in the dirt where the neighborhood kids played.

It's amazing now to look at those patches of ground in cities. They had been so tremendously valuable to my generation of suburban child as places where we could play according to our own devices. And typically it would be baseball or if there wasn't room for baseball it'd be a fort or simply there would be treasure and mystery in such a place where the lawn wasn't kept trimmed and holes weren't filled up.

This vacant lot was overgrown with plants I didn't recognize. I wandered through it looking to see which of these plants I would want as a companion.

In Colorado, I was putting together a greenhouse on the roof. It had been a mad impulse based on practicality. It was one of those houses with added-on rooms and then the roofs going every which-way had formed a trough and in the winter the trough had filled with ice and then when there was melting around that ice, the water would seep upward under the roofing – the miracle of capillary action upward in every direction – so that at one point I had twenty-two pots and bowls here and there around the house catching drips and I asked the local guy what would be the solution to such a problem and he said, "build a room over the trough!" and he and his cronies guffawed. But I was delighted and thought for a while what room would I like up there? And it didn't take long deciding. It was a greenhouse.

And soon the greenhouse was built. My design was simple – a roof pointing upward where the trough was pointing downward – a diamond-shaped room and I would build a big container in the trough and two others, large trays, on the sides and I would fill all three with dirt, a lot of vermiculite mixed with light compost and I hauled bucket after bucket up the ladder and eventually filled the trough and the trays with it and as it happened then I went to Riverside, California.

THE PALM TREE

"Take me!" "Take me!" all the baby palm trees seemed to be saying. All around me in the vacant lot were hand-size palm trees. I realize that sensible people consider interspecies telepathy a doubtful supposition at best or a totally foolish fantasy. But I've always not only assumed it, I've lived by it. Oh, I don't go down the street making up conversations with trees or cats, well, not all the time, but sometimes there will be an occasion when I will "hear" a "shout" – well, it's not with the ears, it's more like how everyone feels eyes looking at their backs – everyone. I've tested it out. People feel eyes on the backs of their heads and they turn to look – it's hard not to. Why resist? I'll feel the eyes of a cat just as well or a squirrel or a horse. And in the vacant lot I felt the awareness of dozens of infant palm trees, all of whom wanted to have a life.

"Take me!" "Take me!"

"I simply can't take you all," I said, probably (regrettably – and unnecessarily) aloud. "It has to be a smallish packet, it has to fit into my suitcase and I have to take some of you and be out of here soon before I get chased away."

And then after some thought, I said, "You have no idea how inhospitable Colorado will be! It's not southern California!"

In the end, I took a dozen tiny trees, took some dirt with each one and put them all into a clean plastic bag with the damp soil, sealed it up into my suitcase and prayed for luck.

I got all the plants home in good shape. I was obliged to give away my new trowel at the airport.

When I got to Colorado, I potted all of the palm trees and gave away eleven, keeping what seemed the healthiest one for myself.

The central trough of the greenhouse was two feet deep and across the trough on either side I had two 2x6 bridges. Directly between those two walkways I put the twelfth palm tree, which consisted of two or three palmate leaves smaller than my hand and a good-looking set of roots. A small beginning of a tree. No trunk at all.

The leaves seemed to have a few dry ragged threads hanging off from them but I watered it well and left the threads alone. It was Springtime.

By Autumn, every one of the eleven palms had died in their pots and mine, in its two-foot-deep trough of compost and vermiculite, was growing very well.

I imagined it might grow up to the roof in a couple of years or so but instead it squatted there enlarging, widening, each frond bursting out of the center, bigger than all previous fronds. I became inordinately fond of it.

Around it I planted tomatoes and lettuce as well as many horticultural oddities and herbs and overgrown houseplants but the palm was a miracle friend.

When one is depressed is the great time for discoveries, it seems to me. And there is good reason for it. Depressed, one drifts about staring, semi-comatose, with an energy-field of tender, pallid sorrow. Again and again, I have in a depressed state found small animals not only fearless but actually consciously reassuring.

264

I don't know what the case was with the palm, nor why I did what I did — perhaps there was a bit of whimsy to my semi-coma.

I sat on the 2x6 beside my friend the palm and I held a sip's-worth of water in my hand. And as it seemed that the frond-threads appeared to be thirsty, I raised my hand toward one of the threads extremely slowly and as I did so, it seemed to me that the thread sank slowly to reach for the water in my hand. Then there it was lying across my hand, sopping up the water and it seemed to me that I saw, felt, could almost hear a thirsty, delighted gratitude.

Oh, of course it was my overactive imagination. I told no one. And the next day, I sat again on the little bridge. I held the water in my hand some two or three inches below the thread, keeping my hand steady, making sure I didn't cheat by holding it down on my knee, my foot solidly on the dirt. I sat for some few minutes as still as I could, watching with intense excitement while that thread moved slowly, excruciatingly slowly, down to that dab of water in my hand. And then again it lay across the water and again I felt that joy, the delight of thirst being quenched emanating from that thread.

Again and again I did this. Naturally I watered the palm and the tomatoes beside it and all, but those threads always seemed dry. And always grateful for a drink.

And then I brought in a few chosen friends, starting with my children, to see if I was in some way fooling myself. They each had to be people who could sit still. And noisy ratchety people weren't allowed in the greenhouse while the experiment was being performed.

I worried that perhaps the palm might trust only me but this was not the case. Person after person sat on the 2x6 bridge and watched wide-eyed as a brown thread slowly moved toward his or her hand and then with a touch too light to feel, lay draped across the water in that hand, drinking it in grateful ecstasy.

The palm lived summer and winter in my somewhat heated greenhouse until one winter night the temperature outside dropped to forty below zero Fahrenheit and the great palm -- which had by then reached five feet in height and leaves about two feet across sideways -- died, along with a lot of other plants, and I mourned its loss. I mourn its loss still, these thirty years later, along with all of my other great friends who have died.

CLOWN

"Hey, Mister Clown!" came a high voice from the sidewalk.

I had given up on the possibility of staying with and dancing to the music of the marching high school band. Such stirring music, and I loved to dance to it in a syncopated off-step, but always the children wanted special attention – and a clown is burdened with responsibility to the children above all.

"Hey! Mister Clown!"

High and strident. I turned to look. It was a little fat boy, age perhaps seven, with round glasses partway down his nose. He was standing alone, and he looked to be having serious thoughts. In fact he looked desperate to understand how to think about things. Why he asked a clown is a question that I think I have answered to my satisfaction across the years.

I knew that this was an important moment to him. And because of that, it became important to me too. I bent down and shook his hand. He solemnly shook mine.

"Aren't you embarrassed," he said, "to be so undignified and everyone looking at you?" He pushed his glasses up his nose and his big distorted eyes glowered at me through them.

"No, indeed I'm not. Don't be embarrassed to be a child," I said. "Everyone should be somewhat of a child always and play and laugh and not be

embarrassed. Sometimes it's nice to be dignified,
too but one should have humor with it. Be always a
child!"

I couldn't believe what I was saying to that
little kid, a total stranger, but the fact was that
he smiled up at me with deep intelligent eyes and
said, "Thank you very much. I think I see what you
mean." And he looked greatly relieved.

And I danced away, shook hands with fifteen
children all in a row across the way, their
delighted open smiles contrasting with the worried
thoughtfulness of the little boy all alone. I
hugged the next cop along the route, exchanged big
smiles with a very drunk man at a corner, had my
picture taken by the local newspaper riding in the
rumble seat of an antique car, found another band
and danced jubilantly to it, waved at old ladies
who smiled and waved knowingly back at me, and all
the time, that kid was in my mind.

I never did like kids because they were
always mean to me when I was little. If I wanted
someone to play with, I'd find a dog. So that's
when I started walking, because dogs like to go on
walks.

Everything seems to contribute to whatever
follows.

Then I did get married and become a mother. So
I learned a little more about kids from a different
angle. But I just thought that my kids were okay
and the others were still mean.

Then one day my old friend Clancy came. He was
a puppeteer and he was to do a puppet show for the
school kids of my little town. And he said that I

had to help. These were hand puppets. And so
without any warning or much preparation, my left
hand became Elsie the cow. It was a small part with
only a few lines to memorize. I was very nervous
but Clancy was not.

Fifty kids in a little room and the show went
without a hitch. I watched them from behind the
curtain as they absorbed the puppet show as though
it were mother's milk. And then came the reception
line. And I watched wide-eyed as one after the
other, those kids solemnly and respectfully shook
my thumb, which represented the right hand of Elsie
the cow. By the time fifty kids had shaken my
thumb, I was struggling hard not to cry.

So then I realized how human kids can be and
how much can be accomplished by treating them with
respect. I had already learned all that about dogs
long ago. And my own kids.

Then there was the evening when I went to folk
dancing and I was watching all the couples dancing
and my cousin Betsy and her husband Arden swirled
by and Betsy called out, "How would you like to be
a clown?" I don't know why it sounded so good.
Maybe it was because I had no partner to dance
with. But the fact is that for the next twenty-two
years, Betsy and I were clowns in parades and it
changed my outlook on life.

I made a costume in considerable haste – one
of those huge baggy costumes with the stiff
accordion collar – and I wore it almost exclusively
for the entire twenty-two years. Betsy had a couple
of costumes and she alternated between being a
roly-poly duck and a clown chambermaid with a

feather duster.

There's a strange thing that happens when you become a clown. First of all, you stop being yourself. And this is extraordinarily refreshing. It was so refreshing that I found myself making changes, deliberately or not, keeping something of that clown perspective in my everyday life.

It always began for me with a twenty-mile drive, watching the sunrise. In Betsy and Arden's back patio, the table was already set up. The tall mirror was laid on its side to accommodate the clowns putting on makeup. My costume was in its box beside the table.

Essential things were heaped onto the table: makeup in white, red, blue, green, and black rubber bands, spirit gum and giant bobby pins and big red noses.

There were numerous things one had to bear in mind. One had to consider the vigorous activity of being a clown and attach everything to one's person very solidly. It was essential to give a lot of consideration to the feet. Everyone looks at a clown's feet and they should be wonderful. But at the same time one should consider that one will be extraordinarily active for about an hour or two on an asphalt or cement street and one should always be kind to one's feet.

Then of course there's the hair. So troublesome. One can't just have one's own hair: It has to be transformed. The simplest thing is a rag mop, firmly attached, or a store-bought clown wig. We've been known to make hair at the last minute out of felt cut in strips. One problem with a wig or a mop with a hat on top was the intense heat in most Summer parades. And it is so warming to have the head that thoroughly covered.

What I always did from the very start was to fill my own hair with powdered blue tempera paint. This caused it to stand out very satisfyingly; so much so that children had repeatedly pulled on my hair and I had said, "Ouch! That's my real hair!" And they wouldn't, of course, believe me.

For some years I wore various hats, mostly of straw because one could put bobby pins through straw. Or plastic flowers. The plastic flowers seemed more stout than the straw hats and in the end they were all that was left. I would pin the flowers firmly to my bright blue hair, a huge stalk of red roses and perhaps some yellow chrysanthemums, and go down the street like a walking shrub, bobbing, smiling, waving.

However, with the flowers, I was seldom called "Mister Clown," and although I naturally liked the cheerful feminine prettiness of the flowers, I rather missed the gender confusion that happened when I wore the hats.

It isn't only one's identity that is lost when one becomes a clown. One can lose gender too. But most shockingly, one loses humanity. A clown is not a person. A clown is something beyond being a living person, I think. I have tried to figure it out all these years.

Some people, especially adolescents, like to see that one is just a person dressed up as a clown. One young girl reached out her arms, as many did, to give me a hug and then I heard her shy brother beside her ask her "Is it a man or a woman?" "It's a woman," the girl informed him.

Another girl, somewhat older, asked me: what did I use in my hair? And I told her "tempera paint" then wondered if I shouldn't have said, "powdered tempera."

As a clown, one takes the role I think of one of the oldest gods, like Pan or Coyote. It's a peculiar part to play. Many clowns like to just walk along tossing candy to the children. I think those are playing the part of the aristocracy tossing coins to the peasantry. This activity has always appalled me. Older children would ask me for candy. One boy graciously handed me a piece of candy that another clown had tossed to him. I thanked him graciously back and tucked it into my glove. But the dancing clown who then smiles into the child's eyes does magic – gives that child something special.

I was never so blessed myself as a child but if I had been, I might have grown up with more self-assurance.

Very often horses will shy at a clown. And one time, a caged mountain lion snarled at me and upset his keepers quite a bit. I saw one of them reach in through the bars and pat the lion on the head. Animals generally like me quite a bit but with the startlingly made-up face and the outrageous costume, conservative-minded and visually oriented domestic creatures can be frightened at the unusual appearance of a clown. Almost all children under the age of two are horrified at the sight of a clown. And visually oriented dogs. But a dog who recognizes by smell can relate to a clown with ease.

People who go to a parade often watch from the same spot year after year. There was a drunk who was always at a certain corner. He had a formidable face, very handsome with well-shaped bones. But every year he was more drunk than the previous year and then one year he was sprawled on the ground and after that I never saw him again.

Parades are set up in an order. Each group goes at its proper time. Before the parade, they're arranged along side streets with markers so that they don't interfere with each other too much as they go along. Bands have to be well spaced. But two or three clowns can forgo the order and just be floaters, dance along awhile with the high school band, then get involved with some kids along the side and find that the band has marched on. And what is now there to be dealt with is a large truck full of children or a flatbed trailer decked out with straw or perhaps a politician riding on the back of a convertible waving and smiling. If the politician is friendly and quick, I could shake his or her hand, could shake hands with some of the kids in the truck or perhaps only wave.

Or it would be old cars and I would jump onto the running board or into the rumble seat and ride awhile. Once a great front-end loader stopped for me and I got onto the shovel and clung precariously with one hand, waved with the other, smiling as I was hoisted up and down, twenty feet into the air, then brushing the ground, then back up again, everyone very satisfyingly wide-eyed. But the fact was that the shovel was built to spill out what it held and I clung and leaned, hanging on with my toes and one hand, unable and unwilling too to signal the driver to let me down — unwilling because it was such a great ride. Finally they stopped and let me get off and I bowed and thanked them and they thanked me. If you have a clown involved, people will surely look, and they surely were looking.

I wish I had half of the pictures that were taken of me. I have one that Arden took early on as I was putting on a straw hat, my big red rubber nose central, and it's a great picture somehow, like a Degas, catching the meditative transformation of making up. The Parade of Lights in December evenings was another thing. No rides on front-end loaders there. And lots and lots of scout troops. But there was still magic.

"What happened in your parade?" Arden asked.

"Oh, nothing much," I said. "There was an Eskimo watching the parade with his kid and a big smile. And the hot-tubbers in their bathing suits even though the temperature was nine degrees. Then there was a beautiful mulatto princess surrounded by a covey of ladies-in-waiting. The princess reached her hands out toward me and I saw that it was important to her that she receive a magical blessing. As it happened, I was alone on the street and I crossed the street to her and gave her my best and deepest bow, took her hands and smiled into her eyes. One of the ladies-in-waiting whispered, 'He knows!' in a great theatrical whisper. The princess smiled back at me, totally gratified and I leaped and cavorted away.

"After that, my costume started falling apart my collar broke and I had to tie it up again. Then a piece of my shoe came off and I gave it to a tall young man who was all alone. There was a hippie who was standing alone too, but he looked like he was wanting to prove that he was a totally unloved misfit so I danced around him, smiling at him, and thereby took the wind out of his sails and cheered him up, both at once."

The princess returned the following year and I could see she was looking for me — tall and stately, a queen now, and not needy, but perhaps she wanted to thank me. I was however, wearing another costume this time and I passed her by, incognito.

"Would you like to be Majordomo in a May Day parade?" asked Jennifer.

Of course I would. What a question. What a dream come true. But for this I was to dress as Green Man, the god of the woods, and Nancy made my costume, and such a costume — green, all shades of green shags all over me. Then on my head a wreath of greens and berries and on my feet (for which I sacrificed a pair of old but comfortable shoes) grapes and flowers and green leaves.

Nancy didn't much want me to wear white-face but I swore it was important — I couldn't be a clown with my face hanging out! So I covered my face with white and filled in the shadows and laugh lines with green, got green tempera for my hair, and we gathered at the library. Nancy had also made King Arthur and Queen Guenivere and they were ten feet tall and were carried on long sticks. Beyond that, I don't remember much. There were some great big stuffed animals and there were groups of children.

There was no music at all. "Jennifer! I must have music!" I exclaimed. The thought of a May Day parade shuffling silently through town was appalling. Besides, I needed it to animate myself. And so Jennifer heroically fetched a lady with a drum.

But she couldn't send away the clouds and the cold. And so I led an incredibly magical parade through the parks and around the old train with no one there to watch us.

Morris dancers danced gloriously beside us. A photographer from the local paper took an amazingly exquisite photo of us - the Green Man, god of Nature emerging live out of the mythical court of Arthur and Guinevere. Smiling.

It was that costume that I wore in two other parades before I gave it back to Nancy. And it was when I was wearing that costume that a clump of ghoulish-looking people were watching the parade and "Hey you, Clown!" I heard from a young man who looked like Mac the Knife called me over. He said, "We want you to know we love you. You are so beautiful!"

So many sets and levels of society that would normally not look at me, not give me the time of day, open to the clown.

After the parade is over, unless there are children present, people look away. And a lassitude and exhaustion overwhelms the clowns so that we don't easily find each other, wander in confusion, staggering in thirst and sore feet, walking blocks and blocks looking for where the car is parked, our costumes crumpling to ruin, our faces smeared unattractively. The make-up is hard to get off, the tempera paint gets all over Betsy's bathroom and lethargy bordering on depression is inevitable.

Fifteen years after that little fat boy had called, "Hey, Mister Clown!" a fine-looking young man leaped out in front of me as I danced with the high school band. "Be always a child!" he called! And I knew it was he, that little questioning boy, grown up.

Why then didn't I stop and say, "It's you!" I knew him. I remembered him well. Oh, for years now I go over possible conversations we might have had.

"There you are!" I could have said. "I've been looking for you!"

What bothered me was that I feared he would unmask me and then be horribly disappointed at the reality of me. But I could have stopped as I had stopped for the princess -- I could have told him he was special, could have given him more advice: "Don't forget to laugh!" "Don't get into a rut!" Maybe I would have heard something brief, personal, intense. But instead I simply echoed him, turned, and over my shoulder as I cavorted on said: "Be always a child!"

SUET

I used to bring up suet, carry it up wrapped in plastic in my backpack, worrying about bears each time, fantasizing about them. I carried a stick then for the bear, not a walking stick but only a foot or two long and I would imagine a bear coming for me because of the smell of the suet although I had wrapped it each time so thoroughly in plastic and buried it in the backpack. Bears' smelling ability is ten times greater than ours. The bear would come and attack me and I would jam the stick into his mouth. I never decided quite between jamming it horizontally down his throat or whether it mightn't be better to stick it in vertically as I think I've heard works well for alligators, you jam a stick into the wide-open jaw so that the jaw can't open any further to make the stick drop out.

If I ever did either of those I'm sure I'd worry for the rest of my life that the bear wouldn't be able to get the stick out and would starve to death but the fact was that no bear came to me for the suet.

I would tack it then on the side of the window and then I'd have the pleasure of watching the birds come to take it by chunks. I could see them waiting in nearby trees like cars at a four-way stop, ready to leap, hoping to make the goal.

Then an ermine came to the suet and I had the inordinate pleasure of observing him through the

278

glass — I could get up to within inches since I was on the dark side of the glass and I studied his teeth and his gums and his fingers and the way the skin stretched at his elbow, the way he stretched his legs out in back, how the eyelids went around his eyes and a little scar on his side. It was always the same ermine.

He came and licked and licked passionately, his eyes half closed. He did that again and again so often that I wouldn't always look at him doing it, would just do other things while he was there, licking and licking.

Then it came into his mind that the suet could better be used as bait. Perhaps he had become satiated with the pure fat. After that, he would hide on the roof waiting until some foolish bird managed to miss seeing him there and went to get some suet, at which moment he would leap out to catch the bird.

And so it was that with a mixture of regret and relief, I quit bringing up suet for the birds.

THE BEAR

I had met her mother two years before in the middle of the night and watched as she, with sensuous concentration, cleaned the table scraps and bird seed from the downstairs windowsill, even pulling up the two-by-four I had nailed on with sixteen-penny nails to keep the bird food from spilling, pulled it up and licked up the millet and sunflower seeds that had slipped underneath. My flashlight batteries were about gone and the light very dim but I had gotten a good view of her face very close, just through the window, before the flashlight faded out. Then I had gone upstairs and had seen her dark mass pressed up against the downstairs window, had then seen that dark shadow move back and sit and watch for a while after the windowsill was all cleaned off.

Until I had quietly said, "You run along now."

At which she had stood up on her hind feet and looked up at me for a full five or ten seconds and had then trundled off into the woods.

And I had, with regret, never seen her again.

It is a strange thing how trained our reactions are. I watched her with intense joy at her calm and logical vitality while at the same time, as though hearing voices in my head: "I can't believe they let these creatures run loose in the woods!" "She might be dangerous!" "Why am I not protected?" I realized that I knew nothing of bears at all beyond the scary stories I had heard or read

- stories presented to children to keep them from going out into the woods alone.

However, I have gone out into the woods here in the Rocky Mountains and other places too since I was a child, alone or in company, usually the company of other creatures like dogs, goats, donkeys. And in decades of such walks I had never seen a bear. This place where I live now is the furthest from town of any place I've lived. And a few years ago a law was passed that bears would not be hunted and killed in the Spring, thus allowing the mother bears to train their cubs for a few months at least before being shot and killed.

This must have been what happened to this bear. She had had a cub in the Winter , had raised and trained that cub across Spring and Summer, and was then shot in the Fall. How that cub fended for herself across that following Winter and Spring, I can't imagine.

But I saw the cub in June, maybe sixty or eighty pounds and thin, but her shaggy black coat looked healthy and her brown-muzzled face looked the dead spit of that other bear's face I had seen through the window two years before.

The bread was rising in the pan on the windowsill. I had naturally moved the bird feeder to the upstairs window in April but the little bear was there outside my door, looking for scraps. I put the bread into the oven and watched her out the window till I couldn't see her anymore.

Then I opened the top half of the Dutch door for air and sat down a while to read. But suddenly and without warning, her head appeared in the open door, her head and one paw, low down but massive, and a curious amiably startled expression.

I moved my book and she vanished. I went slowly to close the door and she was standing on the trail looking over her shoulder at me, sheepish.

It took me the whole hour that the bread baked to realize that the smell of the bread baking was holding her to me like a leash.

I didn't see her again that summer.

In the following year, in July, I walked away on a five-day backpacking trip and she must have broken into the cabin early on in those five days because if she had eaten all that she ate at one sitting, she would surely have died. However, she did not disturb my ham radios nor my books, did not go upstairs to rummage at all. She only ate, poking a claw into each container to sniff the contents and decipher if it was worth opening, tearing open plastic bags to eat the contents, climbing onto the counter to reach containers on the high shelf.

The way she broke in was with her claw as a pry. She got her claw under a small pane of glass through the old framing on the door and the old window putty. And she pulled that pane of glass out. Three out of the four panes she pulled out didn't break. The fourth had to break since it was well seated on one side. But all the glass was on the outside.

This was so in the car also. I had left the car window open a crack on the drivers side so as to let out the heat of the afternoon. There was a large jar of Cajun-flavored seed mix in the car and so she pried again and broke open the window, climbed in and scrounged among the considerable mass of camping gear I always keep installed in my car.

I replaced the car window, cleaned up the cabin, put an old piece of half-inch plywood up over the windows on the door with deck screws, brought up a large container with the last of my dried fruit from the storage shed, and waited.

And on the third evening at twilight, she came. And the munching sound of her efforts to break through the plywood resonated through the cabin. I had already planned out an escape route - out the upstairs window, across the solar panels and down the ham radio antenna mast. I yelled out that upstairs window "Gwan! Geddouttahere!" But she was concentrating on chewing her way through that door and didn't hear. Finally by banging a metal bar on a rock, making a ringing sound, I got her attention and she came around the corner of the house, looked up at me, and then she was simply gone. She didn't return again that night.

I estimated her weight at this time to be maybe one hundred fifty to two hundred pounds. "Claim your property with urine!" everyone said, so I dutifully peed twenty feet on either side of the cabin every day.

And every evening I listened for her, and soon she came again. The moon was approaching the full and very bright. When I heard a thump, I looked out the window at the foot of the stairs and saw her shadow - round body, round ears- and she seemed to be sniffing from a distance at that urine.

"She knows I'm here," I thought. Very quietly and slowly I opened the upstairs window and shone my brightest flashlight onto her. With a really gentle voice, I said again, "You run along now."

And she tore off into the woods as though she had been shot. And I got a good view of her -- plump and agile, very fast, and more than a little spooked by me. I had a distinct feeling that she stopped in the trees then beyond the reach of my flashlight beam. I don't know how I got that feeling but the next morning I went to check, to look for a sign. She was obsessing me. And sure enough, there was a fresh bear turd in the middle of the path. I kicked it off the path and made sure to deposit my own fresh urine between it and the cabin. "I am in communication with a bear," I thought proudly.

On the night of the full moon I was in town and didn't return until midnight. And somehow I couldn't face walking the few hundred yards steeply uphill to my cabin through those woods. It could have been some psychic knowledge of where she was or it could have been panic. Or it could simply have been logical probability. I felt that if I walked to the house, I would encounter her and I was not prepared emotionally or any other way to handle that.

"I'll just sleep in the car," I thought. I put the sleeping bag onto the folded back passenger seat and made myself comfortable.

"But she broke into the car," I said to myself. "There is no food in here now," I argued back. "What about air? I 'll have to leave the window open a crack."

Well, in answer to that one, I told myself to jump up at the slightest sound and close that window. And I went right to sleep.

I can tell you what she did by the muddy paw prints on the roof of the car: She came to the driver's side where she had broken in before. She looked in and saw my sleeping bag laid out flat on the passenger side with me in it. She went to the window behind the driver's window and somehow I had neglected to roll that one up completely. She must have sniffed through that tiny crack and from sniffing I'm sure she knew everything - knew that there was no food - knew that I was in there asleep. Knew who I was too, the woman of the cabin. And who knows what else. Age, gender, state of health, what I had for dinner, etc. etc. etc. She then walked around the back of the car and rose up again to look at my face close-up through the back window on the passenger side.

And finally she made a noise.

At which I woke and madly rolled up the window while looking at her close-up through the glass. She turned and vanished but not before I got a very close view of her face.

And I was astonished.

It came to mind immediately the phrase, "a profound intelligence." But that wasn't all that struck me. There was, of course, that tremendous vitality that you often see in a healthy wild creature. But there was also unmistakably, a tremendous joy. She was looking at me with intense delight.

From that moment on, I have loved her.

By that time I felt quite assured that she wouldn't return that night and I slept until dawn. And when I got to the cabin I saw that she had chewed through the plywood and gotten in again. And even with my poor nose I smelled her scent, and thought it was surely, from the scent alone, a female bear. But this time she made very little mess. She pried open the container full of dried fruit, carefully removed all of the plastic bags, and ate every raisin, every apricot, every slice of dried banana. She took the butter crock full of butter and carried it beyond her turd - i.e. into her territory - and licked the butter out down there.

She also left another turd within ten feet of my door.

I believe my first act was to get the shovel and move that new turd down to the other one in the trees, then empty the chamberpot into the hole that was left by the house. I had no intention of allowing her to claim territory that near to my cabin.

On the following day, my son-in-law Ethan brought up and installed a stout bear-proof door. A few days later, The Denver Post published an article on the front page with a color picture saying that if a bear damaged your property, you could send a bill to the Fish and Game Department and they would reimburse you. And then hidden on page twelve it said that if there were two complaints over the same bear, that bear would be removed. I announced as publicly as I could that if "my" bear were killed, I would send in a bill, but not before.

It may have been a week later that I smelled her scent when I got out of the car - smelled it so strongly that I felt she had to be within a few feet of me. She had just been there a moment before. She was gone. Her face kept haunting me, that intelligence. What was she thinking about looking at me? What was it that so delighted her? Finally I told the story to a man I know who used to work with bears and who has thought a lot about animal behavior.

"What was she thinking?" I asked him. "What was she thinking, looking at me with such delight on her face?"

"You must realize," he said, "that she is a lot more sophisticated about people than you are about bears. She has watched people drive up and get out of their cars and toss their leftover food into garbage cans and then sleep in their cabins or pitch a tent. Then here you are, she's just eaten your food at your cabin and she finds you asleep in your car. So she's saying, 'Look at that! She's asleep in her car! I never saw that before! She's asleep in her car!"'

Well, that made sense. It made some sense. It didn't account for the intensity of her expression nor for the immediate recognition I had of a profound intelligence, but it seemed to be in the right direction.

Then days went by and weeks and I commenced to worry that perhaps two people had complained about her and she had been removed. I found that I cared a lot about her. I found myself even regretting that I had now got that bear proof door because now I missed her, worried about her a lot.

But then one morning I saw a fresh muddy paw print on my car window - that same window through which she and I had looked at each other's faces with such mutual recognition and mutual delight.

"Don't worry about me," that paw-print seemed to say. "And I'm still thinking of you, too."

MOON-TREE

Yesterday, Moon, I looked east and over on that barren ridge was a light like someone's yard light. "Nobody could be over there," I thought. "It must be a planet." Then a slender white tree grew fast like in a mad dream of ancient days, pierced the sky then sailed up into it, saying, with open arms, "Here comes the sun!" And I watched you rise higher, turn rosy and then vanish in all that blue. After all that, I didn't expect to see you this morning, but then, down the ridge from where you appeared yesterday, there you were, a thin white line, not really a light at all, a thin line of white in the early dawn.

BUNION

My mother never succumbed to her bunion as I've seen other women do, getting lame with it, but even in my early childhood I remember her having it, that misshapen knob on her foot; usually it was red and very often painful. It looked to me to be one of those things that happen to old people and so, since I was young, was not of that much interest to me. When I was young, I lived in denial about the inevitability of time. I was so very much in denial that I mixed youth very heavily into my self-image and was arrogant about being young.

Then the awful day came when I was forty and I felt an ache in my foot and looking at it, realized that I had acquired the bunion.

I didn't take well to being forty because I could see it in the mirror – little lines and the effect of forty years of gravity on the flesh under the eyes, the bags. I was horrified and became embarrassed about my appearance, hated the thought of being seen, kept away from people and became quite depressed.

It was because of the identity I had formed for myself in my early teens, the hierarchy of qualities I felt I had carried was, most particularly, the one about being young and how superior that was to age.

Then here I was now with these signs of age in my face. I had been enjoying a pair of shoes that molded tightly to my feet and have always blamed those shoes for the arrival of the bunion. Growing older is full of regrets. Why did I turn left on Third Street that time? Say no? Or yes? Why did I do what I did? Why did I wear those shoes?

Then one day my parents dropped in and I was barefoot. My observant mother walked into the kitchen, "Oh, you've got the bunion!" she said cavalierly, almost joyously, as though she were glad of the company.

Naturally I expressed my distaste for joining her in this way, having all my life felt superior to her in some part because of her bunion and the fact of my apparently perfect feet.

"Yes," she said, "I complained to my mother when my bunion arrived and she said she had complained to hers and that her mother . . ."

Within seconds she had taken the bunion back five or six generations into the horse and buggy days and I could see that it went back for centuries, perhaps even millennia, back, back through history; I could ride my bunion into the past like a time machine — peasantry and aristocracy back through the ages, the Norman Conquest, wandering tribes, the cave-painting days, Homo erectus, each daughter complaining to her mother, "Why did you give me this?," each daughter feeling in her foot the ache of time.

MRS. LEFEVRE'S END

She lived pretty close to town, up Travis Gulch just a little way. Less than a mile. She had been a schoolteacher years ago but now she was old and thin and she was lonely so that on many an evening she'd walk down to the Stage Stop Inn and drink with the folks down there for awhile then walk back home to her lonely treeless little house up on the side of the hill.

Sometimes when it was cold and snowing someone in the merry crowd would offer to drive or walk her home to see that she got there alright, and some folks whispered how lately she did seem a bit more unsure on her feet as she walked home. But whether it was modesty or shyness or not wanting to be indebted, no one now knows, but she always adamantly refused any help and after downing a few, she'd totter out into the night, no matter what kind of night it was.

And on that night, a blizzard came and the wind cut into her face as she walked toward home. She was dismayed at the severity of it, pulled down her cap and bent into the blast as she crossed the bridge, swayed as she broke trail through several inches of accumulated snow swirling around her thinly-covered legs, wetting them, chilling her feet.

By the time she turned off the highway onto the Travis Gulch road, she was sobbing and her feet kept slipping in the snow. Twice she fell and twice she got back up. She turned automatically to climb, bent and shivering up the hill to her house, standing dark and stark on the hillside above her, stopped every few steps to sway and catch her breath. Not far from her doorstep she raised her head and saw her house a few yards away. "I'm home!" she cried out into the wind, and then for the third time, she fell.

She thought she'd just lie there awhile until the pain went away in her knee. But what she didn't realize was that the chill had crept into her and soon, very soon as she lay there, that sweet peaceful sleep they talk about, the one that comes when you're dying of cold, came to her and she froze to death at her doorstep.

FIRST PRESENCE

In the beginning, I was alone and there was the wind brushing the buffalo grasses and jerking creosote bushes around. I was content.

But then, some several creosote bushes over, I saw a lumpy darkness lumbering slowly through the buffalo grasses.

I rose to my feet. I'm not sure what I thought it was at first but when I walked toward it tentatively, I soon deciphered it – it was a desert tortoise of considerable size.

I moved very slowly. I tried to project a kindly image, gentle vibrations. The tortoise was huge, bigger by far than a man's head, perhaps the size of a steering wheel in circumference but then the thickness raised the top of it about a foot above the ground.

I got quite close and the tortoise seemed to stop moving in confusion. "Hey now, there now," I said, as I crouched to get down to his level.

And the eyes looked at me in a sort of horror. The claws seemed clumsy, ineffective; they didn't grasp the ground but only scrabbled and shoved him along. The shell was grand. Sinfully, I wanted it for a salad bowl or a guitar: The desert tortoise is an endangered species and I had all the salad bowls and guitars I needed.

The eyes looked at me and I saw that it was I that was exotic. He was primordial and he looked at me out of the days before our days and I found myself now kneeling at his side in some kind of penance.

HOWLING UP THE SUN

I camped there by the dry creek for a few
weeks. Weekdays, I had a nice mesquite tree with
spreading branches for shade just before the little
dirt track crossed the dry creek bed. The loose
sand of the creek bed seemed too much for my little
economy car and so I never drove across the creek
but parked beside it and walked across when I
wanted to explore.

It was the lush and luxurious Sonoran Desert.
Saguaro cacti towered, their branches going
vertical along with the massive central trunk.
Organ pipe cacti competed gloriously in great tall
succulent bushes. There were Joshua trees, great
yuccas gone on up to make trees. There were cholla
and ocotilla too, big healthy ones. And all
interspersed with the ubiquitous creosote bush.

Along the creek bed, palo verde grew tall and
other bushes too. I forget their names.

Red-tail hawks flew high. A crowd of ravens
roosted along the creek and also a flock of
Gambel's quail. There were tiny trails between the
creosote bushes and holes to match in among the
roots of the bushes. Perhaps it was the antelope
ground squirrel or maybe the kangaroo mouse. I
never saw them, never saw the owls that hooted
occasionally either. So much in any place we miss,
only pick up a few things, even if we try hard.

And every morning, the coyotes howled up the
sun.

295

Weekends, I would leave the mesquite tree because on weekends the little dirt track was used – a few partiers would come and camp under the mesquite tree. I didn't want anything to do with them, so on Fridays I drove the car up a tiny track that dead-ended at some kind of tank. I found a nice spot there beside a huge saguaro and very near the bank of the dry creek bed just where a tiny island was thick with shrubbery. My fire here was very discreet, a small notch in the bank of the creekbed, and I could lounge over breakfast, keep my coffee warm over the dying coals of the fire while I heard the ravens sing their morning song then fly off to scavenge in the desert. Then the Gambel's quails would chatter among themselves where they roosted in low branches near me. Then they'd march out to graze or look for seeds on the ground together, their multi-colored curled forelock feathers bobbing as they marched. I got involved in the coyotes' morning howl. They'd howl in concert for awhile – one howling high, one low, one yipping fast and hysterical, one barking and yowling in turns. But they finished too soon for me. So I started tentatively to howl too – about the time they'd finish up, I'd commence. The sun, I felt, had not quite emerged on the horizon and so the work was not done. I practiced the howls and the yowls and the yips and the barks by turns, taking lessons from them all. And they very graciously commenced another verse in response to me.

This happened again and again. I became quite involved with the coyotes then, following their tracks when I'd find them, noting that they were coming closer and closer to my camp.

Then one morning after the howl, I went out to my cooking spot and found that the coyotes had been there in the night, had picked up some crumbs and had then played tug-of-war with my handkerchief that I had left out there for a hot pad, tearing it nearly in half. I considered it a greeting. Coyote the Trickster saying hello, saying they know all about me and about my howling with them.

I always wanted to stretch out the howling and one day we howled up the sun and then the ravens joined us and the Gambel's quails too before the concert ended.

When I finally left the place, I found myself driving along worrying about the sun – would it come up all right without me there to help howl it up?

THE SUNFLOWER

It was early Spring. I remember there was snow melting. Two or three chickadees were making a rumpus in a tree by the side of a little road so I tossed a few sunflower seeds down and walked on.

I don't know why it didn't start growing until late July. I noticed the first real leaves then. It was a place where there's always a puddle in the Spring. I suppose it was waiting for warm weather, a rare treat here at nine thousand feet in the Rockies. There was a lot of rain in July, and then at the end it warmed up and that's when I noticed it. I remember I "tsk"ed and shook my head. It was one of those great big sunflowers that grow in Kansas to be twelve feet tall and two feet across. We don't have anything like that here.

It grew fast through August. The temperature never got below forty at night and the sunflower got up over two feet tall and started budding. That's when I began getting emotionally involved. "I hope you don't expect to go to seed," I said.

It was a single stalk, maybe half an inch thick, broad pointed leaves coming out alternately, each one with its little bud above, then the developing mass of the great bud on top.

It was well into September when one day there was a tongue of yellow hanging down and the bud had turned to face the rising sun. The bud opened over the next four days. The first day the tongue was wider, the next it was half done, then most of the way, then full circle. And every day that flowerhead faced the sun and

298

followed it across the sky, and always the leaves reached upward.

Big golden presence glowing there by the side of the little road. It must have been lit from inside. Wildly, shaggily, intensely alive. It was breathtaking on a misty mountain morning in September to see that brilliant splendor. Gradually, the flower's rays deepened to orange. And in the composite flowerhead, the flowerets gradually opened from the outside in, their little tassels of golden petals sprawling across the pale yellow-green of the inner buds. For four glorious days that sunflower shone and moved and opened and gleamed.

Then came the first frost. The next morning I went out to face the sunflower with a good deal of apprehension, but the sunflower looked worse than I could have imagined. The head no longer faced east. Though the morning sun was filtering through to it, the head of the sunflower pointed straight to the ground. The leaves were dark and they, too, pointed to the ground. The gleam was gone from the rays. Every part of the plant was dark and wrinkled and dismal. What had been, twelve hours before, the utmost exuberance was now the utmost dejection.

The following night the wind rose and I woke to see pines waving crazily in moonlight. When I came out to the sunflower, it had blown over. It didn't look so sorrowful lying on the ground. Six days later, I bent to look at it -- its rays were dull yellow, brown-edged; its leaves and sepals were greenish-black. A bee was crawling across the flowerhead. She seemed to be finding something of interest. She stayed there a long time.

THE OLD ONES

I look at my peers, I am amazed. They're in their fifties and sixties, and sometimes I think something is wrong. They don't look like they used to look. And I don't either. We're in this together.

I know. It's only Time ticking along, creeping up on us. We get together sometimes and talk. We don't go on much about changing the world anymore or about how life is going to be better for one of us than for the others. We each have our projects and we each struggle along with them and things change and we like to think the changes are improvements. Sometimes we'll sing old songs, or sometimes we'll get to laughing. Usually we laugh at ourselves struggling ineffectually to maintain dignity.

Each one values certain traits and at this age those values show. And we work hard at them. One values useful poverty, another a certain aristocratic style, yet another emerges like Houdini still alive from various horrible situations. With me I think it's my stamina. Maintaining these values becomes more difficult every year. Each one has her self-image mixed up in whatever value she's chosen. When these values break down, then perhaps we will become more purely old.

Keeping in touch with old friends makes poignant what everyone knows like they know the world is round. That is, that people start out young and then they become old. And it's the same people all the way, but the roles change. One plays different parts across the years, even if one is not ready to change. Sometimes the desperation to cling to the old part becomes the new part.

Turning thirty, one is no longer one of the young.

Turning forty, one realizes that one's life is going on and one had better get at it.

Turning fifty, one finds loose ends flying all about, like a rag-tag fringe in the wind, and is looked upon by older people as a young old one.

I know what it is at sixty. Doing things becomes more and more troublesome.

One step at a time. One decade. One role.

You young people, you have your youth and that is very nice. But we old people, we have our age. We are in it at this very moment! We know that it happens. At this very moment we know being a child and we know having a child and we know being discarded. We know surviving beyond the end of the story. We know how to play the game and we know the freedom of not playing it.

At seventy, it comes to seem as though the rhythm of the people is too fast.

At eighty, one sees that the now never becomes final, and therefore all that effort was only dust in the wind.

At ninety, one is amazed to have lived for so long, and wonders why.

Old age is not a spectator sport, old ones watching young ones have their lives. We're not just remembering old times. We are composites of everything that has occurred to us.

301

VISIONS OF MY DEATH

My dear friend Lucia Berlin came from
California to teach a course in prose writing at
the Buddhist-inspired school called Naropa in
Boulder and she let me sit in on a class. There
were whispers going about this year that a famous
movie actor's daughter was taking this course and
as it happened I sat behind her and noticed that
she wore her t-shirt inside out, had short hair
like a boy's and a rebellious attitude. Tom, a very
handsome shy young man sat beside her. Her name was
Vanessa. "Poor princess," I thought. Lucia very
thoughtfully of me suggested a topic for us all to
write about, a topic upon which I would shine –
"Now I want all of you to write about a stump," she
said. "In eight minutes, write about a stump." And
she worked on papers while the students and I wrote
furiously about a stump.

Now, as it happened, and she knew there was a
high probability that it would be so, I could
easily work up a sketch turning a stump into a god,
and thus at the reading of a few of the student's
papers she chose me and I raised a very satisfying
gasp from the students with my story about a stump.
(I believe that story is truly lost.)

A week or two later, another dear friend,
Bobbie Louise Hawkins whom I've known since 1961
was showing her old movies from 25 years before and
there were pictures of Lucia beautiful as a model
and pictures of me too, young and straight and slim

(at a rare moment between pregnancies) in a red dress I didn't remember, holding a baby, smiling. I noticed my teeth seemed big because my face was so thin.

That night as I lay down to sleep in my little car, I thought of that young woman with the red dress, myself in another time in my life, wondered if she could have seen me now as I had seen her then, what she would think of me, what she would think of becoming me a quarter-century later. Would she like me? Would she approve? I had no doubt she would have shouted for joy at the beauty of the land I had just bought. She would have been more than a little bit horrified at my being middle-aged (with a middle-aged spread) and especially shocked at my being alone. But once accepting all of that, she would have had little trouble with my sleeping in my car. She would have applauded my courage and resourcefulness. She would have been very happily proud that I was known as a writer.

I wasn't making these things up; I was in an interesting state of mind in which I was virtually being her, looking at me. I realized that having for the moment achieved this state of timelessness, I could look at something else if I wanted to, as though I had been given a wish. And I considered what I would like to see. There were many possibilities to choose amongst but I chose to see my death.

And there, walking along a path in Autumn sunlight was an old woman, skinnier even than the young woman in that red dress. She was bent and her elbows went up in back to compensate as she walked.

303

She was wearing an outfit that she had recently made, herself, a tunic and pants made of silk in an autumnal pattern, autumn leaves on a silver-gray background. Her hair was long and straight, held away from her face, hanging well down her back. At one moment she stopped and turned to look behind her, back down the canyon. Was it this canyon? I couldn't be sure. Some of the autumn leaves seemed to be maple and oak. I saw her big teeth like those of the young woman in the red dress and I saw her eyes with a sort of mad gleam, a tremendous inner intensity, and in those eyes I saw that she had her own worries that I didn't know anything about. I saw also that she remembered the occasion when she had been me looking at her now and she knew, as she had known when she was buying the silk, making the tunic and pants, putting them on in the morning, that this was the day of her death.

She walked on up the path to a place where a cabin had been, no walls or roof in sight but two levels of floor, two or three steps between them, autumn leaves covering all. She sat down on that floor to wait. She had an appointment to meet a man here who was to bring her food for the winter. It was one of those exquisite autumn days, the clear sunlight, yellow aspen leaves rattling in a light breeze. She sat, leaned back holding one knee to luxuriate, intensely loving the sweetness of the day, the clouds rolling across a deep blue sky, loving life on earth. Time and beauty were immeasurable. At one point she just tipped over and died among the leaves, her clothes fluttering in the light breeze.

No one came except for the Winter, a dry one. Snow covered her and then blew off again more than once. In the Spring my son Bear came and found her there. He knew he would because I had told him this story. Her body had flattened out and dried up so that it was like carrying a poster, the silver-gray silk dappled with orange and brown leaf-images fluttering in the lush greenery of Springtime as he carried her away through the woods.

Epilog Written Twenty Years Later

I knew that I wanted to know all and that in some way I could know all. And I knew that to know all seemed to demand that I be in some way cognizant after I die or cognizant of that part of time -- the future -- that some sense of it would be available to me. How I envision it was this:

I had a sort of vision once of my death, and I remember in that vision I was sitting alone in the wilderness. It was autumn and I was very old. I was sitting in glorious sunlight and beauty all around me, and I was beaming out love in an ecstasy, knowing that it was my last moment of life and knowing that words were too narrow to carry what was going on between me and Nature. So I couldn't really tell what I knew or what I found. And I knew that that was as it had always been.

In that vision, at one moment, I dropped and was dead. But then, in this vision going on beyond that vision, at one moment, I just jumped out and let the body drop and I danced through trees and felt the leaves falling through me as I touched one tree after the other, recognizing that the senses

305

of my life were now replaced by full knowledge without substance as revelation.

I danced and danced, going about the world timelessly, to visit friends and places that I loved and places that I had always dreamed of going to and loving.

And then later, in this second vision, I watched as all of that world that I had loved, beautiful places that I knew or would have loved to know, they all died – every bit, even in the end, the shape of the land – and then in suspense, I watched the birth of what followed – slowly at first, then more and more, all strange to me, strange but indescribably wonderful, a new world of life.

I PUT THE WATER ON FOR TEA

I put the water on for tea and stood in the back door to look out. It was Autumn.

The neighbors to the north were nice enough people but invasive, watching my gardening technique with a critical eye, and the kids tirelessly on the trampoline. I wanted to raise the five-foot fence another five feet.

There on the south side of the house where the rain spout came out were quite a few weed trees popping up, the ubiquitous cottonwoods, elms, poplars, lilacs, ornamental cherries, I don't know what. "I'd better get at those pretty quick, "I thought, "or we'll have a forest for a yard."

I looked with distaste to the north, then at the trees, and I thought, "Why not plant all these trees along that north fence?" Not the cottonwood, of course, but I could plant the others every few feet apart along there and the neighbors wouldn't know what hit them.

I walked along the fence. I'd have to put the trees between the hollyhocks of course – funny to think of trees spaced by hollyhocks. The hollyhocks, short-lived, would most probably be long forgotten while the trees grew and grew. If the trees actually lived past transplanting.

I got the hose out and a shovel, dug some holes along the fence, dribbled water into them, added some compost for each. Then I dug carefully around the trees one after the other. They were small, two to four feet

high, so their roots didn't amount to much, didn't
break much as I transferred them from their shady
nursery under the rain spout to the new home along the
fence where they would hopefully settle in across the
Winter and burst forth in the Spring.

Nine holes I dug, composted and watered, nine
trees transplanted to the north and settled in. I
watered them once a month across the following Winter.

Now, a year later, seven of those trees have
held on, grown leaves anyway in spite of the
bindweed and the fairly severe competition from the
hollyhocks. I've kind of whimsically put in some
peach pits and a couple of acorns in the gaps. I
don't suppose they'll come up, but on the other
hand, that is what trees come from.

The tea kettle was ruined of course. And I felt
terrible. So irresponsible, just went without a
thought from one world to the other and stayed
there, enjoying myself. Unforgivable. I remembered a
character in an Agatha Christie book; a duchess or
some such who'd wake up early and put on a pot of
tea then go back to bed. No, she didn't burn the
house down; everyone loved her just the same. And
they bought tea kettles by the dozen, not bothering
her with it. But she was clearly over the hill.

Carlos took me down immediately to the store
and we bought a new kettle, and it was there at that
store that I realized that what I wanted was one of
those foolproof tea kettles for old ladies, the kind
you plug in separately and it turns off by itself,
keeping the water warm for an hour or two while you
go back to sleep or plant a few trees or whatever.